Jason and Anna

Irwin Sadetsky

Also by Irwin Sadetsky
Iraqi Rebound
A Terrorist on Every Block
Honorable Choices

For Rick & Sandi, Steve & Laurie, Joe & Flora, Herb & Rose, Dave & Kathleen, Pat & Joan, Bob & Vi, Marty & Mickey, Bob & Peg because they have demonstrated their love, fidelity & partnership to each other over many years!

For Mary, my endeared other, who has been my best friend, sweetheart, supporter, cheer leader, confident & editor. My everlasting unconditional love to this remarkable woman.

Prologue

Noise, the type of noise that starts as insidious, the type of noise that keeps you awake, the type of noise that makes your innards shake, the type of noise from a Boeing C17 Globemaster that shakes you constantly — hell it was constant!

Ensign Jason Darvish looked outside the small window and contemplated his situation. He really was a researcher, not really a nerd, not really a warrior, certainly not a SEAL! Jason looked around and observed six men in full battle gear. These SEAL's were combat ready, the cutting edge of the military of the United States of America. A bead of sweat ran down Jason's face.

"Hey newbie, drink some water," yelled Chief Master Petty Officer Dugan, "that's a request!"

"Thanks Chief. I really don't want to be a pain in the ass or trouble for you."

"Sir, you have the talent we need to make this mission a success. The Navy would not have sent you to us without checking you out. Just do your job and be our translator. Got it!"

"Got it Chief!"

The mission was to rescue two CIA agents who were captured by the Taliban in the far reaches of Afghanistan. They were too valuable to be left to the torture of the Taliban who knew many techniques to get information out of any person. It was vital to the United States that they be rescued. There were satellite pictures of the camp as well as a promise that a drone would be overhead to insure up to date surveillance. Jason knew that if the agents were not captured the drones would fire their hellfire missiles and destroy the camp.

They landed at Bagram Airfield, near the ancient city of Bagram. It was the busiest and largest airfield for the United States Airforce. The team headed to a small building carrying their gear with them. Jason had no problem with any of the weight since he was twenty-two years old and worked out every day at a local gym near the Office of Naval Intelligence where he worked.

At three in the morning the Blackhawk helicopter settled behind a large hill two kilometers from the Taliban base. Modern design minimized the sound and the landing was flawless. Master Chief Dugan gave the high sign and the men started their advance to the base. Jason's role was to be behind the team with one of the SEAL's. He would be used, if necessary, if they came upon any person they found. Within twenty minutes they found an Afghan man who had an AK-47 in his hand. He was taken down and Jason was asked to question him.

The man spoke Darsi and was surprised that Jason was fluent in the language. "Why are you here carrying a gun?"

"I get paid to watch out for people who want to come to the base."
"How many more guards are there?"

"I don't know?"

Jason turned to the Chief. "He's lying, there has to be guards around the base."

The Chief hit the guard in the face and the man went down to the ground. He was held by his collar and slapped. "Sir, ask him again?"

"How many more guards?"

"Two more. On the east and west sides. I'm in charge of the north."

Jason relayed the information to the Chief. The man was gagged and tied, Another SEAL gave him an injection that would keep him knocked out for four hours.

Upon entering the Taliban base the team spotted a small hut that had bars in the window.

That had to be where the agents were housed. They approached the hut when Jason heard shouting behind him. Two men were running towards him with their weapons poised. Jason took his short stock HK 416 and squeezed off three shots. Both men fell.

All hell broke loose right after that. The SEAL's blasted their way through ten Taliban fighters and rescued the two CIA agents. On cue the

Blackhawk helicopter came down with two machine gunners blasting away clearing a path for the team. Jason was sprinting alongside Chief Dugan when Dugan tripped on some debris. He fell on his face and Jason stopped to help him up. As the Chief was getting up a solitary Taliban fighter came out of a large bush and aimed his rifle at both men.

Jason knocked the Chief to the ground, twisted around in a pirouette and got off a shot killing his enemy. His single shot went right between the enemy's eyes. Dugan managed to get up and said, "Man, you've got great balls, let's get out of here!"

Flying back to the States Jason thought about his parents and Great Neck, Long Island. *Nobody would believe that I could have done what I just did. I can't believe it.*

Chapter One

Great Neck Long Island is a community on the north shore of Long Island, New York. It has outstanding schools, outstanding stores, outstanding restaurants and is considered by many an affluent community. This is where Jason Darvich grew up.

His parents emigrated to the United States from Iran in 1979 due to the possibility of a war with Iraq plus the emergence of Saddam Hussein. His first cousin sponsored Farid and his wife Dorri as well as giving Farid a job.

Their life was limited because they were Catholic. Most of the Iraq people were tolerant. Yet, the Darvich's community was only made up of church goers. Dances, parties, celebrations were always held at church and low key in nature.

Farid Darvish had studied pharmacy at the university and worked for a large drug store in the outskirts of Teheran. He excelled at his position and kept a quiet, low profile.

Dorri Darvich held a Masters Degree in library science and converted to Catholicism in order to marry Farid. She never regretted it and was pleased that they were able to go to the United States to start a new life. When Jason was born in 1998 she was forty-one years old and then she gave birth to Melody a year later. The Darvich's felt it was divine intervention since Dorri was told that she would not be able to have any natural children by reputable doctors. Both parents loved and cherished their children.

Farid worked for his cousin who was a pharmacist for a few years and saved enough money to open up a small drug store in1985. He worked sixty hours a week and was able to purchase a fixer upper house in Great Neck in

1995. His store was only a few miles away in Lake Success. It was a financial struggle, yet the couple loved the area.

Dorri Darvich made sure to teach her children Farsi. Jason picked up the language easily, but Melody had no interest in learning the language. At times his parents talked to him in Farsi to keep up his skills. Jason enjoyed the dialogue and excelled in the language. Melody just wanted to be the "All American Girl."

When both children entered public school Dorri Darvich took a part time position at the Great Neck Library. She loved books and felt that she could contribute to the family income since the budget was always tight.

Jason's high school career was outstanding. He was very bright growing up in a school district with many bright and talented students. Jason graduated fifth in his class of twelve-hundred and received a Varsity Letter in Cross Country Track. He won the French Medal at graduation and loved languages, so he decided to study many languages at college.

Jason had a friend whose family owned a boat and because of this he sailed for four years and loved the sea. There was something special about fighting the wind and making it your friend. It was thrilling to estimate the timing of your sail and come into port at the time you planned.

During his senior year in high school a girl called Angie asked him to a party at her house. She was part of the "cool crowd" and Jason felt uncomfortable with her friends who seemed to know the latest songs, their words and all the newest dance moves.

He liked Angie. She was pretty, with blue eyes and natural honey blond hair. She took him under her wing and taught him how to dance and introduced him to petting.

He was new to dealing with girls and asked his sister, "How should I know when to stop when we are making out?"

Melody laughed, "Just keep on going, she'll tell you when to stop."

A week later Angie called Jason. "I'm baby sitting at the Johnson's house this Saturday night. Come over at eight. I cleared it with the Johnson's and they told me it was okay."

When they got comfortable on the couch and started to pet Angie unzipped Jason's pants and started to fondle him. He responded with great enthusiasm and Angie kissed him, "Jason, let me show you what I can do for you and what you can do for me."

He was a good student and since he was a virgin Angie's experience helped him over that awkward period of young, inexperienced love." They became a couple for the rest of the senior year and were inseparable.

Jason enjoyed every minute of it and looked forward to seeing Angie although she did not have a decent intellect. She always wanted to go to the movies, go bowling, have parties with her friends and just hang out. Something was missing. He really wanted to go to some school functions that had a more intellectual bent as watching the Debate Club, listening to a lecture about the space program, and participating in the Advanced Science Fair. Angie did not want to do any of the activities he suggested.

She seemed to control him with his need for sex. There were times that she would quickly give him oral sex if he insisted to go to some activity he wanted. Jason would acquiesce. He was having a great time and did not want to break up the relationship.

Immediately after the senior prom Angie broke up with him, "I honestly like you Jason. You are really a nice guy, but you're not a fun guy and I need that!"

Jason was relieved. He relished the sex, but certainly knew that he needed more than that to have a good time.

Jason applied to five colleges. Two were Ivy League, two were part of the top two in California as well as large University located in Manhattan. He was accepted by all of them. He and his parents discussed the pros and cons of each school. Then one night he heard his parents talking.

"I can't take out a second mortgage to pay for his school because I had to use the money for the store," his Dad quietly said to his wife.

"I can get a fulltime job and Jason can take out student loans." "God, that will burden him for years."

"We also have to consider Melody. She wants to go to college as well." "Perhaps I can speak to my cousin for a family loan. He's doing well!' "Please Farid, we will never hear the end of it if he lends us money!"

"Look at our problems, I'm hardly making a living at the store, we have heavy taxes in Great Neck, the loan we took out for the siding on the house has another two years to go and Melody's dental work is costing us a small fortune."

Dorri Darvish started to cry as she sputtered, "We have to tell Jason." "I'll do that tomorrow night."

Jason realized that his parents truly had financial problems and he was determined to ease their burden. He made up his mind to see a guidance counselor the next day to search for options. There had to be a solution to the problem.

Dr. Greenburg was considered a top-notch counselor. He was professional in his interactions with students, parents, teachers and administrators. If there was a conflict between any of the parties Dr. Greenburg would say, "I am here for the students. What- ever you say, do, or want, it has to be in the student's best interests. Jason respected Dr. Greenburg and always made sure to listen to his career lectures during special senior days. He made an appointment to see his counselor during lunch period.

Dr. Greenburg was short, stocky, had a goatee beard and wore the same clothing for years. He cared about only one thing, his students! In a low baritone voice he queried,

"Well Jason, what's up?"

"Dr. Greenburg I won't be able to make it to college because of financial concerns. Are there any special scholarships that might help me out?"

"How bad is it, Jason?"

"Dad already second mortgaged the house, there are other loans and expenses. It's not good at all."

"Jason, what did you want to study at school?" "Languages, I love languages."

"Do you like the sea?"

"I love to sail, I love the sea."

"Would you consider an opportunity to have all your books, supplies, tuition, fees and other expenses fully paid?"

Jason laughed "Who do I have to kill?"

Dr. Greenburg stroked his beard, "Are you Catholic?" "Yes, although we only go to church on special holidays."

"Fordham University has a Naval ROTC scholarship program. After you graduate you will have to serve in the United States Navy for five years. You will have to give up your summer vacation time in order to go on cruises and special training. There will be special subjects in calculus, seamanship, naval engineering as well as your full- time studies. It is quite a load to carry."

Jason thought for a minute, "I have to talk to my parents. May I see you tomorrow?"

"I'll get some paper work ready for you. I'll see you here at the same time tomorrow. Okay"

"Yes sir!"

Farid Darvich finished his dessert of citrus rice pudding, an Iranian favorite. He wiped his mouth and looked directly at Jason, "We have to talk. Let's go into the living room. Melody, you are excused."

Jason's parents sat down on the love seat opposite Jason who sat on the edge of his chair.

Before his father could say anything, Jason exclaimed, "Mom and Dad I would like to go to Fordham University. It has a Catholic orientation, run by the Jesuits, but open to all faiths. They have a Naval ROTC program that will pay for my books, tuition, courses, fees, housing and supplies. I have to give them five years of service as a naval officer after graduation. What do you think?"

His father looked stern, "Why don't you want to go to that Ivy League school? They wanted you."

"Mom and Dad, I heard you last night. I wasn't trying to, but when I heard how tough things are right now, I spoke to my Dr. Greenburg, my counselor and he suggested this opportunity."

Mrs. Darvish started to cry and Jason came out of his chair and put his arms around her, "Mom, I love you and Dad and I know that this will really be okay. I'm smart and I know I can do it."

"But you will be a sailor!"

"Yes—and you know I love the sea. I'm looking at this as an opportunity to serve my country and get a quality education. It is a win, win, for all of us."

"Son, my dear son," Farid's voice quivered, "is this what you want!" "Dad, this is what I want. Please say yes."

The family came together and hugged as his mother whispered, "Jesus, keep my son safe!"

The next day Dr. Greenburg set things in motion. He said, "Make us proud Jason.

I'm rooting for you!"

Chapter Two

Anna Mason always knew she was going to go to Columbia University. She saw pictures of her at the age of two wearing a "Columbia University" tee shirt. Her father, Dr. Henry Mason, had started as an instructor and worked his way up, after fifteen years, to a full professorship at the University. He was a talented writer, taught journalism and was on many television shows as an expert on journalism and the free press. His magazine articles were used as models to new writers entering the field.

Anna Mason was born in 1999 in Teaneck, New Jersey. Teaneck could be described to people as an affluent community with a broad spectrum of professionals, and business people living there. It is in Bergen County, New Jersey, a very short distance to New York City. Many people consider it as part of the greater metropolitan area in terms of transportation to the city and opportunities for music, art and recreational opportunities.

Anna's mother, Jacki Mason had her own fulltime business as a commercial office designer and interior decorator. She had an office in New York City, but worked out of her home four out of five days in the week. She believed in women's rights before the movement became popular and made sure, as she raised Anna, that her daughter would be a free thinker and independent.

The family went to the United Church of Christ, a liberal religious denomination.

Many projects centered around civil rights, women's rights, LGBT rights, and abortion. Anna had the opportunity to study about other religious faiths and understand what main stream Protestantism means in the modern world.

Anna had twin brothers who were five years older. When Anna graduated high school her brother Joel graduated medical school and her brother Mark opened up his second pizza store in New Jersey. They were as different as night and day except for their fierce independence.

Attending Teaneck High School was a sheer joy to Anna. She had many friends who had the same interest in music, plays, museums and intellectual pursuits. Anna hung out with her group of friends, had sleep over parties, shared their interests in the world around them and confided about their feelings about boys. They were called the "Nerdy Girls'" because they were all members of the National Honor Society. Yet many of the high school kids looked up to them because of the many community projects sponsored by the National Honor Society.

Anna was on the Debating Team, Associate Editor of the school newspaper, and had fifteen advanced placement credits for college. In her senior year she won the National Council of Teachers of English Achievement Award in Writing. Her thematic paper was entitled, "How Valuable is the United Nations?"

She graduated Salutatorian and won the medal for Writing and Literature. Anna was offered four scholarships, two to Ivy League Schools and two to prestigious smaller schools. There was only one school she wanted to go to and that was Columbia University. Her tuition was paid 100% because of the "College Tuition Program" for dependent children attending the University. Having her father as a teacher paid off—big time!

Her first boyfriend was a kid called Chuck. He was on the staff of the school newspaper and had a great sense of humor. They hung out a little, but never became serious. They were both sensible kids so they necked a little but did not go all the way. Anna felt that it was important to protect her virginity until the right man came along. Some of her friends were looser and discussed their sexual adventures, yet Anna was not ready or even interested in considering losing her virginity.

She had a frank discussion about her decision with her mother who hugged her, "Sweetheart, you will know when you are ready and who it will be. It will come onto you as a revelation and I guarantee you will be very happy when it happens!"

"Thanks Mom, I really needed to let it out and I love you and trust you with any confidences I have."

Henry Mason as a father was a bit distant to his family. He always seemed to have a project, a deadline to finish, papers to mark, a conference to go to, a paper to edit or a television show to attend. He did have one passion and that was the New York Yankees. He would take Anna and some of her friends a number of times during the baseball season to Yankee Stadium. At that time he was the perfect father having fun with his daughter. Anna relished those moments. She enjoyed his enthusiasm and when the Yankee's won he was on top of the world. When they lost he would squeeze Anna's hand and say, "Okay, tomorrows another game and we're going to win it. I feel it in my bones!"

It was fun being with her dad.

As soon as Anna graduated high school she registered for summer school classes at Columbia University. She was seventeen years old and ready to conquer the world.

The poetry class was fun, but with a great deal of reading. She felt a bit inadequate. Anna seemed to have problems with meter and rhyme.

Along came Brian. He was from Dublin and attended Trinity College. He was twenty years old with flaming red hair, green eyes and a brogue that was lovely to hear. He offered to help Anna with her poetry and after three weeks they became close. Anna felt attracted to him. She liked the way he moved, she liked the way he smelled, she liked his courtesy given to her and the respect he showed to the people they met.

One evening he invited her up to his apartment and when they settled on the couch he kissed her. Anna kissed him back with her mouth wide open and her tongue and lips inviting him for more. She thought, *I am ready and he is the one!*

Without a moment of hesitation Anna took off her blouse and her bra. Brian responded by kissing her all over. A few minutes later, although it seemed that time stood still, they looked at each other stark naked.

"This is my first time Brian, please be gentle." "I will not hurt you, but I cannot do this." "Come here and kiss me Brian."

Anna hugged him, teased him and finally positioned herself to a lover's position.

She wanted him badly and her independence took over. Anna pulled him into her and smiled as she looked at his beautiful green eyes.

Brian responded gently and carefully as their excitement grew. Anna's new joy filled her and finally they both lay spent.

The couple had a summer romance albeit too short. Brian kissed her goodbye in September. He flew away and out of her life. At the airport she said goodbye and continued to smile. She thought, *I am happy it happened with him!*

Columbia University is located on an island in the borough of Manhattan in New York City. Most of the studies take place in and around an area called Morningside Heights, an area described by most people as the upper westside. It is an historic university going back to 1754. The school is identified as an Ivy League research university. The original name was "King's College" and after the Revolutionary War it was renamed Columbia College in 1784. It is highly competitive with an acceptance rate of under six percent.

The thirty-two acres of land covers more than six city blocks and contains seventy-eight-hundred apartments, two dozen undergraduate dormitories, large academic buildings, classrooms and a huge library It has a large underground tunnel system that was built more than one-hundred years ago. The borders are Broadway on the west side, Columbus Avenue on the eastside, West 120th Street on the north side and 110th Street on the southside. There are additional properties located in and around the city as well as a medical Center on West 168th Street.

Anna knew the University since she had numerously visited her father who worked there for many years. She completed registration for her first semester very quickly and focused on her major which would be English. She took a minor in writing and hoped that she would be worthy of getting into the full program as a Junior.

During her Junior year she had enough credits and faculty support to transfer her major to writing. She was thrilled. Her father and mother shared their enthusiasm with her at a celebration diner.

Her mom lifted the glass of wine, "My darling daughter, to a successful writing career. It may be hard with rejections, but I know you will be a star!"

Dr. Mason lifted his glass, "If you think you are going to outwrite me then I accept the challenge. After all, I can't make pizza and lost that battle with your brother Mark— and I don't know a damn thing about being a doctor as your brother Joel—yet I am so pleased and happy that you have chosen writing as a career. May your words inspire or at least entertain the people who read your work product!"

Anna completed her degree in three years and won the Philolexian Prize which was established in 1904. The prize is awarded to Columbia College students for essays, short stories, and poetry. Since she graduated at the age of twenty Anna decided to take six months off and visit Europe

Anna heard the constant steady noise form the plane's jet engines as she headed to Europe and thought, *I feel excited and am blessed that my parents gave me the courage to be independent. I have a lot to learn and write about!*

It was a valuable experience where she gained insight into the different customs, attitudes and values of the many people she met. She managed to get to know a few people quite well.

Chapter Three

Fordham had its beginnings in 1841.The Catholic Diocese of New York founded it and quite quickly it became a Jesuit independent college. Even today the basis of its curriculum is based on educational concepts laid by the Jesuits. The religious requirement are two courses in theology during the student's undergraduate years. There are many students who have different religious affiliations who go to Fordham and some controversy revolves around the secularization of the school.

Jason's orientation to Fordham was given by the Dean of the school. It took place at the Lincoln Center campus located on West 62nd Street between Columbus Avenue and Amsterdam Avenue.

The Dean waived his arms in a circle and said, "Welcome to Fordham. Your campus is New York City. Enjoy our art, music, museums, theaters, sports, entertainment and of course don't forget to study!"

There was another campus in the Bronx called Rose Hill. It was walking distance to the fabulous Bronx Zoo. Yet another campus was in Westchester County and if courses had to be taken there would be busses available to take the students to any campus. The Navy ROTC unit was located in the Bronx at the State University of New York Maritime College.

Jason was housed in a small apartment with two other students. The building was owned by Fordham and of course he was on a free ride because of his ROTC scholarship.He couldn't wait to get started.

Jason called his mother, "Mom, it's everything I wanted. I'm going to be very happy here!"

"Don't forget to come and visit us. I miss you already." "Love you Mom! Say hello to Melody and Dad."

Jason thought, *This is the first time I am really on my own. I know I can make it!*

He met a number of students from Afghanistan and seemed to understand some of their language called Dari. These students were children of high ranking government officials or millionaire business men from Afghanistan. Dari is also known as Afghan Persian, East Farsi, and Eastern Persian. He learned from his studies that is spoken by seven-million-six-hundred- thousand people in Afghanistan. Jason became *proficient* in Dari.

Jason enjoyed his course work and excelled. There was never an assignment he did not tackle and by the end of his first year the professors in his language studies were quite impressed. The talented student had the natural ability to remember vocabulary and nuance based on slang.

He understood jargon and had perfect pronunciation whether it was in Chinese, French or Advanced Farsi.

Once a week Jason had to report to the Maritime College in the Bronx for drills. The instructors made sure that all of the candidates were physically fit. At times special programs were set up to have candidates lose weight. Hardly any candidate had to gain weight. Jason was fortunate to have been a cross country runner and was in good shape, except his instructors felt he needed more strength training and he started lifting weights.

Every summer Jason had to go on a summer cruise. During that experience he was professionally trained to be an officer in the United States Navy.

During his four years at Fordham he had to take additional courses in calculus, naval engineering, seamanship and navigation. He loved the challenge and by the end of the normal school week he was exhausted, yet quite happy.

He participated in summer cruises between the Spring and Fall semesters. Jason studied as a Midshipman being introduced to four warfare areas: submarines, aviation, surface warfare, and Marine training. Jason also studied leadership training and protocol. The young Midshipman evaluator's, at all his cruises, gave him superior ratings. He scored top grades in written work and was outstanding in critical thinking skills, logic, agility, strength and problem solving. The Marine Corps Commander at his Summer Cruise in Quantico asked Jason to consider becoming an officer in the Marine Corps

"Thank you for the invitation sir, but my first love is the Navy!"

"Too bad young man. If you ever want to change I certainly will recommend you. You have the right stuff!"

Jason saluted smartly, "Many thanks sir!"

Jason's heavy schedule prohibited any meaningful relationships with women. One day in his sophomore year he became sick & reported to the Health Center. He was treated by a young nurse called Sharon. He was nineteen & she was twenty-three.

"Okay Jason, you have the beginnings of a possible flu. I suggest you go back to your apartment and rest for a few days. Take some Tylenol, drink plenty of fluids and take it easy. There is a twenty-four hour virus around the campus. Perhaps you will be okay sooner than later."

He looked up at her from the examining table and smiled. "You are an angel of mercy.

Thank you."

Sharon squeezed his arm as she helped him up from the exam table. I'll call your Commander at the Maritime College and get you a clearance. I've done this before,"

Jason thought, *Here is a woman who I can relate to. I like her.*

The day after he received a call from Sharon asking him about his health. He was improving, but Sharon told him that she lived near him & would drop over to check him out.

When she arrived to his apartment he was alone. His roommate was in class and would not be back until the late evening.

"Take off your shirt I want to listen to your heart."

Jason complied and when she came close to him she smelled wonderful. He looked into her eyes and Sharon kissed him. He responded with vigor and became immediately aroused.

Sharon did not hesitate at all. She kissed him again, "I want you now!"

They had sex promptly and a short time later they did it again. He was nineteen and in great shape. Sharon responded to Jason in an open and mature manner. There was nothing she would not do for him and he felt the same way about her.

The affair was physical with not too much companionship due to Jason's schedule and Sharon's work schedule. It worked for both consenting adults. Jason never mentioned his affair with any of his friends or associates. This was private.

Sharon was an open book to Jason, "Hon, I am dating other men and want you to know that. You are a very busy man, but I just can't sit around and wait for you to take me to the movies."

The relationship lasted until Jason's senior year. Sharon told him that she was quitting the job & getting married. Jason was happy for her and pleased that he did not have to make a commitment in any manner to Sharon.

The four years at Fordham seemed to move quickly. Jason majored in Chinese, French and Psycholinguistics. He graduated with a BA in Language Studies with a Grade Point Average of 3.94. Jason won the Guardiani Award for the Study of Modern language & won the Mandarin Achievement Award at graduation. His parents were thrilled with his accomplishments and so was he. Jason thought, *I am pleased that my parents are able to share this joy with me.*

The very next day his parent attended the ceremonies at the Maritime College. The Admiral who was in charge of the third Naval District was in charge. He was erudite as he congratulated the NROTC staff and instructors at the college. The Admiral pointed out that the

Midshipmen had received the best training in the world to become Naval Officers.

There were fourteen new Ensigns and the Admiral congratulated every officer and their loved ones. After saluting the Admiral Jason went back to the group of new officers and listened to the Admirals speech.

"When you join the United States Navy you join the men and women who protect our nation. You are subject to the Uniform Code of Military justice which in many ways control your life. However you have been trained to be leaders, you have shown excellence in terms of your proficiencies in seamanship, you are now professionals and I congratulate you! My advice is simple, Your values as officers and as citizens of the United States will be paramount"

He snapped off a salute and left the podium yelling, "Remember that!"

Ensign Jason Darvish was assigned to a Destroyer. He was to report in two weeks. Jason went home to visit with his parents and a week later he received a phone call from the Office of the Chief of Naval Operations (CNO) to report to the Office of Naval Intelligence located in Suitland Maryland.

Jason thought, *Now, what is this all about.*

Chapter Four

Anna spent a very exciting and valuable six months travelling in Europe. She realized that the same motivations that drove people in the United States were similar to those in Europe except for one major difference. Health care was considered a right not a privilege in terms of everyday living. She saw the same passionate love of mothers and fathers as they raised their children. Anna realized that the social fabric of society had basic norms that crossed all national boundaries.

Anna spent a month visiting England, Scotland and Wales. London was her favorite city since it compared to New York City. Cardiff impressed her with the punk rock kids as she compared them to the hard-muscled older population who worked as fishermen and factory workers. She enjoyed Glasgow with its tremendous music, theater, design, creative arts and innovative cuisine.

When in Ireland she was enchanted with the folk tales, history and friendliness of the people. Her journey through the country included kissing the Blarney Stone as well as seeing the Bay of Galway. She decided to look up Brian, her first love who lived in Dublin.

She approached an attached brownstone building that had six steps to climb. She used the old brass knocker and it had a solid sound. A few moments later a red headed woman of fifty or so answered.

Anna smiled, "I used to know Brian when he visited Columbia University. Is he here?"

The woman ran her hands through her hair, "I'm Brian's mother. Please come in." The room reminded Anna of a sitting room she visited in a museum when she was a little girl. It had crochet doilies over the arms of the chairs and couch. There was a fireplace with a lovely painted family picture over it.

"I'm sorry, I should have called, but I'm only in Dublin for a day on my way back to London."

"Are you Anna?" "Yes I am."

"Brian told me about you when he came back from the States. He was pleased to have met you."

"I'm so happy to hear that."

"My dear, I'm afraid to tell you that Brian joined the army and was killed in Iraq.

It was quick and he did not suffer."

Anna started to cry and the woman came to her and held her. They both cried for a short time. Finely Anna said, "We had a romantic relationship and he was so kind and gentle to me."

"That was my son. He loved the world, he loved people, he was so gentle. Yet he felt it was his duty to join the army."

They talked a bit more and Anna left with a lump in her throat. She took the first plane out of Ireland with a heavy heart. She thought, *War is futile. Men die for no good reason. Bless you Brian.*

Anna spent a month in France using the wonderful rail system as she visited all of the cities she used to read about. Her favorite city was Vienne. It was located in southeastern France about thirty kilometers south of Lyon on the Rhone River. The Roman ruins and standing buildings impressed her. She had the best food of her life in small mom and pop style bistros. Anna needed to let go of her depressed feelings about Brian's death. She let it all go away in Vienne.

The cities of Amsterdam, Prague, Munich, Berlin, Vienna and Budapest were visited as well. Anna decided to go back to Prague. She felt very comfortable there and decided to spend a few weeks exploring the countryside and its people. She though, *I think I could live in Prague. It is comfortable.*

After a little over five months of travel Anna decided to come home. She was satisfied that her trip had helped her into adulthood. The twenty-one year old was ready to start her writing career.

Her parents invited her to stay home until she got a job and settled in. Rents in New York City were quite expensive. Anna took them up on their suggestion with the caveat that as soon as she could afford it she would move out.

Anna tried to get a number of writing jobs, but to no avail. The Columbia University Placement Bureau sent her on interviews that did not even come close to her needs, yet she took them for experience. After two months she spoke to her parents.

"Mom and Dad, I better start looking for college graduate jobs. I can't break into writing."

Mr. Mason sat next to his dejected daughter, "Anna, would you mind if I made a few calls for you. I know some people who might have something."

Anna gave a quick sob, "Yes Dad. I need your help."

Anna's interview at the "Bronx Dispatch" was short. It lasted twenty minutes. The owner was a woman named Margaret Jones. She was about sixty years old and had worked as an assistant editor for the New York Times for twenty years. Margaret Jones asked questions in a staccato manner and Anna answered them as quickly as she could.

The last question was a doozy,

"If you had to choose between saving a box full of pictures or a box with a lot of cash in a burning house, which would you save?"

"Pictures, of course, pictures."

"Report to work tomorrow morning at nine a.m. I'm going to work your little tail off. I hope you really can write. We will see!"

Anna was elated. She never discussed salary, benefits, hours or position. She was going to be a writer. That was the most important thing. When she got home she called for a pizza and bought dinner for her parents.

Toasting Anna as he held up his glass of diet soda Dr. Mason said, "Work hard, take any assignment, be productive, enjoy the story, be truthful, never fudge, accept your editor's comments, changes and suggestions. Here's to you my dear daughter. You are now a professional writer!"

Anna jumped into her father's arms and hugged him. "Thank you, Dad. Thank you!"

Chapter Five

The Bronx is a world onto itself. Yes, it is part of New York City and the people as well as the businesses pay New York City taxes. The structure of all the boroughs of New York City is unique.

There are five boroughs in New York City. The citizens elect their own borough president. The president is concerned about the interests of the citizens residing in the borough. He or she may introduce legislation through its own Borough Board and then given to the New York City Council. The borough president can hold public meetings, make recommendations to the mayor, make recommendations to other public officials, plan for land use, check on contracts, and in general make sure the interests of the people of the borough are represented.

Each borough has a board consisting of the borough president and Council members from the borough. There is a close connection between the board and Community Boards. Community Board members represent a distinct political-community district. Community board members are volunteers appointed by the borough president.

They advise upon matters of budget requests, zoning, borough projects and citizen concerns.

Perhaps one of the most important aspects of each borough is the election of its own District Attorney. There is great power in this seat and the borough citizens take their voting seriously.

Into this political arena entered Anna. She was a neophyte and perhaps her newness gave her the ability not to be too jaded. She reported on births, deaths, elections, zoning, protests, building developments, murders, rapes, robberies and court cases. By the end of her first year she was called into the owner's office. Margaret Jones was reading the news when Anna walked in.

"Ms. Jones, did you need me?"

"Ah, Anna. I just realized you are here one year and I haven't evaluated you as yet. Are you satisfied with your position?"

"Most of the assignments are fair, except I spend a great deal of time writing obits instead of me being out there reporting."

"Well that will change. I'm making you our feature writer. I want you to do feature stories about politicians, musicians, sport figures, community heroes and community goats. In other words, you are going to have your own special by-line as our feature writer. What do you think?"

"I'm grateful that you have the confidence in me. I won't let you down!"

"Oh, I'm giving you a three-thousand dollar raise. I thought you wouldn't stick it out so I really low balled you. Sorry, that's business."

"Ms. Jones, I'll make you proud of me!"

Anna's second year was dedicated to good reporting and good writing. She was able to enhance her income by writing feature stories to trade magazines. The research was all on line as well as conducting phone interviews. Anna was able to get six feature stories sold to the airline industry, motorcycle enthusiasts, foodie magazines, auto dealership newsletter and she broke into the big leagues with a feature article in Money Magazine.

During her research on the District Attorney of the Bronx she met his assistant. Tom Pride. He was tall and carried himself as an athlete. The fact was that he played quarterback for Yale. They seemed to hit it off quite well and Tom asked Anna out for a date.

"Tom, I don't have much time these days to go jumping around to see plays or even see a movie although I do enjoy a decent meal."

"Anna, that's what I like about you. No bull, just tell it the way it is."

He viewed a beautiful woman with jet black hair and coal black eyes that would mesmerize a fierce lion. She had curves on top of curves, yet hid her femininity with bulky sweaters, puffy blouses, sweater sets and soft, non-clinging dresses.

They ate dinner in a small restaurant in Greenwich Village. The food was superlative and Anna had three glasses of wine. She felt happy, loose and was quite talkative.

"Do you like working for the D.A.?"

"Anna, I don't want to talk about work. Let's talk about ourselves. What we like, what we hate, who are our heroes, what values we can agree to, where we would like to take vacations, and how we know that a relationship can really work?"

"Tom, we will have to see each other a number of times to cover what you just said. Right now I'm a bit tipsy. Let's get an Uber because I have an important interview set up for tomorrow. Is that okay?"

"How about getting together this Sunday. I have tickets for Yankee Stadium and the Red Sox are in town?"

"Okay, it's a date!"

After three months of dating Anna took Tom to bed in her small furnished apartment in the Bronx. They seemed to fit well together and they became an item. They were together for almost a year and it was comfortable. However there always seemed to be something missing in their relationship. Tom did not want to take it any further. Anna. felt she was ready.

"Tom, do you want to get an apartment together?"

"Hell no! I'm not ready for that at all. Can't we just have it this way?" "Do you see us eventually being together permanently?"

Tom rolled his eyes, held Anna's hands, "I just want it this way. No strings, no major worries, just this way."

Anna let go of his hands, "That's not what I invested almost a year together to hear. Sorry Tom, I'm letting you go!"

Instead of hearing a plea, Anna saw Tom get up, wave goodbye and leave. That was the last she saw of him. She felt used.

One month later Ms. Jones asked Anna to be the Editor of The Bronx Dispatch. "Anna, I'm setting up a digital copy of our newspaper and I can't do two jobs.

You have proven yourself in every manner. You will get an additional two-thousand

dollars since the work is tedious and time consuming. What do you think?

"I'm willing to give it a try and I'll let you know if it is okay. My dad will be pleased. He is one smart cookie and his eleventh commandment is: 'Be specific!' I use that commandment."

Margaret Jones roared with laughter. "I love your dad as well!"

Anna went to see her parents to tell them about the new position. She was elated and wanted to share her happiness. As was her modus operandi she brought pizza with her to share with her parents.

Jacki Mason lifted her glass of diet soda, "Here is to my very smart and talented daughter. Well done!"

Henry Mason wiped a small tear from his eyes, "You graduated with honors at age twenty, you spent about a year overseas, you got your first job at twenty-two, and now at twenty-four you have been made an editor. Your brother's have enjoyed success and I guess you follow in their footsteps. I am so very proud of you!"

"Mom and Dad, I feel so happy/ The only problem is that I can't seem to get a man to really commit to me. I thought Tom was the one, but he failed me."

Her mother took her hand, "Sweetheart, you will have to kiss a lot of frogs to have your prince emerge."

Anna started to laugh as she wiped away a tear, "I don't like frogs!"

They all started to laugh. The evening with her parents was therapeutic. It made her feel happy that she was able to share with them.

"I love you so much, but I have work tomorrow. I'll call you later in the week. They hugged and kissed goodbye.

It was not a simple job. The tasks were multiple from editing articles, giving assignments to the staff, working on design, layout and handling some advertising copy. She was happy that her experience at the university, editing a newspaper, gave her a full understanding of the position.

Anna was always one step ahead in her planning and thinking. Although she was young the experienced staff respected her judgment and there was hardly any in-fighting. During the year she became a superior editor and felt that editing would be a wonderful career for herself.

Ten months later Margaret Jones called a meeting of all staff members. She got on a small step stool so the staff could see her. "Ladies and gentlemen, I have sold my business to a large private combine. It consists of some bankers, some investors and a new team to oversee the newspaper. This will take place in two weeks from now. Any questions?"

A reporter with fifteen years on the staff nervously queried, "Do we keep our jobs?"

"I don't know. Why don't you wait and see what happens? I'm sure they will want to evaluate everything."

Anna was stunned. She waited until all the staff returned to their positions and then walked into Margaret's office.

"In your experience Ms. Jones, will they keep the editor on?"

"I'll be very honest with you. I think they will bring in their own leaders."

Anna felt betrayed yet outwardly calm. She looked at her boss, "Thank you for the experience, you have my two week notice as of today!"

Anna thought, *I'll get an editing job somewhere!"*

Chapter Six

Jason's flight from JFK to Dulles International Airport took one-hour and twenty- five minutes. He hardly had enough time to drink his diet soda. He rented a car to get to his interview at the Office of Naval Intelligence which is located in the National Maritime Intelligence Center (NMIC). It is a restricted federal installation, located at the Suitland Federal Center in Maryland. The center is located about ten miles from Washington DC.

He wore his summer white uniform which was a bit creased from his journey, yet he felt calm and looked forward to the interview. A young woman escorted him to a security desk where he had to produce his military identification. A picture was taken of him and almost magically a stick-on paper pass with his information was given to him.

"Please wear this pass throughout the day. When you are finished make sure to give the pass back to the security officer right here. We are very security conscious and run a tight ship."

"Are you Navy?"

"No, I'm civil service with a high security clearance." "Okay, what next?"

She did not say anything but ushered him into a large office that had two officers and a civilian. Jason snapped to attention and one of the officers smiled.

"Sit down Ensign Darvish. I'm Captain James Duncan and I run the operational unit in this facility. May I introduce Commander Felicia Cummings, who would be your boss if you are successful in this interview.

That fine looking civilian is Dr. Peter Wong who helps us in our evaluations. Any questions before we start."

"Yes sir. Why was I selected to get this interview?"

Commander Cummings looked at Jason in an unrelenting stare, "I ran the criteria I needed for my office through our computers and your name popped up. We checked you out with your ROTC trainers, your summer cruise officers and a preliminary FBI check. You seemed okay so you are here. Do you know what we do?"

"No ma'am. Only what I have read in novels." All of the interview team started to laugh.

Captain Cummings stood up and nodded his head, "I really like your honesty Ensign. Here is our mission. We collect, analyze and produce all important naval and maritime information to make sure that the United States of America will hold an advantage over possible adversaries. Tactical decision are presented to the Department of Defense and the Navy in terms of planned operations We are key to the strategic combat missions overseas as well as other activities that may be considered part of our national defense."

Jason snapped, "Got it sir!"

Commander Cummings stood up and pointed her finger at Jason, "If you work for us you will have tons of reading material to know who we are. We employ over three- thousand military and civilian personnel. They work for us all over the world. Further we use scientists, engineers, analysts, and computer specialists. At times we will even utilize Naval Reservists is necessary. We have four centers of excellence and you will learn more about them if you are successful in this interview."

Jason queried, "What Center do you work in and will I work for you?" "We call it the Kennedy Irregular Warfare Center. Are you interested?" "I certainly am interested!"

Dr. Wong grinned, "David do you think you are patriotic?'

"Yes sir. If it wasn't for this country my parents would have been stuck in Iraq— and I would not have gotten an ROTC scholarship to go to school."

"No, I mean patriotism in the purest sense. Do you understand?"

'Sir, I understand the psycholinguistics element of your question. I am willing to give my life for my country although I would reject any order that would be immoral in terms of my values."

Dr. Wong put his hand on his chin, "Now let me see if I get this right. If we ordered you to assassinate a woman would you do it?"

"Did this woman cause death to any citizen of the United States?" "Let us assume she did."

"Then I have the duty to protect citizens of our country as well as our military and I certainly would go after her."

"Would you kill her without knowing the situation?"

"No sir, not at all. If it was combat then it is a different situation."

Captain Duncan interrupted Dr. Wong, "Psycholinguistics is beyond me. Ensign Darvich, what languages are you proficient in?"

"Sir, I am proficient in Farsi, Dari, Chinese and French— all psycholinguistics is the study of the link between the brain & language."

"Okay, what the hell is Dari?"

"Dari is a language spoken in Afghanistan by some seven and a half million people. It is also known as Afghan Persian, Eastern Persian and East Farsi"

Commander Cummings quickly asked, "Do you have any girlfriends or attachments that would hinder you from working many, many hours a day?"

"Unfortunately, no I do not."

All of the people in the room started to laugh.

Dr. Wong stood up and approached Jason, "Do you consider yourself a scholar? After all you graduated with high honors, you are proficient in four foreign languages, you scored top grades on all of your summer cruises, and you usually use three and four syllable words."

Jason studied Dr. Wong for a moment, "Kindergarten is a four syllable word."

All of the interview team as well as Jason started to laugh loudly. The ice was certainly broken.

"Ensign Darvish, welcome to the team!" Captain Duncan verbalized.

"Ensign Darvish, I'm going to work your tail off. You are going to be assigned as a language expert and possible planner," said Commander Cummings.

Dr. Wong put his hand on Jason's shoulder, "I have a daughter who I want you to marry."

There was even more laughter after that statement.

Commander Cummings smiled, "You are to report back to this office in one week. The FBI has to finish their report. Then it will take a few days for us to process you. Good luck Ensign."

Jason stood up and shook Commander Cumming's hand as well as Dr. Wong and Captain Duncan's. He was very pleased and thought, *I can be of value here!*

When Jason left Dr. Wong told the group, "We have a winner here. Use him wisely.

The Handbook of the Office of Naval Intelligence was given to Jason as he signed out of the facility. It was thick and divided into sections. On his plane trip back to his home he read the section on new military members. It gave specific instructions in terms of communication with family members, friends and strangers.

His mother and father greeted him warmly with hugs and kisses. They thought that he would be leaving immediately to some foreign land.

"Mom and Dad I will be working in the Office of Naval Intelligence as a language specialist and planner. The work is very serious and at times top secret. It is important that not too many people know where I work. May I suggest you tell every person who asks that I am a language expert working for the Navy in Washington DC. If they ask where you could say any facility where he is sent."

Mrs. Darvich held Jason's hand, "Will they send you overseas?"

"I doubt it. At least for the first six months I'm sort of on probation. They will consider me a real rookie and will carefully train me."

"Where is the facility? Where do you work?" Mr. Darvish queried.

"It's a large complex in Maryland about ten miles from Washington DC." "Will they let you come home on occasion?"

Jason kissed his mom's cheek. "Of course. I get thirty days of annual leave a year.

I'll have to earn it since I am brand new."

At that moment Melody came into the room. She had a young man beside her. "Mom and Dad, John and I are engaged."

The family surrounded the young couple and wished them well. John removed himself from the group hug. "Melody wants to get married in six months. I'm anxious as well. Is that okay with you?"

Mrs. Darvish approached John, "How are you going to support my daughter?" "My father wants me to join him as a partner in his automobile business. I'm his top salesperson right now and I earn in the low hundred-thousands."

Mr. Darvish hugged Melody, "What about school?"

"John wants me to finish my degree. It's in early childhood education and I just got a job, working part time at a nursery school."

Jason was elated, "Melody and John—I am so pleased with both of your plans. If I can help you in anyway let me know."

John looked at Jason and saw a young man with straight black hair and hazel eyes whose posture was perfect. "Yeah Jason, when Melody and I start a family I want our kids to get the color of your eyes!"

That caused an hilarious uproar from the whole family. Jason quickly answered "Only God can decide that!".

The rest of the week was dedicated to Jason clearing out his room by donating a great deal to Catholic Charities at St. Vincent DePaul in New Hyde Park, Long Island. He wanted to make sure that his parents would not be stuck with that chore. Then he decided to talk to his parents about finances.

"Mom and Dad, I'm a single man with not too many commitments. My salary as an officer will be close to four-thousand dollars a month. I am going to send you one-thousand a month for you to do as you wish. As I improve with rank you will get more. That's the least I can do for you!"

His parents remained silent and finally his mom said, "Thank you son. Melody's marriage will be a financial burden, but now this will help us greatly."

Jason's Dad had tears running down his eyes. He nodded to Jason who nodded back. No words had to be said. There was respect, love and admiration between father and son.

The rest of the week whizzed by as Jason said goodbye to some of his friends.

When questioned he remained guarded. Another highlight was his visit to his old guidance counselor Dr. Greenburg. Jason decided to wear his uniform.

"You look good Jason. I guess the military regime works for you."

"I just wanted to thank you again for your advice. This career that I am embarking on seems to fit me well. I have a great posting in Washington DC as a language specialist."

"It seems to me you have a little more on your plate than that. The FBI visited me last week to get my impressions of you as a young man."

"Oh that. It's just standard procedure."

"Standard procedure my foot!"

"That's all I can say Dr. Greenburg—you know the way it is?"

Dr. Greenburg went into his file drawer and pulled out a large envelope. He withdrew a certificate and showed it to Jason. It read, *Army Security Agency. Meritorious Award to Major Nathan Greenburg for his heroic duty in Vietnam.*

"Wow. That's something."

"No Jason, it was survival. Keep your mind sharp and make sure your six is covered. Got it."

"Thank you, sir."

Later in the day Jason looked up "Army Security Agency." It basically was an intelligence gathering and communications group that was a holdover from the late 1940's. It morphed into the National Security Agency that is operational today. Jason was impressed.

Chapter Seven

Jason was early. He arrived at 0700 hours or as civilians would say, seven in the morning. After showing his identification to the guard on duty he was given directions to the cafeteria. It was housed on the lower level of the building. When he arrived he smelled the coffee, looked around and noticed the cafeteria was relatively small. It reminded him of the hospital cafeteria in Roslyn, Long Island. St. Francis was a renowned heart hospital as well as serving the north shore community.

He ate his toasted bagel with cream cheese at a table near the coffee station.

About fifteen minutes later he saw Commander Cummings. She walked over to his table and sat down.

"The coffee is the best I've had in this Navy!" Commander Cummings said as she placed her tray on the floor. "The eggs are so, so—but what the hell—the price is right."

Jason looked at her and saw a woman about forty years old with strong features.

Her nose was pronounced and her hands were large. On her left hand she wore a marriage band. She had nicely groomed short brown hair and piercing brown eyes.

"Do you come here every day for breakfast?"

"Almost always. The prices are so low since the Navy doesn't have to make a profit. At times I work at my desk during lunch. When I make lunch for my daughter I make lunch for myself. It's easy that way."

"How old is she?"

"She's eleven going on one-hundred." They both started to laugh.

Commander Cummings finished her meal, "I'll see you topside in fifteen minutes."

"Yes Ma'am."

It took a full day for the personnel department to do their thing. There was a one hour video of the ONI mission; a walk around orientation through the massive complex; paperwork in terms of his current status; pictures of him naked and details of any scars or birthmarks; eye scans; new fingerprints, DNA samples; and the signing of three different security forms. Jason was told he would be advised when he got "top secret" clearance.

A Chief Petty Officer who controlled most of the day looked at Jason, "Any questions?" "Will I be able to get housing at Bachelor Officer Quarters?"

'Let me make a call for you, Sir."

Fifteen minutes later the Chief came back. "They are full and will be full for the next few months. I suggest you go to a motel tonight and start looking around for an apartment. Don't forget to tell personnel since you will get extra pay if you live off base."

It was past nine pm before Jason sank into a bed at a nearby moderate motel. He was tired, forgot dinner and really had no appetite anyhow. The paperwork was tedious and all the tests were onerous. He set the alarm on his phone for six am and as a good measure called the desk for a wakeup call. Within ten minutes he fell asleep.

The second day Commander Felicia Cummings told him he had been placed in Section One. The overall assignment of his section was to utilize standard intelligence protocols to gather information. The most important was that it is most often utilized by UNSC forces. UNSC is a cutting- edge combat group called Spartans who were similar to the SEALS. Jason would be part of a team that provided information gathering, codebreaking through, language deciphering and at times planning for military espionage. That includes spying, infiltration, eavesdropping, surveillance, reconnaissance, intelligence, undercover work, black operations, known as black ops. He was introduced to Lieutenant Commander Eric Long, who would be his supervisor.

Lieutenant Commander Eric Long was built like a fullback. Later Jason found out that he was a fullback at Michigan State. He was a no-nonsense boss.

Jason's boss took one look at him and said, "You may be bright, your scores on top of the heap, but you start at ground zero with me. Everything I say will be a learning experience to you. I hope you have a good memory because I really don't want to repeat myself. As far as I am concerned you are a Plebe, a rookie, a newbie—got it!"

"Aye, aye Sir."

Jason went back to the Personnel Office to see if there was any room at Bachelor Officer Quarters. The petty officer there chuckled. "It will be months before you get anything. Here is an information sheet that covers most of the apartment houses, furnished rooms, and houses with rooms that you may use. Good luck!"

"What about my housing allowance and food and drink?"

"Here—fill out these forms. Let me see. You're an Ensign. You better figure that you will get a combined total of about fifteen hundred a month. It's not much, but it's a start."

It took him a week to look for and find a place that would be in his price range. He found a small furnished studio apartment five miles away in a 1970's style garden apartment complex. Not too fancy, but clean, within budget and efficient. The owner was on assignment overseas and would be back in eighteen months. There was a nice sized bedroom with a queen bed and dresser; a work kitchen; a dinette plus a small family room. Luckily there was a large color television set mounted on the wall in the family room. Looking around he felt that it would be more than adequate.

Jason bought a small Japanese used car and within a week he settled in and looked around the area. He was pleased with the shopping and all the support services in and around his place. It would take him about fifteen minutes to drive to work and that was a lucky break since many of the employees at ONI travelled over an hour from their homes.

Jason was informed that he would spend the next six months with different mentors who had expertise in different areas of intelligence work. He was to learn and apply the skills taught. At the end of the six months he would be sent on at least one covert mission to make sure that when he planned missions he would realize the mortal danger he was placing the SEALs or a Spartan Group.

Jason was ordered to return to Quantico for additional training in hand to hand combat and weaponry skills. The young ensign became very proficient in killer Judo, knife fighting and guns. His Marine instructor said, "You may be a NERD, but I'll go into combat with you any time"

Chapter Eight

Anna had saved some money in her years at the Bronx Dispatch. She thought, *I have enough to last me three months, if I stretch it, maybe four months.*

Her first move was to go to a headhunter in New York City. She had prepared an extensive resume with her magazine credits and sample work from the newspaper. Anna was confident that she would be able to get a position as an editor.

Lifting up her glasses, Maureen Gallagher looked at Anna. "Hon, you are too young to be an editor anywhere in New York City. I might be able to get you a job in south Jersey or Maine, but a New York City editor—you've got to be kidding!"

Anna spat out her words, "I'm tough enough. I bossed men twice my age and they listened to me!"

"Yeah kiddo. They knew if they didn't your boss would throw them out on their ass. Look kid—you were playing in the minor leagues. Sorry, can't do anything for you right now."

Anna tried another headhunter with the same results. She took some interviews for assistant editors in some local magazines, but the pay was too low. Anna was frustrated. Two months of trying with absolutely no results. She was tired and depressed.

One day her father called. "How is it going?" "Lousy—nothing there!"

"Why don't you go up to Columbia University's Placement Bureau?" "I thought it was for mainly teachers."

"No, they may have something. It's worth a try." "Okay Dad, I'll try."

After filling out the proper paperwork Anna was interviewed by a graduate assistant who knew less about editing and more about dog walking. However, he gave her a dozen sheets of paper for open jobs. Anna went to a cubicle on the side of the office and reviewed the job opportunities. The first seven were not even close to what she was looking for in terms of editorial work. Number eight was a winner. The United Nations needed two editors. She had the qualifications and decided to apply.

The initial job process was done on line. There were numerous questions including references, education, background, language fluency. When it came to language Anna decided to check fluent in French. She was quite comfortable in France and was told her accent was more than acceptable by French friends.

One month later Anna received a call from the Human Resource Department to come in and take a test. They told her it would be at least a four-hour examination. True to their word it was that and more. By the time her paper work was filled out Anna was at the United Nations for six hours. The proctor told her that she would be notified within two weeks if she was to move up for an oral interview.

A week later Anna received another call. She was to report to another office to be evaluated by a team of people. The interview was long and tedious. Midway through the interview she was asked a question in French. Anna answered fluently in French and the conversation took place for fifteen minutes. She was told she would be contacted within a week for the next step.

Five days later Anna came into a different area of the United Nations. It was housed at the General Assembly Building located in the Turtle Bay neighborhood of Manhattan. The grounds stretched from First Avenue on the west, East 42nd Street on the south, East 48th Street on the north and the East River to the east. It consisted of some eighteen acres of land. It was huge!

Anna was escorted by a guard to a section of the United Nations that had signs all over that read, *Restricted to Authorized Personnel Only.*

She was introduced to a small woman named Iris LaBelle. Ms. LaBelle was dressed in a smart black suit with a fancy white blouse and wearing very high heels.

"Ms. Mason, this test will be based on your competency. I will give you two United Nations texts. Text one is the format we like to use as we edit all the work from our delegates. Text two is an unauthorized, yet legitimate speech given by an associate. You are to study text one for ten minutes and place it in the shredder. You are then to redo the speech, making sure to maintain the context, but putting it into our United Nations format. Are you familiar with Word?"

"Yes. I used it at work as my tool." "Are my instructions clear?

"Very clear Ms. LaBelle."

The woman took a look at her watch and said, "Go."

What helped Anna was her writing for different magazines. Every magazine wanted their feature stories written in a certain format. Anna was successful in her writing because she complied with the format requested. This held true to the format of the United Nations. In fact the format was simple once you followed the model. Anna's good memory helped her as she quickly rewrote the speech. She really did not care about the context, it was how the context was presented. It seemed simple to her. Forty minutes later she looked up and told Ms. LaBelle, "I'm finished."

"We will get back to you either way within a week Ms. Mason. Good luck."

The two women shook hands and Anna went home. She called her father and told him about the experience.

"Anna, it doesn't sound too creative. Perhaps it's not for you."

"Dad, it pays over seventy-five thousand a year. I'll take it for a short time if offered. Who knows, I may enjoy the international aspect of it!"

Six days later Anna received a certified letter from the United Nations Human Resource Department. It indicated that they were prepared to offer her a position as "Editor – Full Time" at the General Assembly with a starting salary of seventy-eight thousand dollars a year plus a host full of perks. If she was interested she was to report to the HR Office within three days of receipt of the certified letter. Anna returned it in one day. She was thrilled!

While filling out her paper work Anna thought, *I hope this is the start of something good in my career!*

Anna was helped by a supervisor who showed her what she would be doing by mentoring her. At times Anna would sit alongside Thomas as he edited speeches by delegates or edited reports from United Nation Commissions. He was not afraid to pick up the phone and call a translator or the person who originated the speech or the report. The most important thing was to get it right and in the proper format. He sat in his office with two large computer screens. On one was the original copy and on the other the edited copy. Anna was a quick study and within two weeks she was doing editing on her own. At times she would call Thomas with a question.

"Thomas, I have a translated article written by a Chinese person who is a member of UNICF. In it the translator wrote that UNICEF only works for third world countries. I personally know that is not true. What do I do?"

There was a short pause, "Call up the translator and make sure that he meant what he wrote. If he did, then ask him to call the originator of the copy to make sure that it is what they meant to say. Prudence is important in our work and accuracy is as important."

The issue was settled in three days as the translator called Anna.

"You were spot on! Our writer made a serious mistake and he would have been truly embarrassed. He asked for your name so he could send your supervisor a letter of commendation. Thank you, Anna."

At times the reverse happens where the document is reviewed by an editor before it is translated. Accuracy, appropriateness for the readers, consistency and intelligibility were the hallmarks of anything written.

Anna found herself correcting factual material, spelling, grammar, and format all the time. It was a tedious yet rewarding job. Over ninety percent of all drafted documents were written in English. Anna had an advantage over some foreign-born editors.

When Anna started working she was told to use "The United Nations Editorial Manual" which was online. It gave guidance in terms of policies and practices and set standards which remained consistent.

Thomas had told her in no uncertain terms, "Become political sensitive when you suggest anything to change a text. The important thing is there are committees that will discuss a resolution. You don't have to make that decision."

Anna seemed to be always on a timeline. When she checked with the other editors they felt the same way. The volume of work presented for review was enormous and the work seemed to be endless. Yet Anna felt rewarded when a particular piece was given the okay to be published.

Anna lived in Flushing, in the Borough of Queens New York. She rented a downstairs one-bedroom apartment from an Asian couple. Mr. and Mrs. Sun requested the rent be paid in cash. Anna agreed and the couple made the rent reasonable because of this. She enjoyed furnishing her apartment by going to estate sales and flea markets. It took her a month or so to get it right, but she was pleased with her decorating and felt very comfortable in her place.

The good news was transportation. There was a subway station only five minutes away on Main Street. She would take the train to Grand Central at 42nd Street and walk for about ten minutes to get to work. Most of the time it took about thirty to forty minutes for the train and the good news was that the trains ran every five to ten minutes. Anna bought an Unlimited Ride MetroCard for her transportation. The cost was $121 per month instead of the $165 she would have had to pay without it. It was a good deal.

After a few months of work Anna informed her parents that she was satisfied.

"Mom and Dad, I really like my work. I see history happening in front of my eyes. It is exciting. I work with a group of dedicated people from all countries and I am excited to go to work every day. It looks like I have found something that makes me happy!"

She thought, *If only I can find a man to make me happy!*

Chapter Nine

Captain James Duncan had his office strategically placed in the center of his team's complex. He would have a daily briefing with Commander Felecia Cummings who in turn would make sure to pass the word to Lieutenant Commander Eric Long. Ensign Jason Darvish on occasion would get some information given to him by Lieutenant Commander Long, but most of the time it was filtered through the lower Lieutenants, to the Lieutenants Junior Grade and then to the bottom of the ladder, meaning the Ensigns.

It didn't bother Jason at all. The manner of the military was the chain of command and he learned that very early in Navy ROTC. So, when he was told to report to Captain Duncan's

office in one hour he knew something was up. He thought, *Well, I'm here six months—perhaps they want to get rid of me or maybe give me another assignment.*

Captain Duncan motioned Jason to sit down. He opened a file and read it for about thirty seconds, closed it and stood up. Jason immediately stood up as a courtesy to his superior.

"At ease sailor. Take a seat. I'm just thinking about something." "Aye, aye Sir."

"Jason, you have shown incredible skill working here. Your supervisor is quite pleased with your work as well as all the men and women who have worked with you. It has been six months and we would like you to be a permanent part of our team. How do you feel about that?"

There was no hesitation Jason's part. "I feel as if I can contribute and use my talents to help our country. I'm all in Sir!"

"Okay. Speak to the Chief about getting you special gear. Son, you are going to war.

There is a SEAL team that needs a translator and you are the man. Good luck!" Captain Duncan shook Jason's hand and that was the end of it.

On the C-17 Globemaster returning from the mission Jason stopped thinking about Great Neck, Long island and started thinking about the three men he had killed less than two hours ago. *I can't believe it. I'm not a warrior, I'm a translator—hell I'm a desk jockey. What am I doing here—what the hell— I can't believe I did it.*

Chief Dugan looked at Jason and went over to him. He knew the look of panic and he saw it in Jason's eyes.

"Sir, I have a spare chocolate bar. Are you interested in it?"

That broke the ice. Jason looked kindly at the man whose life he had saved. "Chief, does it ever go away? I mean killing your enemy."

"No sir, it never goes away, but it gets better. It's the job we chose to do for our country and we have to deal with it. I tell myself that on every mission. I understand!"

"Thanks Chief."

"Sir, I owe you one. You saved my ass out there today. There was no hesitation. You acted bravely without any concern of your safety to save me"

"Would you have done it for me?"

'Hell yes!"

"Well Chief, case closed."

They both started to laugh. Jason took a bite out of the chocolate bar and it tasted like home. He was finally able to sleep on the noisy plane.

The SEALS gave him their thumbs up and when they came off the plane. They gathered around Jason and yelled "Hooyah" which made him feel part of the group.

During the individual debriefing the Chief reported to the Intelligence Officer in Charge of the action Jason took in the mission. The Officer in Charge recommended that Jason receive the Bronze Star for his heroic actions. It would take a month for it to go through the Chief of Naval Operations.

Jason was debriefed by an Intelligence Officer in another room at Andrews Airforce Base in Maryland. He gave his version of the story which was basically the part about translation and the fire fight. He did not mention his role in killing three Taliban fighters. Jason was told to go to a specific barrack to clean up and then go to the base cafeteria to get some chow. He found clean clothing waiting for him. After his shower he felt relieved that it was over. He thought, *How could these men go on these missions over and over again. They are certainly brave.*

Two hours later Jason was finishing his second cup of coffee when a hand touched his shoulder. It was Dr. Wong, the ONI psychologist.

"May I join you Jason?"

"Hell yes. I was looking for the team, but they seemed to disappear."

Dr. Wong quickly responded, "After their debriefing they took a helicopter to their station in Norfolk. They were anxious to see their families."

"Oh, I see."

"When was the last time you saw your family?" "Oh, we facetime a lot."

'No, I mean when did you last see your family in person?" "I guess it's about been six months."

"Well, that means you have earned fifteen days of leave. Why don't you take some days and visit your family?'

"Maybe."

The cafeteria was just about empty and Dr. Wong whispered to Jason. "How do you feel about killing those men on your mission?"

Jason looked up at him and whispered, "Lousy, but it was necessary. I'll get over it."

Dr. Wong said, "If you have any dreams, shakes, regrets or shitty feeling let me know, it could be post- traumatic- stress- disorder. PTSD works in strange ways. You are to take tomorrow off and return to ONI the next day. We have a lot of work to do!"

"I'll do that."

Dr. Wong shook Jason's hand and thought, *This man is made of the right stuff. He will make it with no problems!*

When Jason came back to work he requested leave for seven days. Lieutenant Commander Long denied the request.

"Sorry Jason, we're getting a new computer program and all of us have been assigned to go to class to learn the system. It will take about three weeks. As soon as the classes are over I'll approve your leave."

"Aye, aye Sir." Jason said in a disappointed voice.

During the three weeks that followed Dr. Wong asked Jason to come and visit him. They had a few sessions and Jason felt pretty good about talking with the doctor. It really wasn't more than talking about his feelings and making plans for the future.

"Jason, you don't have to see me anymore, that is professionally. I still like you and we can share a lunch or coffee together."

"Sounds great to me."

Commander Cummings called Jason into her office. Sitting alongside her was his boss and four other officers from his unit.

She opened a drawer in her desk and gave Jason two boxes.

"Jason, I want to congratulate you on receiving these two awards. The first is the Global War on Terrorism Medal and the second is the Afghanistan Campaign Medal. The Chief of Naval Operations has waived the sixty-day waiting period because you were in combat. Yes, we have read the sanitized After Action Combat Report. The SEALS want you to join their unit as one of them. In fact, one Chief said, 'any time, any day, any hour, he is one of us!'—that tells us a great deal."

The men and women applauded and Jason was embarrassed. He looked at all of his co- workers, "Thank you so much. I just sort of fell into it. What the hell did I know?"

They all started to laugh.

The following week Jason applied for a seven-day leave. It was approved and he was to go home the following Saturday. He called his parents and told them that he would be home next week. They were elated. Then he got a call from Lieutenant Commander Long.

"Jason, your leave has to start on Monday. You have to attend a meeting with the Admiral on Sunday. We all have to wear our dress uniforms."

"What is this all about?"

"I have no idea, but when the Admiral says do it—we just say aye, aye sir!" Jason called his parents who did not seem that concerned. His mom said, "Another few days will be okay son."

On Sunday the crowd gathered in the large Lecture Hall at ONI. Sitting in the front row was Jason's mother, father, sister and her fiancé, as well as Chief Dugan, his wife and two children. On the platform were the Admiral, his aide, Captain Duncan and Commander Cummings.

As Jason entered the hall all Naval personnel stood up and started to applaud. The Admiral's aide took Jason's arm and led him to a chair on the platform. Jason looked down at his parents who were beaming.

Capitan Duncan approached the microphone. "Ladies and gentlemen, we are here to honor Ensign Jason Darvich for his heroic actions in an operation that occurred last month. The dates and times are confidential, but the country and the action took place in Afghanistan. May I present Admiral Johnson, the Commander-in-Chief of the Office of Naval Intelligence.

A silver grey haired man speaking in a gentle voice greeted everybody and finally said, "Ensign Darvish, front and center!"

He gave his aide a folder and the aide began to read.

"The Chief of Naval Operations is pleased to recommend the award of the Bronze Star with a "V" for valor to Ensign Jason Darvish for his heroic actions on a mission of great importance to the United States of America. During the action Ensign Darvich provided necessary technical skills to help the mission and when fired upon he dispatched the enemy as he was in the line of fire himself. Near the completion of the mission Ensign Darvich saved the life of one of his team by again facing the enemy head on and dispatching him as he helped his fallen comrade to safety. Because of his actions the mission was a great success, helping the cause of freedom."

The Admiral placed the medal around Jason's neck and said, "Well done sailor, well done!"

Jason responded, "Thank you sir, but it really was team effort."

"Son, the team wanted to let you know how much they appreciated your efforts."

There was a reception in the foyer after the ceremony. Jason's parents were very proud as many people congratulated them. They finally were able to hug and kiss Jason.

"Mom and Dad, it was expensive to come down here."

"No son—the Admiral sent tickets to us. He said he had a special fund for heroes." Jason's mom hugged him, "Oh my God, I thought you were a language specialist?" "I am Mom, but sometimes you just have to do the right thing."

Master Chief Dugan and his family approached Jason. Both men hugged in front of everyone. Mrs. Dugan kissed Jason and said, "Thank you for saving my husband's life. He told me what you did over there. Thank you."

The rest of the day was a blur, except when Jason saw Dr. Wong.

"Mom and Dad, may I introduce Dr. Wong. He keeps everybody here sane. I needed him and he came through for me."

Dr. Wong was gracious, "Your son is a special man and I want to thank you for raising him with such fine values. I call him a friend."

Jason flew back home with his parents. He had four ribbons on his chest within six months of active service. Many people on the plane looked at him and some said "Thank you for your service." He felt honored and humble.

The decorated ensign enjoyed a week's leave. There was a great deal of family stories to catch up with, as well as planning for Melody's wedding. He went back to Fordham to visit with some of his professor's and saw a few plays on Broadway. Jason had no regrets going back to work.

On the plane back to his Washington DC he thought, *I've had enough action. I really want to concentrate on my work—planning and organizing is plenty to do.*

Chapter 10

Anna and her best friend Susan Han were sunning themselves on the sundeck of a huge Carnival Cruise ship. They decided that it would be great to take a vacation in February since New York City was just about snowed in.

The women knew each other for two years since both of them worked at the United Nations. Susan's department was in public relations. She wrote short, yet comprehensive copy for the many brochures, pamphlets, and press releases issued by the General Assembly of the United Nations.

"I wish I had some guy come over and offer to put suntan lotion on me," whispered Susan to Anna.

"God Susan, you are such a whore!"

Both women started to laugh until it became a roar.

Susan Han was Eurasian. Her father was a career diplomat in the service of the Queen of England and her mother was a Professor at Cambridge. Her mother had a PhD in International Relations and a Masters Degree in Criminal Justice. The diplomat and the teacher got together at a seminar and were married within three months.

She was born a year later and one year after that her parents divorced. Since Dr. Han had to make a living she became a consultant to Scotland Yard and then became a mid-level administrator at Interpol. Dr. Han was invited to take a position as the Director of the Investigation Department at the United Nations.

Susan had made a name for herself in England as a teenager by writing articles for teenagers. She had a following and was paid well for her articles.

When her mother "crossed the pond" she followed and was hired to write copy for the General Assembly. Susan was beautiful. Her jet-black hair was long, flowing and silky. Susan's curves were in the right places and she attracted many looks from men. Her slight almond eyes were so hypnotic that if you looked at them too long you would be mesmerized.

Anna had met Susan in the cafeteria and they became buddies quickly. They both were the same age, single, educated and loved all of the cultural aspects of New York City. Both women made sure to watch out for each other and double dated frequently. They worked out a code if one of them was truly interested in a guy. The other woman would make sure to separate from the party in order to give more space to their friend. They were close.

Anna had become more sophisticated during the few years working in New York and dated a number of men. On rare occasions she would go all the way, but not too often. There was one man who had come close to making a commitment, but after six months backed out of the relationship.

Anna was frustrated and she and Susan tied one on over a long weekend. Anna in a drunken voice blurted out, "Why the fuck are men such wimps? They love to love, but not to commit. God, I don't think I'll ever get married!"

Susan hugged her friend, "You are twenty-six years old and beautiful. Give it time."

They fell asleep in Susan's apartment and woke up with hangovers that were immediately treated with aspirin and tomato juice. Both women had a bond that was strong. It was important to have this type of relationship in the big city and at work as well.

A few days later Anna received a phone call from her mother. "Anna, will you please come to dinner tomorrow night."

"Sorry mom, I have a date." "Break it. We need you." "What's wrong?"

"Your brothers are coming in as well." "What time Mom?"

"Get here at six!"

Anna started to think about possible scenarios that would cause her mother to call. It was obvious that it had something to do with her father. She started to think of problems, *He must be sick— yet looked okay last month when I visited.* She did not sleep well that night.

Anna arrived early. It was 5:30 pm and her mom was still cooking. She kissed her mom, went to the closet and put on an apron and started to help cook. Her mother looked at her, started to sob and Anna held her close. "We will work it out. I'm here for you Mom!"

"I better clean up before your brothers come. Oh Anna, he has prostate cancer and he will be operated on tomorrow. The PET scan showed some problems and his doctor described it as stage 3A."

Anna looked deeply into her mother's eyes, "Mom, they are doing some marvelous things for men. Let's find out more before we bury dad. Okay?"

"Anna, you are such a comfort. We have to see more of each other. What's happened to us?"

"Life has happened to us Mom—just living!"

The dinner was stressful. Her brothers put on a good show, telling funny stories and just fooling around. Anna tried to laugh, but it was really hard. Her dad was silent except for a toast as they started their meal. He looked at each person and said, "May we all have good health and good times!"

During dessert Dr. Mason stood up, "Kids, I have Stage 3A prostate cancer and I'm having a radical tomorrow. My doctor has told me it is treatable. We'll know more later."

Joel clinked his glass, "Loosen up gang, here are some of the latest statistics that I know. After all I'm a doctor." He took out his cell phone and after fifteen seconds he read, *According to the most recent data, when including all stages of prostate cancer: The 5-year relative survival rate is 99%.; The 10-year relative survival rate is 98%.; The 15-year relative survival rate is 96%.*

Mark went over and hugged his father, "Dad, if you get too frail I'll hire you to make pizza boxes for me. Let's see, in fifteen years you will be eighty-two."

That broke the tension. The rest of the evening was spent talking about vacations, ball games and family good times.

Anna promised that she would see her parents much more as well as both brothers verbalizing the same thing.

Her mom wiped the tears from her eyes, "I'll hold you to it."

Mark looked at everybody, "I'm staying here tonight and will be with mom at the hospital. Keep you cell phones on and I'll text you."

Anna said, 'I'm sleeping over and will be with you as well!"

Joel shook his head, "No good for me, I have patients to see tomorrow." Anna hugged him, "I'll keep you informed."

Dr. Mason's operation was a success and he was back teaching in three weeks. He started a regiment of chemotherapy that did not cause him to lose his hair or become debilitated. Anna visited one weekend and found her father in a lounge chair with his feet stretched out.

"Dad, how do you feel?"

"Not too bad. My question to you is—how are you doing?"

"I love my position. It is exciting although very stressful at times." "Let me rephrase that" her Dad countered. "How is your social life?"

"Not that great. I had a few guys who I really could relate to — yet nothing happened. I am dating one interesting man and I'll see how that works out."

"Perhaps your standards are too high?"

"Dad, I love you. Perhaps my standards are too low!"

They both started to laugh. It was one of those precious moments that was spontaneous and Anna knew that her dad loved her very much.

Anna's work was intense. The General Assembly of the United Nations produces volumes of written reports, resolutions, speeches, position papers, and many other items that have to have the correct format and structure. Editors are charged with putting the written document in its final form to be read by all one-hundred-ninety-two nations.

Anna thrived on dealing with solutions to editorial problems. She would talk to authors, diplomats, committee secretaries, and of course to the translation department to resolve issues. Her supervisor would bring sensitive issues to her and she loved the challenge. At times there were political issues that could not be resolved and her suggestions were not taken.

Anna realized that the General Assembly utilized a process called "concordance" to make sure the final product was within the agreement of the various countries involved. She dealt with linguists who were fluent in Spanish, Chinese, Arabic, Russian and French in order to make sure there were no mistakes. Anna thought, *Six official languages makes my head spin at times. Yet, I love the challenge.*

The next week Anna and her best friend Susan sat in the United Nations cafeteria talking about their next planned vacation. The decided they would fly to London and enjoy the sights, shows, music and sounds of England.

Anna blurted out, "Perhaps I can find an Earl or at least a Baron. I've decided to look for men in higher stations."

Susan giggled, "I lived in England as a teenager. I'd rather enjoy a conversation and then have sex with a miner from Wales. They're more interesting!"

Both woman laughed again.

Chapter Eleven

Jason was dedicated to his work. He enjoyed being a translator using his skills to decipher certain messages. The Office of Naval Intelligence at times had Jason work with various intelligence agencies. His keen knowledge of Darsi was unique among translators and because of this the CIA, NIA as well as the FBI requested his services.

After two years of active service Jason became a Lieutenant Junior Grade. The promotion helped him send a little more money home to his parents. He was too busy to spend any large sums on himself. Lieutenant Commander Long insisted that Jason take some leave time.

"Jason, I don't want you to burn out. You are very popular with all of our intelligence agencies. Time for you to take some leave."

"Thanks Eric, but I'm okay."

Jason and his boss Lieutenant Commander Long had become close over the two work years at ONI. When they talked in front of other staff members it was formal, but when they talked together it was on a first name basis.

"I don't want to give you an order—take some time off!" 'Okay, I will."

The Caribbean has some of the clearest water in the world. Jason was on his first solo scuba dive some fifteen feet under water. He was told by the Dive Master, Chelsea Bremmer that it was critical he go down no further. Some beautiful yellow and blue fish past him by as well as a thing that looked like a small squid. He was enjoying himself immensely. There was a tap on his shoulder and as he turned he saw Chelsea. She motioned with a thumbs-up and Jason started to ascend.

Jason wanted to do something completely different and he felt scuba diving would be completely different. He signed up for a two week package which included a bungalow, a full morning breakfast and scuba lessons. He was enjoying himself. As he looked at Chelsea he enjoyed himself even more. She was tall, muscular, well-built and young. Her eyes were shaped in a slight angular position and that made her absolutely beautiful. He thought, *I've been with her for three days and I am attracted to her. Wow!*

Chelsea's father, John Bremmer, owned the dive shop and gave scuba instructions to intermediate divers and advanced divers. He let his daughter handle the kids and neophytes as Jason. Yet, when he met Jason there was something about Jason that that he couldn't place. He resolved to take a look at Jason's application to investigate.

There were additional lessons on taking care of your equipment; training to utilize a buddy system; understanding safety procedures; understanding and using dive charts; and open water dives. Jason thrived on learning new material. He had taken two more dives before Chelsea called it a day. Jason was really into the mechanics of the diver and wanted more dives.

That evening Jason sat in a small restaurant near his bungalow. He loved conch chowder and the chef made it hot and spicy. The grouper was always good and Jason ordered tacos along with some ice cold beer. He saw Chelsea come through the door with her father. She was radiant in a sun dress that was multi- colored. Her chestnut hair glistened in the light of the restaurant and if someone saw her they would have thought her to be a movie star. Her dad looked neat with a short sleeved print shirt and a pair of clean jeans. Some couples at the bar greeted them warmly. They immediately had beer in their hands and started to chat.

Jason waved to them and motioned to them to come over. Chelsea pulled at her father's sleeve and they both walked over to Jason's table.

"Please join me for dinner. You have been so kind to me and I have enjoyed the course and your company so much."

Chelsea's smile was radiant, She sat down next to Jason as her father sat across from him. "Jason, you have qualified as a Beginner-Open Water Scuba Diver. Congratulations.

Tomorrow I'll give you your, Diving certification and C-card."

John Bremmer extended his hand, "Congratulations Lieutenant Darvish!" "How did you know I was Navy?"

"Jason, I called your work number and asked for you. The receptionist said, 'Lieutenant Darvish will be back in one week'. Kind of simple to find out information about you."

"I hope you don't think I was holding back. Sometimes I want to look like a civilian." "Son, the moment you walked in and introduced yourself I knew you were either military

or involved in some form of law enforcement. You carry yourself in a special manner."

Chelsea took Jason's hand, "You haven't made one move to flirt with me, or come on to me, or anything. My first thought was that you are gay, then I figured you just did not like me."

"Chelsea, I'm not gay. I don't have a girlfriend. I'm not committed to any woman. I'm quite solo. The fact is that I respected you so much as my teacher and I didn't want to screw up the situation. Got it!"

"Aye, aye," she squeezed his hand.

Jason went back to his bungalow and took a shower. It was late in the evening and he was ready for some sleep. Suddenly there was a steady knock on his door.

"Hi Chelsea, kind of late. What do you want?"

She came through the entrance, pushed his chest with her hand, "You have a choice. You can work on your scuba skills and try to qualify for an intermediate certificate or you can hook up with me for the next week. I'll show you the Bahamas the tourists never see— and I will be your constant companion, friend and lover. What do you want?"

Jason took her by her shoulders and kissed her. She kissed him back. They stumbled into his bedroom and made love into the early hours of the morning. It was something that Jason needed and obviously Chelsea wanted badly.

Late the next day John Bremmer gave Jason his C-Card. The Diving certification or C- card usually comes as a plastic wallet sized card. It is a universal document that recognizes and certifies the level of diving of the bearer of the card. Only recognized companies or agencies may issue the card. Jason received a log book with all of his dives already logged in.

He shook John's hand, "Thank you, John. It was a privilege to be a student at your shop." "Jason, I hope you come back here again. Chelsea has really taken a liking to you. She never mixes business with pleasure, so I assume you will treat her with respect and kindness?"

"No problem John, But, don't forget I'm out of here in six days.

The Out Islands of the Bahamas are untouched and barely populated. Jason was amazed to see the beautiful beaches, unique wildlife, and the natural tropical beauty of the area. Chelsea handled her thirty foot sailboat beautifully.

When Jason asked to take over she looked at him and said, "Hey sailor, do you have the right stuff to handle this boat? It took me a year to save up to buy this beauty."

Jason took over and tacked beautifully into a small cove. He remembered all his sailing skills when he and his friend, Gary sailed on the Long Island Sound. They anchored close to shore so they could swim to the beach.

Chelsea was a fully grown woman with many likes and not too many dislikes. She was a free spirit in her lovemaking and Jason discovered areas of eroticism that he never knew before.

The days seemed to merge into each other as they dove, fished, explored and sailed to very special islands that Chelsea knew. It was a magnificent vacation.

The last day of his vacation they returned to have dinner with John Bremmer. John was sitting at the bar when Chelsea and Jason walked in.

John said out loud, "Attention on deck. We have a hero approaching!" "Come on John, stop the joshing."

"No sir. I researched you and I know about your bravery. Jason, I was a full Commander in the Navy and I retired after twenty years."

He saluted and rushed over to hug Jason. "Jeez John, I'm embarrassed. Please!"

"Jason, you can come back here as my guest any time.!"

They had a great dinner. John Bremmer told Jason stories of his service in the Navy. It seemed that he was the Captain of a destroyer and had great experience in his service in Vietnam. There was a special bond that developed between the men.

Jason flew back to Washington the next day. *He thought, Lieutenant Commander Eric Long was so right. He needed the vacation.*

Chapter Twelve

Jason was working in his office when Commander Felecia Cummings walked into his office. He started to raise out of his chair, but his boss waived him down. She was carrying a small box. "J.G. Darvish you are out of uniform."

"Excuse me Ma'am?"

"Congratulations Jason. You are now a full Lieutenant and I have a gift for you."

She handed Jason the small box. "These are my pins when I made Lieutenant. I thought you would enjoy them!"

"Commander—"

She cut him off. "Call me Felecia. I really think it is okay unless, we are in a formal situation. You have certainly earned my respect. That's why I really feel good that you will wear my pins."

"Felicia, this is an honor. Thank you."

She came over to Jason and hugged him. "Let me tell you, I really feel close to you. You have made a huge difference in my command as well as being a really stand up man. Thank you for all you have done."

She smartly turned around and left the office. Jason opened the box and saw the pins. He knew that he had four years of service and that he was on target to become a Lieutenant. His rank now would be equal to an Army or Marine Captain. Jason looked at the pins again, he smiled and thought, *I've got to get to the tailor to change my uniforms.*

Jason was really tired. The fact of the matter was that he had put in fourteen straight hours planning a raid for SEALS that was paramount for national security. Then suddenly, before being able to go home, he had been lent out again to the CIA to translate some Darsi. It was written in some colloquial form. The CIA Officer in Charge stated that the translation had to be made as quickly as possible because lives were at stake. Jason worked until two in the morning to get the document translated. He finally was able to drive back to his apartment and fell asleep at four in the morning.

The next day was Saturday and Jason slept in until one in the afternoon. He had planned to do some shopping and later in the day experiment with some new recipes. Jason yawned and knew that he needed more sleep. He sat in a comfortable chair and fell asleep again. The weekend was a bust and Jason just wandered around listlessly for rest of the weekend. When he woke up on Monday morning his first thought was, *I like my job, but I'm tired of the constant pressure and responsibility. Maybe there is something better for me.*

Jason had made it a habit to go to the cafeteria almost every morning to have coffee and a donut. During that time, he usually saw and talked to Commander Cummings and Lieutenant Commander Long. Once in a while Dr. Wong would show up and share some jokes with Jason and they would share family stories. He really liked Dr. Wong. Today Dr. Wong came over to his table. "Jason, how are they hanging?"

"Slightly tired Dr. Wong. Actually— really tired. They've got me burning the midnight lantern!"

"Ah, that's the way it is in the service. We are in a shooting war over there!"

"Hell yes!" exclaimed Jason. He finished his coffee, looked at his watch, "Got to go Doc."

Dr. Wong reflected, *I wonder if he is getting too much pressure. I'll speak to Felecia.*

The rest of the week was hectic since Jason was the lead planner for a SEAL mission that was aborted last week. He had to redo all his research and get the information out to the proper channels by Friday. He put in twelve hour days to get it right. Jason knew that any planning for this mission was a matter of life or death to the heroic members of the SEAL team. Finally, Jason was able to go to sleep satisfied.

Jason received a phone call at three-thirty in the morning from the ONI. The duty officer said, "Lieutenant Darvish, you are directed and instructed to report to the Operations Center as soon as possible."

"It's 0330 now. How much time do I have?"

"Sir, you have forty-five minutes. I was told to tell you this involves national security."

When Jason reported to duty he was met by Captain James Duncan. He was dressed in civilian clothing and looked a bit disheveled and angry.

"Lieutenant Darvish. Here's the scoop. The lead officer for the special-ops mission you planned in Yemen has come down with food poisoning. And the next officer in command just broke his leg in a freak automobile accident at the base rushing to take over. There is no officer in charge to take charge of the mission."

"Will they scrub the mission?"

"Hell no young man! The Chief of Naval Operations demanded that the mission continue and not be scrubbed. Jason, you planned it, you organized it, you weaponized it, you know more about it than any person—and you are qualified to lead it! You fly out of here in one hour to meet your SEAL Team in Jian, Saudi Arabia. They will then fly you to your mission! Good luck in Yemen".

Jason was shocked, yet stoic. He was in the service and shit happens. Jason had observed situations like this before, yet he felt that perhaps it was an omen in terms of deciding on a Naval career. The mission was a screw up from the get-go. The Chief Petty officer resented Jason and just about spit in his face. The rest of the SEAL Team hardly acknowledged him. Jason called a "time out" on the C-130 Hercules Troop Carrier about two hours before landing.

Looking around he said, "If you think you are pissed off it's nothing like my feelings of being the odd man out. I designed this fucking mission and the CNO wants this done. So, lighten up, put on your big boy pants, and do your job. I promise you one thing, I have your backs and when we debrief I'll let you call the shots on how the mission went down. I'm your boss right now, that's the way it's going to be!"

They all nodded and the Chief said, "Okay, it's a deal. Let's do the job!"

Yemen was a hell hole. The civil war had killed more than ten-thousand people and displaced more than two and a half million people. The nation was involved in a calamitous cholera epidemic. According to the United Nations it was one of the poorest countries in the world. A large group of Al-Qaeda fighters remained in southern Yemen. That was where the team was headed. They were to take down the leader of the group and capture important intelligence.

Jason's team was sitting on seats as the Bell Boeing V-22 Osprey flew to its landing zone in southern Yemen. The Osprey is a unique aircraft. It was planned to do multiple missions since it had vertical takeoff and landing capabilities. Jason thought it was a sort of a long-range helicopter that could fly faster and hold more troops. It was a turboprop aircraft and noisy. The noise was diminished since all of the men had helmets with noise suppression headphones.

They landed right on their targeted point and the Chief, whose name was Carson led the group. Jason stayed with a SEAL called Harvey. Chief Carson made sure to give Petty Officer Harvey his instructions.

"Harvey, I don't want Lieutenant Darvish to get killed. Got it." "No problem Boss. He'll be treated like my old lady!"

The team advanced quietly covering one kilometer and entered a small village. There were one and two story houses along a narrow street where the suspected Al-Qaeda leader was supposed to be housed. Finally, Chief Carson gave the go ahead sign and three SEALS broke into a shabby two-story building. Jason heard some muffled shots and a piercing woman's scream. The rest of the team rushed in.

Jason observed two men, on the ground, dead, at the end of the second downstairs room. He moved upstairs and saw a woman bound and gagged. She was sitting next to a large man who bound up as well. Carson looked at Jason.

"That's Abdul Nek and his wife. It looks like we hit the jackpot!"

Jason gave Chief Carson the thumbs up. He felt a great deal of pride that his planning made a difference. Some of the other SEALs were carrying files and placing them into large duffle bags. Three computers were taken as well.

Chief Carson led his men downstairs. The SEAL who stayed downstairs said, "We are good to go. Our transport will be landing right outside the village in ten minutes"

The group with their prisoners started to move towards the landing spot when all hell broke loose. Several fighters came into the street and started to fire their weapons. Three bursts from the SEALs compact MP5 finished them off.

"Carson yelled, "Get your asses to move—make it fast!""

Fifty yards from the Osprey another group of Al-Qaeda fighters came out of the east. There were about twelve of them. Three SEALs set up a large spread of automatic fire as the enemy approached. Two other SEALs escorted their prisoners to the plane. Chief Carson and Jason moved quickly toward the plane when another group of four fighters attacked them. Carson's machine gun was knocked from his hands. He was able to get his pistol out and shoot one of the attackers. Another attacker hit Carson over the head with his rifle and Carson went down.

The three attackers turned to Jason. Jason took out his pistol and wildly shot at the three approaching fighters. He finally hit two of the men as the last fighter approached him with a knife. Jason took aim and shot. He was out of ammunition.

The knife fight lasted for thirty seconds thanks to a grizzly old Marine Sergeant who trained Jason in hand to hand combat. The enemy closed on Jason waving his knife. Jason waited until the man was close enough. He dropped kicked him with a Judo move and the man went down. Jason grabbed the knife and plunged into the side of the man.

Chief Carson was up and observed the scene. He was groggy, but he realized that he was observing a warrior handle a bad situation and turning it into a victory. He finally got to Jason as the Lieutenant was standing up looking down at the dead fighter.

"Let's get to the plane sir. Our job is finished."

The SEAL Team deposited their prisoners at the designated base and returned to their airplane. They remained very quiet on the way back until the Chief loudly said, "Lieutenant Darvish, I'll serve with you any time, any place, and on any mission. You better believe it.!"

The rest of the team yelled their approval. "Any time Boss, any time!" Jason responded, "My honor to be part of your team, Hooyah!"

Nearing the end of his five years of service Jason realized that he was no longer conflicted. He had done his duty and was prepared to become a civilian. Jason did not want the Navy to be his career.

He left the service not only with the Bronze Star, but with another medal. The Yemen mission was reported by Chief Carson and one month later the Chief of Naval Operations awarded Jason the Silver Star.

Immediately after the awards ceremony the CNO said, Jason, "I know you want to leave the service, but here is my deal. If you stay with the ONI I will give you a spot promotion to Lieutenant Commander immediately. That's pretty good for five years of service. You could have a brilliant career in the Navy!"

Jason declined gracefully. He thought, *I'm ready to become a civilian. I served my time.*

Chapter Thirteen

Anna met Dr. Neil Roth when he left the operating room and walked into the patient's waiting room. He walked directly over to her mother, held her hands and said, "The procedure was a success. I got everything I could. Your husband is a strong man and with the proper treatment plan he will have many more years of successful living!"

Mrs. Mason hugged the doctor and took his hand to introduce her family to him. Anna noticed a tall man, about six foot two inches, with dark brown hair and the most beautiful hazel eyes that shone green in the sunlit room.

"Thank you for your words Dr. Roth. I'm grateful."

He looked into her eyes, "Oh, all it took was thirteen years of study and a gallon of coffee a day. It was nothing."

Anna laughed and hugged the handsome doctor. I'm so happy that we selected you."

Two weeks after her father's operation she received a call from Neil Roth.

"I called you mother to get your number. I hope that it is okay?"

"No problem. How may I help you?"

"I'd like to take you out to dinner. Would you consider it?"

"Sounds like a great idea."

The next few weeks were wonderful. Neil Roth was thirty-six years old and kept in very good shape. He worked out every morning and watched his diet. Dr. Roth had a great sense of humor, loved romantic comedy movies and shared funny stories with Anna.

Anna was enchanted with the assurance of himself, the politeness he showed to people around him and the respect he had for her. He had not tried any physical moves on her and kept his hands to himself. That was a change of pace for her since most of the men she dated wanted oral sex on the third date and coitus the sixth date.

The sixth week together they went to a posh restaurant. Neil took her hands, looked deeply into her eyes, "Will you be able to take a long weekend with me. I'm off on Friday. It's the Labor Day weekend and I have a condominium in the Berkshires. Some of the trees are beginning to turn and I know of some great sites to see."

Anna immediately said, "Yes. It sounds marvelous!"

It took Anna some clever finagling to get the long weekend off including Friday, but she succeeded. During lunch she shared her enthusiasm with her best friend.

"Neil is the consummate professional. He writes articles for medical journals, is a great surgeon, has a great bedside manner and seems dedicated to his patients."

Susan loudly laughed, "How is he in bed?"

Anna turned red, "We haven't even had any heavy petting, or necking at all. He is a perfect gentleman, but I suspect he will be a tiger when we go on our trip."

"Look girl. You have been disappointed too often. Please don't get your hopes up. This may be just a roll in the hay for both of you. Enjoy it as long as it lasts."

Anna put her hand on her chin, "I want more. I want a commitment!" Susan nodded, "I love you little sister, but be careful."

"I will, I promise."

The four day weekend was perfect. Neil drove a Porsche Panamara. It was sleek and fast with plenty of luggage room and comfortable orthopedic seats. They got to the condo in the early afternoon and Anna looked around.

While she roamed through the rooms she kept on thinking about her situation. Many of her friends had either hooked up with boyfriends, married or at least had a permanent relationship. She started to count them in her mind and realized that almost seventy percent were in positive relationships. Of course, there were some of her friends, as Susan, who really liked to play around and had no concept of settling down with one man.

Anna had read some articles in women magazines and had little respect for their conclusions. A great deal of articles challenged the idea of getting married young. They suggested that women become involved with their careers and have sex whenever they wanted and with whoever they wanted.

It seemed to Anna that the right man would eventually come around if he was given a chance. She felt that women had to take a chance with men and encourage relationships without pressing the men.

Anna really liked Neil. She respected his intellectual curiosity, his sense of humor and the manner he treated her. He was a gentleman and she liked it. However, he never really made a sexual move and that concerned her. She thought, *Perhaps this weekend. That really would be nice.*

Neil had made sure that housekeeping took care of clean sheets, towels and stocked the refrigerator with all sorts of food. Anna was impressed with the size of the condominium which was just outside of Pittsfield, Massachusetts. There were three bedrooms, two baths with a built in jacuzzi. The great room overlooked magnificent trees on one side and the mountains on the other side. It was beautiful.

Anna hugged Neil and said, "I'm going in for a shower."

As she was soaping herself Neil knocked on the shower door and queried, "May I join you?'

Anna opened the door all wet and soapy—"As long as you do my back."

Neil laughed, "I'm going to do you all over!'

And he did!

There was a great deal of laughter during the weekend. Neil shared funny stories about medical school and Anna shared funny stories about her work in the Bronx. They seemed compatible in many respects. One of the areas of concern was religion. Anna made sure to tell Neil that she was Christian and would not deviate from her beliefs.

I believe in one Lord Jesus Christ, the Only Begotten Son of God, born of the Father before all ages. My love of Jesus is part of me and when you take me you take that as well."

Neil did not say anything and it seemed a bit awkward. Yet he remained loving and communicative.

Later in the day Neil said, "I'm an agnostic. I was raised Jewish, but all it means to me right now is celebrating some holidays with my parents. I don't like gefilte fish, but I love corned beef and pastrami!"

The rest of the weekend was perfect. Anna felt that she had found a person who she could spend the rest of her life with, at least she prayed she could.

During their time together over the next five months Anna and Neil worked at the problem of scheduling. Anna's work schedule was very heavy and Neil's surgery and patients were many. Yet they were able to capture moments together that were passionate, talkative and sincere. Anna did not care about the inconvenience of his schedule because he was saving lives. Neil told her that he respected her work.

One evening at her apartment they were talking about some serious world problems when Neil said, "Anna, I love you. Let's make this relationship solid. I will not see or think of any women. How about it?"

"I will on one condition. That— being that— we tell the truth to each other about everything. It means present, past and hopes for the future!"

Neil kissed her. "You have my word."

Two weeks later Anna was given half a day off because the Information Technology Department had to install new fiber optic wiring and computers in her department. She had an idea. She looked at her watch and it was noon. Anna decided to make a surprise visit to Neil at his office. Perhaps she could take him out for a late lunch.

Dr. Neil Roth's office was on East sixty-sixth street in a large thirty story building. The Uber driver knew exactly where it was and even in heavy traffic arrived in less than fifteen minutes. Neil's office was on the fifteenth floor.

When Anna arrived, and before she could check in with the receptionist she observed a pretty little girl of seven with her mother. The little girl had curly brown hair and green eyes. Her mother was smartly dressed and had blonde hair. Just then the doctor's office door opened and the little girl yelled, "Daddy, daddy!" she jumped into Neil Roth's arms.

Neil hugged her and kissed her cheek. The little girl's mother stood up and approached Neil. She whispered something into his ear.

Anna felt as if she had been stabbed in her heart. She thought, *He lied! He lied big time! That son-of-a-bitch—he conned me. I hate him.*

Anna ran out of the office and yelled for a taxi. She got to her apartment and cried for the rest of the day. She thought, *I can't trust any man at all. They are all after one thing and when they get it, they just enjoy it. No commitments at all! Shit!*

Neil tried to call her. She would hear his voice on her answering machine. The same message was repeated three times that afternoon. *We are going to be separated. I don't love my wife—I love you. I'm sorry I didn't tell you about her and the child. Anna, pick up, pick up.*

On the fourth call Anna picked up and quickly yelled, "If you don't stop calling me I will get a restraining order and call your medical association about you harassing me. Get the hell out of my life!"

She heard the click when he hung up.

Chapter Fourteen

Jason finished his five year commitment to the United States Navy and returned to civilian life. He was given a small going away party by his department. The Admiral came to the party to say good-bye.

"Lieutenant Darvich, you have served most honorably and I am proud to have served with you. The SEALs still talk about your guts and they have sent me a small gift to give to you."

He gave Jason a small box. In it was a fourteen karat gold pin that had the American eagle with a trident crossed over an anchor; and an old fashioned pistol crossed over the other way. It was the Navy SEAL pin. The Admiral stepped back and saluted Jason. "It was a pleasure serving with you!"

Previously to leaving the Navy, Jason had some major sessions with Dr. Wong. The reasons were numerous. Since his last combat Jason had slept poorly, upon awakening he felt severe anxiety, and felt as if he was in a full state of panic. He sometimes felt that the world was spinning around him.

Dr. Wong explained, "Jason, you are suffering from 'Post Traumatic Stress Disorder'.

PTSD is a problem that many men and women have after combat; and your combat was belly to belly and eye ball to eye ball. When you get back to New York sign up with the Veteran's Administration and you will get some very needed therapy. Have your therapist call me, please."

Jason moved back to Long Island, New York. He rented a condominium near his parent's home in Great Neck. The veteran had problems sleeping, felt anxious and seemed despondent.

Jason took six months off and used the time to enjoy New York City seeing plays, ballgames, swimming on the beaches and just hanging out with a few close friends. He needed the time to relax and get back to civilian life.

Jason saw a therapist, Dr. Blackman, at the VA weekly to discuss his feelings as a warrior and his combat experiences. She was a wonderful and skilled therapist. The therapy process seemed to be helping.

During a therapy session Dr. Blackman suggested that Jason's should get to work. "Look Jason. You are used to being busy and living a meaningful life. You've had your

rest and rehabilitation, or as other's call it, your "R-and-R. Now go ahead and get a job!"

"What the hell should I do?"

"Come on Jason—don't be a prick. You have a background in languages, in intelligence, security, in surveillance and in research. Hell, any corporation would hire you! Use your background and skills. You are a born leader, at least that's what your service record says and that's what Dr. Wong said as well!"

Jason talked to his mother about his situation. "Mom, I really don't feel like working for a corporation. All they think about is the bottom line. I'm not into that."

"What are you into?"

"Well it's not into making any money and joining the corporate and business world!" "Perhaps you might think about public service."

"Thanks Mom, that is a good idea."

On his way home to his condo he thought, *I gave service to the USA, perhaps it is time to give service to the rest of the world. Sure, why not?*

The next day he called Captain Duncan at ONI and asked if he could put in a good word at the United Nations for a job. Perhaps in security. Duncan told Jason to wait a few days and he would hear from somebody.

"Thanks Captain. I think I need a purpose in my life."

Captain Duncan spoke to the Admiral about Jason; who then spoke to the Chief of Naval Operations; who spoke to the Secretary of the Navy; who spoke to the President of the United States.

After reviewing Jason's five year career as a Navy Officer, medals for bravery, language skills, and performance the President spoke to the Secretary-General of the United Nations who told the Undersecretary to move as quickly as possible to interview Jason.

Five days later Jason received a call from the from the Undersecretary of Safety and Security at the United nations. He was interviewed by a panel of five people who were high up on the chain of command.

The interview seemed to be a great success since Jason was able to speak Mandarin to the Chinese representative and French to the French representative. However, he apologized to the German representative since he did not speak German.

The German representative said, "Young man, most of the time we speak English around here since it has become a universal language. We are here because when we want a person with very specific skills, as you have, we sometimes waive the United Nations hiring process. We will let you know within a week whether you will work with us—or not."

Jason shook hands with all the members and left feeling very good about the interview.

Within one week Jason was hired as a mid- level professional employee working for Security Operations at the United Nations in New York City. His group focused on investigations & safety of high level diplomats.

There were orientation lectures, administrative operational practices, United Nations protocol behaviors, human resource paper work that Jason had to experience. It seemed to him it was similar to his experience at the Office of Naval Intelligence. This process took three weeks and finally Jason was introduced to his immediate supervisor, Judy Han.

She was in her late forties, very well dressed with a PhD in International Relations from the University of Cambridge. Jason was impressed that she worked for Scotland Yard and Interpol. She looked carefully at Jason, "I have read about you and find it is hard to believe that you have had so much experience at such a young age. However, I will not hold that against you.

I expect you to be candid with me at all times. If you think I have made a poor decision—please let me know. I want you to be a team player. You are a mid-level professional and I can see you moving up the chain quickly, if you wish to do so."

"Dr. Han, I have a great deal to learn about your operations. I recognize your valuable experience and expect to learn a lot from you."

"Okay Jason., down to work. Review the security operations for the safety of the Vice President of the United States. He will be visiting the General assembly on a tour. His own Secret Service protection will have to be integrated with our own protocols. Are you up to the job?"

"You bet I am!"

"Here is the folder that our people have put together. See if there are any flaws?"

Jason found two problems with the security plan. When the Vice President was to take a bathroom break, the elevator carrying the Vice President was too close to a public entrance. The second was that the Secret Service had too many agents to fit into the private elevator. Jason suggested that the Vice President and his protection take the stairs to have him go to the bathroom. It was only one flight down.

Dr. Han remarked, "Jason, I think your suggestions are valid and I'll pass it along to the proper authorities. May I ask, how did you figure this out?"

"I placed my thoughts on the angle that if I were an assassin where would the Vice President be the most vulnerable. Kind of easy. We did it all the time as we planned operations for the SEALs."

"Good job. Keep it coming. Oh—you are invited to a "Get to Know You Party" that will take place next Tuesday at noon. Make sure you attend. There will be new staff members as well as

different department heads, managers, supervisors, editorial staff, and specialists. We do this every quarter. I'll introduce you to my daughter who works in public relations."

"Looking forward to it."

Jason thought, *I really don't want to go, but I guess I'm stuck with it.*

Chapter Fifteen

Anna felt as if she was living in a dark cave with the knowledge that a large animal was about ready to attack her. She had been despondent for over a month since breaking up with Neil. How foolish she felt being so deceived by him. She had given him her unconditional love which included her hopes and desires for the future, her joys, her sorrows, her soul and her body.

Jerome Lightfoot, the Supervisor of Editors came out of his office and went directly into Anna's area. He said, "Anna, what's this foolishness that you don't want to go to the Get to Know You Party. I see from our rotational list that you and Rosalie are our representatives."

"Mr. Lightfoot, I'm sorry—I just am not ready for any social relationships right now." 'Miss. Mason, you are directed and instructed by me to go to the event. That's an order!"

"I don't want to go and I will not go! Don't treat me like a school girl. It's unbecoming of you."

"Jeez Anna, please—do me a favor. I really am up to my eyeballs — please."

Anna looked at Jerry whose wife just gave birth. He was a good man helping her with all the feedings, taking care of the other two children as well as putting in a fifty hour day since he had lost his assistant.

"Okay Jerry. I'm doing this for you. You owe me!"

Jerry smiled, "Anna, I'd marry you, but my wife won't let me."

They both laughed and Anna felt a little better with the levity they had shared. She started to think about the outfit she would wear. Picking up the phone she called her best friend, Susan.

"Are you going to the Get to Know You Party next Tuesday?

"Yes, I am. I heard that there may be some men there. Who knows, we can share some eye candy."

Anna felt much better when she spoke to Susan. She had shared her breakup with Neil and Susan was very kind and supportive of her. Susan was the type of friend who had great empathy and knew exactly what to do when trauma happened.

Anna thought, *I am blessed to have Susan as a friend!*

The room that the party was in had been decorated with "Welcome" balloons and colorful signs containing many slogans. Some of them Anna liked were: **Your Attitude Determines Your Direction; Do What is Right--Not What is Easy; and To All New Employees--New Incentive Plan--Work or Get Fired!** The last one tickled her funny bone:

She was wearing a new dress because Susan insisted they go shopping for the party. Her friend knew exactly what to do to help Anna get past her depression. After shopping they decided to have dinner at their favorite Italian restaurant.

Susan pushed her lasagna away from her and said, "My mother told me about a cute guy who just started working in her office. He is talented and really smart. Mom told me that he knows French, Mandarin, Farsi and some special dialects that only a few people at the United Nations know about. She is personally bringing him to the party on Tuesday."

"He sounds like a special nerd." "Perhaps a special professional." "No Susan—just another nerd."

"He's a nerd who was recommended by the President of the United States. He's a nerd who has the bronze star plus the silver star and worked in Naval intelligence. My Mom doesn't rave about the average Joe."

"I'm quite impressed!' "So is my mother!"

The party was going on in full swing when Anna noticed Dr. Han walking in with Jason.

She started to introduce him around the room to the various people who represented the many different departments at the United Nations.

Finally, Dr. Han brought Jason to Anna and Susan. Jason Darvish please meet my daughter Susan Han who works in public relations. She writes well and I'm really proud of her accomplishments."

Susan looked at Jason, smiled and said," May I introduce my best friend Anna Mason, she is one of the best editors we have."

Jason shook hands with Anna and they both looked at each other. Jason did not take her hand away from his for an extra few seconds, then said, "Oh, it's a pleasure."

Anna was attracted to him. She could not take her eyes away from his face. Finally, she chuckled, put her hand to her hair for a moment and said, "I hope you will be satisfied with your position. It's security, isn't it?"

"Thanks."

Susan disappeared to get a drink and Jason was alone with Anna. Jason was intrigued. "You have beautiful eyes."

Anna responded, "You have great looking hair."

They both giggled, it turned into laughter and then into hysterics.

Jason composed himself and said," Now that the ice is broken can we get a cup of coffee some other time?"

Anna was intrigued, "Yes, most definitely, yes!"

A few hours later Susan called Anna and joked, "God, I was ready to jump him right then and there. He is so hot! Unfortunately, he looked at you and I knew he's not for me."

"I'm not sure if this will lead to anything, but he really seems nice. And I need 'nice' right now!"

"You got it girl!"

A week later Anna told Susan, "I'm seeing him tonight for our first date. We plan to go to the Village for some Italian food."

Susan advised, "He doesn't look like a man who just wants a roll in the hay. Take it easy with him, don't scare him away."

Quickly smiling, "Yes Ma'am."

Greenwich Village in New York City is centered around Washington Square and New York University which is located on the west side of Lower Manhattan. It is a large neighborhood and has as its borders, on the north - Fourteenth Street, Houston Street on the south and Broadway on the east. There are many restaurants, smart shops, off-off Broadway venues, and many young people. When visiting you can feel a certain vibration or vibe that the community has—more of a special tone since there are so many diverse groups studying, working and living in the area. It is a fun and happy area to visit.

The restaurant had wonderful food and the couple ate with gusto. They shared two pitchers of an Italian style sangria that was delicious. Anna and Jason talked about their childhood and schooling as they were growing up.

"I never felt like a nerd although a lot of the kids thought I was. Anyway, I was able to have some fun in my senior year. Lots of dates and lots of fun!"

Anna kept on looking at Jason as he talked. She liked the way he phrased his sentences, his use of expressions and his sharing of feelings with her. She really liked him.

"I really hung out with the girls at the National Honor Society. It was safe there and I never really had a boyfriend until I got into college. Even in college I was motivated by studies and didn't focus too much on men."

"I assume you have had relationships."

Anna blushed and her face turned red, "Yes, lousy one's."

Jason was shocked because her answer was spit out with venom. "I apologize if I brought up a bad subject. Anna, I'm embarrassed. I am so sorry."

Anna looked at Jason's face and noticed true regret. "I'm sorry for my behavior Jason. It will not happen again."

The weather was perfect and the couple decided to walk through the village. Their conversation continued into their college years. Anna proudly told him about her writing awards and Jason was impressed. Then Jason shared his achievements in college to Anna. They both seemed pleased.

Jason said, "Anna, most of the time I would be too shy to tell you about winning awards in college, but I really feel comfortable telling you."

Anna took his arm and held on tightly, "I feel the same way. I guess when a couple of nerds get together it's okay."

They both shared a funny laugh. Jason felt really comfortable and Anna felt the same way.

Finally, they took a taxi to Anna's apartment. Jason escorted Anna to her apartment's door. She looked up at him, smiled and put her arms around his neck and said, "I had a great time and I want to see you again."

Jason kissed her lips lightly, but Anna opened her mouth and soul kissed him. Their tongues danced together for a moment then Anna broke it off. "I really like you Jason."

Jason slightly separated from her, looked directly into her eyes, "I want to see you again."

They disengaged and Anna went into her apartment. She leaned onto the back of the door and felt her legs trembling. Anna was wet with desire and thought, *Dear God, please, I want this relationship to work!"*

Jason went outside and decided to walk the twelve blocks to his apartment. He smiled, *I really like this woman. Wow!*

Chapter Sixteen

Jason reported to work on Monday to find Dr. Han and two men huddled around a map in the conference room. He walked past the room to get to his office when Dr. Han called him.

"Jason, please join us. May I introduce Jack Van and Saul Rubin. They have a problem that you might help settle."

Jack Van was a well built, fifty year old who had a short beard and wore thick glasses. He was dressed in a checkered sport jacket that went out of style ten years ago. He scratched his beard and said, "The new Iranian United Nations Ambassador is coming to New York next

week. Normally we leave his protection to his mother country unless we learn of something fishy."

"What's wrong?"

Saul Rubin was a pudgy, thirty-five year old, who was dressed in a sweater and jeans. He looked at Jason, sucked in his breath and said, "Through some reliable sources we have learned that some Israeli agents may want to assassinate him We have spoken to the Iranian security people and they laughed at us. Now we know that security people usually cooperate with each other, but Iranians are different."

Dr. Han queried, "Jason, Farsi is one of your specialties—correct.?" "I speak it fluently Dr. Han."

"Good. We think that the Iranian security people will accept one agent to be with them on their trip to the United Nations."

"Will that be me?"

Jack Van quickly responded, "Look kid, it's like this. The name of the new man from Iran is Aram Babar. He lives with his family in Zahedan. It's a city located near the borders of Pakistan and Afghanistan. We have a request to the Iranian President that one of our security representatives meet the new ambassador in his home town and escort him to Tehran. Then he and the Iranian team can fly out together."

Saul Rubin blurted out, "My contacts in Israel have told me that a hit team is already on their way to kill Aram Babar. So, time is of the essence."

Dr. Han showed the map to Jason. "We can fly you out to Afghanistan and we will get you a military helicopter to fly you into Zahedan. My plan is to have you leave as soon as possible and we will let you know in Afghanistan if the Iranians will approve the plan. What do you think?"

"It's part of the job. I'm going home, right now to pack. Text me the information as soon as possible."

Jason stopped by Anna's office area and motioned her to come out into the hallway. She quickly left her desk and met Jason.

"I have to fly to Iran on assignment. Sorry to break my date with you. When I get back I'll make it up to you."

Anna looked at his face. It seemed serene and untroubled. They had only two dates and she felt comfortable with him. "Okay—I'm happy you came to see me face to face. I don't feel dumped!"

"Raincheck?" "You've got it!"

The plane out of JFK was a new Airbus 380 flown by Air India. He was able to get some shut eye and was served some very nice Indian meals. The flight took sixteen hours and during that time Jason read about Iran and its government. It seemed that Iran is an Islamic theocracy. The Supreme Leader has true control over the decisions of the President and Iranian Parliament.

When he arrived in Kabul there was a man waiting for him who had a sign with his name on it. The messenger said, "Excuse me sir, I have a car for you. We have to get to another airport within the hour. Here is an envelope with your instructions."

Jason went into the back seat and read his instructions. They were quite specific. The Iranian government had given permission for Jason to travel to Zahedan and accompany Ambassador Babar to Tehran. There he would meet with Iranian security and travel together to New York City. In the envelope there was a light blue armband with the United Nations symbol on it. It was requested that he wear it all the time.

The helicopter was waiting for him in a remote airport. He recognized it as a UH-60A/l Blackhawk helicopter that had the capacity to fly elven hundred miles without refueling. The distance between Kabul and Zahedan was about six hundred miles. The logo of the United Nations were on the doors of the helicopter.

He threw his light bag into the cabin and climbed in. The pilot looked at him and said, "Hey Mr. VIP, there's a box behind the seat that your boss wants to have. Let's get you to Iran!"

Jason opened the large metal box and found the following items: a bullet proof vest with the United Nations logo on it; a Glock G43, 9mm pistol with three magazines holding six shots in each; a belt holster; a small commando knife with sheath; a LED compass; about a thousand dollars in Iranian rials and instructions on how to get to the Ambassador's house.

Jason decided to get some shuteye. He felt he better get some immediately because the trip may be a bad one. Right before he fell asleep he thought, *I wonder what Anna is doing right now.*

It seemed to Jason that Aram Babar and his family were delightful. Babar was forty years old, a scholar who had written about moderation. He was a devoted family man. His family loved it when they heard Jason speak in Farsi. He had the right sound, tone and his pronunciation was perfect.

When they were alone Jason explained his mission to the ambassador. "We have been told that there may be an Israeli hit team out to kill you. Your government believes it is rubbish, but they agreed that I may accompany you to Tehran. I am armed and trained to defend you.

"I believe that you are wasting your time. My government has very good information. If they thought it necessary they would have sent soldiers to protect me."

"My hope is that we are wrong and your government is right. Let's get an early start tomorrow."

The breakfast they had at six in the morning consisted of honey, naan bread, and clotted cream. They washed it down with black tea and at six-thirty they heard the honking of the private car that would take them to the airport. The ambassador had one valise and Jack helped him load it into the car.

Ambassador Babar said, "It will take us forty minutes to get to the airport and our plane will take us to Tehran in less than two hours."

Jason quickly replied in Farsi, "God willing."

Ten minutes into the drive Jason heard a single shot and the car swerved onto the side of the road. The driver got out and yelled, "We have a flat tire."

Jason took out his gun and motioned to the ambassador to come with him. They immediately went into a clump of trees some thirty yards from the side of the road. The ambassador took his phone out and said, "I'll call the police to come get us."

He tried dialing, twice. "I can't get a line. It happens all the time."

Jason said, "Let's sit down on the ground and wait until the flat is fixed."

Three minutes later two men showed up and spoke to the driver. The driver pointed towards the trees where they were. The men approached the trees.

Jason stepped out of the trees with his gun drawn. "Don't get too close gentlemen!" he spoke in English.

"American?"

"American who works security for the United Nations. Now go tell your boss at Mossad that today is not the day it's going to happen."

Jason shot two rounds about five feet to the side of the men. I mean business. No bullshit from me."

"Okay Mr. Hero. We don't want any trouble with American's. You are a pain in our ass." "Get the hell out of here. We already called the police."

Both men ran down the road and Jason heard a car start up. He turned to the ambassador, "Try the police again."

This time the police answered and in fifteen minutes they came and escorted Jason and the ambassador to the airport.

On the plane from Tehran to New York the ambassador went to Jason and sat down next to him. "Thank you for saving my life. I owe you and you may collect. I pay my debts."

"Sir, this is the job I had to do today. You have a lovely family and your wife served me a wonderful breakfast. That was enough."

The ambassador squeezed Jason's arm and left.

Jason was able to get some good shuteye. He knew he had to write a report as soon as he got back to his office. His last thought was, *I wonder what Anna is doing right now.*

Chapter Seventeen

Anna was asleep when Jason called her. She quickly became alert and picked up. "Hello."

"Anna, it's Jason. I just got back and I'm sorry about the time, but I really wanted to hear your voice."

"Are you okay?"

"Yes, except it was hairy for a little while. I kept on thinking about you."

"Same here. I know you were going overseas and I can put two and two together." "Anna, I know tomorrow is Wednesday, but can we see each other tomorrow

night. I really would like to see you."

Anna thought for a moment, "Jason, come on over to my apartment at seven.

You're going to get a home cooked meal." "What can I bring?"

"Yourself!"

On Wednesday, Jason got into his office an hour before anybody arrived. He had a typed report ready for Dr. Han. She called him at ten to meet her in the conference room.

He arrived to see Jack Van and Saul Rubin alongside Dr. Han. Jason inwardly chuckled because Jack Van had another sport coat on that had so many large checks on it that he looked like a clown. Again, Saul Rubin was in jeans and a sweater.

Saul Rubin extended his hand to Jason, "Nice job —my sources have told me that you took care of a threatening situation quite professionally."

Jack Van was next. He stayed near Dr. Han and pointed his finger at Jason. "My sources told me that you shot at those men."

Jason was cool and looked at Van with distain. "No, I did not shoot at them. They would be dead men if I shot at them. No, I shot five feet away from them to scare them and tell them I meant business."

Dr. Han went over to Van and put her arm on his shoulder. "Sit down Jack. Don't get your underwear all tightened up. Jason knew exactly what he was doing."

"Jason gave his report to Dr. Han. It's all in there, including the breakfast menu that Mrs. Babar served that morning. It was a damn good breakfast, but I wanted out of Iran as soon as I could get out. I missed my date and that's a near tragedy for me!"

They all laughed at his joke and the tension was diminished. Van & Rubin left the conference room as Dr. Han said, "Jason wait for a moment, please."

Jason looked at Dr. Han in all seriousness and said, "Who are those men?"

"Jack Van is a Senior Supervisor of Field Operations and Saul Rubin is the Associate Director of Intelligence. They have been with the United Nations for at least ten years."

"Rubin is kind of young to have that title."

"He paid his dues in the Congo—believe me he paid his dues." "Will that be all?"

"No, I wanted to compliment you on your field work. Nice job! Take tomorrow off, you need to catch up on your sleep."

Anna was humming to herself as she set the table for dinner. She was pleased that Jason immediately called her when he came back to the States. It meant a great deal that he thought of her first. The menu was simple: Green salad with balsamic dressing, garlic bread, linguini with spaghetti sauce, small Italian meatballs, and ice cream for dessert.

There was red wine on the table and white tapers that she would light when Jason arrived.

He knocked on the door and when Anna opened it he looked at her. She was smiling, she was radiant— she was pretty. Anna hugged him and kissed him on the lips, once and then again. "Welcome home soldier!"

After cleaning up the kitchen they sat on the couch holding hands. Previously at dinner the couple talked about the weather, the ball games, the family, but not anything about their relationship nor Jason's trip.

Jason rested his head against the back of the couch and said, "I had to use a gun on the job the other day. I didn't hurt anyone, but I'm not sure if I want to continue with the department. It reminds me too much of my Navy days."

Anna said, "Come here and rest your head on my chest. Just rest, don't talk, just rest."

He put his head on her breasts and within two minutes he was asleep. As he slept Anna thought, *I care about this man. I care a lot!*

He left Anna's apartment after a short snooze. He was apologetic that he fell asleep and Anna just smiled, squeezed his hand and said, "I'll call an Uber for you. Get some sleep."

Jason was so tired that he slept until one in the afternoon. After a very long shower he made coffee and ate some corn flakes. Jason decided to go on the computer and research the different departments of the United Nations. Perhaps he belonged somewhere else. The day turned into early evening and Jason went down to the small Chinese take-out place and brought home his shrimp with lobster sauce, fried rice and some dumplings.

As he was laying out his meal, his phone rang. "Hello."

"Jason, it's Anna."

Jason heard sniveling. "What's wrong?"

"My eighty-nine-year old Grandmother just passed away. I'm going up to Buffalo tomorrow for the memorial service and help my mom sort things out. I hope to be back next Monday or Tuesday. Our Saturday night date is out, I'm sorry."

"Anna, I'm so sorry—is there anything I can do?",

"Just say a prayer for us and see me as soon as I come back. I'm missing you already!"

"I've missed you all day today."

Anna started to sob, "Good bye Jason, I—"

She had hung up after "I"—Jason started to think. *Now what could she have meant?*

Jason called Dr. Han on Friday morning and advised her that he was not coming into work. She was agreeable and did not say anything other than, "Have a pleasant weekend."

Jason rented a car to drive to Great Neck. The drive to Great Neck, from his apartment took over an hour. His parent's house was only twenty miles away from his apartment, but traffic was heavy. Jason resolved to take the Long Island Railroad train from now on. He arrived for lunch and his mother was thrilled to have him .

"Where is Dad?"

"He is with a financial planner. It seems that a large drug store wants to buy the store. His accountant has told us that it's a very good deal. If it goes through then we could sell the house and move to Florida. The winter's have been brutal here. Another thing is that the Great Neck area is considered affluent and we could make a huge profit on the house."

"What do you think Mom?"

"Melody lives in New Hampshire and visits about once a month. Her twins really keep her busy. And you are all over the world, or all over someplace and you hardly visit— so why not Florida. It's really nice in the winter time!"

Jason thought, "It's a plan that can work for you. Sure, why not Florida. I can fly down in the winter time and mooch on you."

They both started to laugh as Jason thought, *Things are changing quickly.*

When his father came back they discussed the pros and cons of the move. The more they talked the more Jason saw the wisdom of the move. His parents were getting old and deserved a good life in Florida.

Later in the weekend Jason spoke to his mother about Anna.

"Mom, I know a woman who is kind, smart, beautiful and really terrific. We 've been on a few dates and I can't get her out of my mind."

"How serious is it, Son?"

"We haven't even made— ah , I mean we haven't—"

His mother cut him off, "You have not had sex with her. Is that correct?"

"I'm sorry mom, we haven't even gotten close to that as yet."

"Well, get to know her and if you think she is the one please bring her to us." "Will do, Mom!"

On his drive back to his apartment Jason thought about Anna, *I miss her!*

When he got home there was a message on his machine from Anna. She gave him her cell phone number and said, "I miss you. Call me tonight."

They talked for an hour on the phone. Anna would be back to New York on Tuesday. They made plans to meet for dinner that night.

Chapter Eighteen

They decided to meet at a Greek restaurant called "Olympia" one block from Anna's apartment. Jason finished work at five in the afternoon and rushed home to shower and change. He knew that Anna had flown back from Buffalo in the early afternoon.

When Jason came into the restaurant he saw Anna sitting in a booth towards the back. He quickly moved to her and kissed her. He looked into her eyes and saw tears flowing.

'Oh Anna, I'm so sorry about your grandmother. I'm sure she was a good person."

"She helped my mother with my older brothers, but by time I came along she had moved to Buffalo. I knew her from a distance, yet she was kind and my mother adored her. My tears are for my mother who started to talk to me about her own mortality even before the memorial service was over. Jason, it was a real downer. I hurt for my mom and her pain.

The waiter came over and they both ordered Greek Pastitsio. It's a baked layer style dish, with a type of a rich white sauce made with milk saturated with herbs and other flavorings on the top layer. The chef's call it "Béchamel sauce." Then they place pasta in the middle and ground meat cooked with tomato sauce at the bottom. It was absolutely delicious. They served it with a side of lemon potatoes and plenty of pita bread. The couple finished with Greek rice pudding. It was thick and creamy and mouthwatering.

Anna said, "Come up to my apartment for a little while. I'm a bit tired, come up for a short visit."

They settled on the couch and Jason took her in his arms and kissed her. She kissed him back and they kissed some more. He lifted her onto his body and Jason started to run his hands over her body and she seemed to freeze. "What is it."

"I'm not ready —I'm sorry Jason—I'm not ready."

"Okay. I thought you sort of gave me the signal that it was okay."

"I did, but I just can't do it. Look Jason, I'm not a tease, I'm not a prude, I'm not a cock teaser. I thought I could do it with you tonight, but I just can't."

"Anna, I really like you. I mean I really like you as in super-like you! Hell, you are the wordsmith—you know what I mean!"

She got off him. Kissed his cheek and said, "We're going to double date with Susan, if that's okay with you. I'll tell you the whole story late Friday night."

He kissed her lips and she kissed him back. Jason realized that he was falling in love with her and thought, *I hope this isn't a one-way street.*

During the rest of the week Jason reviewed plans for the new set of meetings that would be held at the General Assembly. The committee meetings needed security and Jason was tasked with developing the administrative design for security. One of the major meetings was the "Administrative and Budgetary Committee." He was informed that there might be marches and protests outside the building and he had to design the necessary perimeter defense to protect the committee members from being harmed. It was tedious work, but important security work.

His sources informed him that more protests were planned for the "Human Rights Committee"

and that there might be some planned violence. Jason coordinated with the supervisors of the uniformed United Nations guards as well as a number of plain clothes officers. The details were numerous with options planned for all sorts of scenarios.

Jason thought, *"Now this is the type of work that is meaningful. I'm using my planning skills from ONI a well as my brain.*

When Friday night came Jason was exhausted. He hardly said hello to Susan and her date. Anna looked at him. "Are you okay Jason?"

'I'm sorry guys. I'm exhausted from the work I've been doing. Let me just be the ears for tonight, not the mouth."

Susan and her date, Stan Peters nodded. Then Stan said, "I've been there. It's okay Jason, I can carry the ball."

Susan hit him on the arm, "He's not much of an athlete, but he really can dance."

Everybody started to laugh. It was a very pleasant dinner with Susan and Stan carrying the major conversation. It seemed that they have been seeing each other for five months and were planning to take a vacation in the Bahama's together.

Susan asked Anna, "Perhaps you and Jason could go with us. It would be great."

Anna looked at Susan in a hopeless manner, "We haven't dated that much as yet. Going with Jason to the Bahamas would be premature in our relationship."

Jason chimed in, "We're not a couple as yet. There is no commitment as yet. There really is nothing more than being good friends. Right Anna?"

Anna blushed, "Susan, we are not up to being lovers at all. We are just good, loyal friends."

Susan laughed, "Too bad guys. You make an adorable couple."

The main course consisting of New York strip steak came and the two couples started to devour their meal. Not too much was said during the main meal and when dessert time came Susan lifted her glass of wine and said, "Here is to good friendships, good food, and good beginnings."

Anna lifted her glass, looked at Jason and said, "May it be so."

Jason closed the door of Anna's apartment and went into the kitchen. He took a K-cup and made some coffee. A little while later Anna returned from her bedroom wearing a thick terry cloth robe. She had scrubbed off her makeup and looked like a teenager.

She sat down and told Jason about her affair with Dr. Neil Roth. She cried bitter tears as she explained her situation, the manner she found out about the betrayal, her deep depression and her slow recovery.

"Jason, you have been like therapy for me. I love the way you talk; I love the way you walk; I love the way you think; I love your manners and respect you give me; I love the way you show your values; I love everything about you, but I am not ready to commit."

Jason held her two hands and looked deeply into her eyes, "I'm not ready to push you into anything at all. Let's just enjoy each other and let time heal your wounds."

She came around the kitchen table and sat on Jason's lap. "I'm beginning to fall in love with you and I'm scared Jason. I am terrified that it will not work."

"Anna, you have been candid with me so here is my honesty right back at you. I see a therapist about twice a month at the Veteran's Administration. I have PTSD and am being treated by talk therapy and on rare occasion, when needed, anti-anxiety medication. I did some pretty horrible things in my Navy career and it's haunting me. Well, what do you think? Can you still love or maybe like me after what I told you?"

"Oh, my sweet man. Of course I can!"

The couple held each other for a few minutes. Jason stood up and kissed Anna on her cheek. I'll call you tomorrow. I want to see the new Spielburg movie that just came out."

Anna looked up at him, "Of course. I want to see it with you."

Jason let himself out as Anna stayed in the kitchen. Anna had tears streaming down her cheeks as she thought, *What a heroic person he is—he really doesn't know that he is so very special!*

In the Uber car Jason thought, *What a courageous woman she is—she doesn't know she is so very exceptional!*

Chapter Nineteen

Anna and Jason spent a great deal of their spare time together. Weekends were the most precious to them since they were able to have a great deal of uninterrupted time together. They discovered interesting facts about each other.

One weekend they took the Staten Island Ferry. The ferry navigates New York Harbor in its five mile run. It runs every thirty minutes and during peak hours the ferries run every fifteen to twenty minutes. Each ferry can hold from four-thousand to six-thousand people plus thirty to forty cars. The cost has been free since 1997.

The couple had packed a picnic basket and planned a full day at Clove Lake Park in Staten Island. They took the ferry and as soon as they got off they ran to the S61 bus that took them directly to Clove Lake Park in ten minutes. They had a wonderful day hiking through trails and renting a paddle boat. The park was in wonderful condition with clean rest rooms, picnic tables, waste baskets and a kiosk that sold drinks and ice cream.

Anna was very much aware of the newer Broadway shows and she was able to get some "preview" tickets at reasonable prices. She was a member of "Theater Development Fund" that discounted Broadway and off-Broadway shows to people who worked for non-profit organizatons. These discounts saved forty to fifty percent of the price of the tickets. They saw many shows.

They went to movies and restaurants as they enjoyed the sights and sounds of New York City. Anna insisted on paying for many of the tickets and meals. They were very compatible and really enjoyed each other. Both of them agreed to to keep their distance in terms of physical contact. That didn't mean a hug or a kiss was out of bounds. It really was meant for the evenings at each other's apartments where they could have become intimate. She liked his feel against her and hoped he didn't mind her tight body hugs. Jason realized that Anna needed reassurance and made sure to be as supportive as possible. There were times as she hugged him he became excited, but she did not seem to mind it at all. More than once Anna thought, *I really love him, but I'm afraid of getting burned again!*

Anna's office phone rang and the screen showed it was Jason. "Hi, are we on for tonight?"

In a low subdued voice he said, "That's why I called. Dr. Han just gave me an assignment to go to Prague. I have to baby sit a Special Envoy and the Secretary-General directed Dr. Han to put a mid-level administrator to do the job. He didn't want an armed guard—he wanted a diplomatic person who could handle a gun. That's me!"

Jason flew out the very next hour and arrived in Prague thirteen hours later. He checked his gun with Air France security and it was locked away for the flight. He would get the gun after he cleared customs. Dr. Han was kind enough to get him first class tickets on Air France. He was wined and dined including a very friendly flight attendant who told him where she was staying in

Prague for the next few days. Jason smiled and thought, *I am so ready for some loving, but only with Anna. I'll wait!*

He registered at the Prague Hilton Hotel in the heart of the city. Jason was to stay in his room until he received a phone call from the person he would guard. During the next two days he used room service and decided to go first class. It was on the United Nation's dime—*and I'm stuck with this duty,* he thought. On the third day a man called Jason with a short message. "Downstairs bar in ten minutes. Order a Vodka gimlet."

The Hilton bar was crowded. Jason pushed his way to the bar and ordered a vodka gimlet. He was served in less than three minutes. As he started to drink it a man with a grey beard came to Jason's side. "I see you like vodka gimlets."

"First time I ever tried it. A friend recommended it."

The man took Jason's arm and escorted him out of the bar. "I'm Hanzel Bada and I need a ride to the United Nations. A few people are after me. Can you help?"

"Where are you staying Mr.Bada?"

They took a taxi to Hanzel Bada's apartment. It was located at Smíchov, Jižní město, which was in the southern town of Prague. It had the reputation of being a crime ridden area with robberies and some murders taking place. Jason reached back and made sure his gun fit well in his back holster. Bada went up a long flight of stairs and Jason followed. They entered a seedy and smelly apartment. It really was a furnished room with a small kitchen. Bada started to pack his belongings as Jason watched.

Jason was looking out of the kitchen window when a dark van pulled up with two men getting out. As they crossed the street he saw that they had Balaclava ski masks on. Their faces were hidden behind the black cloth. Jason said, "Let's go. We have company. Two men hiding their faces. Is there a backway out?"

They climbed down a rickety fire escape and landed on some smelly garbage. Jason took the man's suitcase and motioned with his hand. They sprinted two blocks and ended up in a local tavern filled with a mixed crowd. Jason spoke up, "If anyone has a car and can take us to the airport I will give him one-hundred American dollars." There was no answer. 'Okay, final offer, two hundred American dollars."

The car was an old, beaten up Russian sedan that sounded as if it was going to die any minute. They finally got to the airport in thirty-five minutes. Jason gave the man two, one- hundred dollar bills and the man said in perfect English, "Thanks buddy!"

Jason checked his gun with British Airways and he and Mr. Buda left Prague.They flew to Heathrow in England where they would transfer to a "red eye" flight to JFK. There was a two hour layover and he and Mr. Buda stretched out on some hard benches waiting for the gate to open up. It was two in the morning. Jason kept his eyes open as he rested. He tried to meditate and relax, but that did not work. Finally he gave up and decided to sit up. Luckily he did at the right time because he saw three men approaching him. He smelled trouble and took out his gun. The men took one look at Jason and split their forces. One ran towards one side of the bench and another to the opposite side, while one man started to approach Jason.

Jason was trained as a warrior and his instincts kicked in. He squeezed off a round from his G42 Glock light weight pistol and hit the approaching man in the leg. That seemed to be enough because the other men grabbed their injured partner and dragged him away. He heard Hanzel Bada crying in fear.

"Calm down man. If anyone comes tell them you saw and heard nothing. Do you understand me?"

The flight was less than half filled and Jason was able to stretch out in the centre row and slept for three hours. He heard a flight attendant asking people if they wanted breakfast. Jason was starving. He enjoyed two cups of coffee and a breakfast that tasted like bacon plus scrambled eggs. He looked at Mr. Buda, "Hey—get something to eat. It's important you keep your strength up."

Later he deposited Mr. Buda to the Czech Consulate General on seventy-third Street in Manhattan, NYC. He left a voice message to Dr. Han that he was bushed and was going to sleep for a day and he didn't want any phone calls. He thought, *It seems I can't get away from trouble.*

The following day he presented a detailed report to Dr. Han. She callled him into her office. "Well, Jason—another job well done!"

"I really don't appreciate the cloak and dagger scenario I was sent to take care of— if you knew Buda was in danger why didn't you send a force to pick him up?"

"Diplomacy my boy. The people after him were Czech citizens and his government had nothing on them. This was a favor given to the United Nations Ambassador of the Czech Republic from the Secretary-General of the United Nations. We had to do it quietly."

Jason stood up and looked at Dr. Han. He felt great anger and was about to say something that would end his career, so he nodded and quickly left the office. He started to shake when he sat down at his desk.

Jason called his therapist at the Veteran's Administration. "Dr. Blackman, I really have to speak to you today. It's urgent. Can you fit me in?

Caroline Blackman's voice was soothing, "Jason, I'm free at noon today. See you then."

Chapter Twenty

Caroline Blackman had worked for the Veteran's Administration for three years as a psychiatrist. She was trained in Birmingham, England and had a small practice for one year before she married an American. The decision to move to the United States was based on the couples income. Her husband was an executive with a major Wall Street firm and made three times her income.

When she settled into the States she applied for a medical license and was told that she had to go through another three years of training, pass all sorts of tests and spend a ridiculous amount of money. She thought it was ridiculous since her training was equal or perhaps better than American schools. Dr. Blackman knew that The Veteran's Administration was in dire need of psychiatrists and they hired her on the spot. There was no need for a State license because she worked for the United States government.

The Veteran's Administration's NY Harbor Health Care System is located on East twenty-third Street in Manhattan. It is a huge facility and is considered by many evaluators as one of the best in the country. Dr. Blackman's office was on the eighth floor of the main building. Her patients were veterans who have PTSD. Some were alcoholic and others addicted to drugs. She was dedicated to her patients and made sure they had her cell number as well as he home number.

She advised her patients, "You better be close to killing yourself before calling those numbers. If not, I'll kill you!"

Most of her patients loved her sense of humor, professional attitude and her deep dedication as she helped them. She used "Exposure therapy" which is based on a straight forward behavioral treatment. Dr. Blackman and the patient would discuss behaviors that they participate in, focusing on avoiding the situation. The discussion would be in response to a set of circumstances, thoughts and memories that are viewed as frightening or anxiety-provoking. At times she would prescribe anti-anxiety drugs, but only if necessary.

Jason arrived and waited in her office for twenty-five minutes. She came out of her office door and he viewed a small, slender woman of forty with honey blond hair cut short wearing a print dress that ended to the middle of her knees. She hardly wore any makeup, perhaps lipstick since her complexion was flawless.

"Jason, come on in. We have an hour before I have to go to a staff meeting."

Her office was painted in foam green. The type of color that made you relax and feel comfortable. She sat down at a small bistro table and motioned to Jason to sit opposite her.

"Okay, what's the emergency?"

"I had the shakes and felt as if the world was closing in on me. I'm really scared Dr. Blackman!"

"What do you think brought this on? You know that we have doctor-patient confidentiality here and my lips would never say anything to anybody to hurt you!"

"I just completed a mission overseas. It involved getting a man out of Prague at the request of the Secretary-General of the United Nations. Dr. Blackman, I had to shoot a man in order to save myself and this man."

"Did you kill him?"

"No, I shot him in the leg and he and his thugs ran away." "Did you succeed in your mission?"

"Hell, yes!"

"Then why are you here? You seemed to function okay!" "I started to shake, so bad I thought I was going to faint." "Did you faint?"

"No."

"Did the shakes stop?"

"Yes—but only after I called you."

"Okay. So by calling me the shakes stopped.'

"That's what I said. Why are you questioning me this way?"

"Because you are using me as your crutch instead of using all your God given talent, your intelligence, your understanding of PTSD to stop from being an emotional cripple."

Jason stood up from the table, he was angry, he was livid, he was pissed off, "You bitch, I'm not using you and I'm not an emotional cripple. I can handle myself almost always. Aren't you here to help me. Goddammit, you are no help at all!"

Dr. Blackman started to laugh, "I guess we'll just have to see you once a month—I think you're getting better."

Jason wiped his brow, "What?"

"Jason, you are in a job right now that is called security. People will always rely and depend on you. My observation of you is that you have the right stuff to be doing what you are doing. I read your total file. The Marines wanted you, the SEALs wanted you, the Navy offered you a very early promotion and a career ladder that eventually would have made you an Admiral. Jason, you are a winner. You win in almost everything you do. The next time you have the shakes and the world closes in on you just think about what I have just told you! The shakes will go away."

Jason sat down and looked at his doctor. "Thank you. Is that really the way people look at me?"

"Damn straight young man! We have fifteen minutes, do you want some coffee?" "Sound great to me Dr. Blackman."

"Call me Caroline. I really want to be your friend, not your shrink." "Thanks Caroline."

"No Jason, thank you for your service!"

On his way back to work Jason thought, *I have to tell Anna about Caroline and what just happened. I guess security is the right job for me.*

As soon as he got back to the office he got a call from Dr. Han.

"Jason, we have been invited to see the Secretary-General. I think he would like to thank you for the work you did in Prague. This is rare and let's not be late. Meet me in my office at four and we will walk over to his office together."

The Secretary-General of the United Nations is the head of the United Nations and is considered the chief administrative officer of the United Nations. He plays a most important role to use his good will, his "good offices" and the manner he takes publicly, and at times in private meetings to prevent disputes by countries. He is considered to have the qualities of integrity, independence and impartiality.

When Dr. Han and Jason entered the office of Mr. Alberto Domingo, the Secretary- General of the United Nations they were greeted by his secretary and brought into his office. She sat them down and said, Mr. Domingo will be in shortly. He is in conference and will be here within fifteen minutes. They waited for another twenty-five minutes until he walked in.

What Jason noticed at first was the amount of grey hair on the man. It seemed to him that he needed a good haircut. He was wearing a well-fitting blue-grey suit with a blue tie and white shirt. His shoes were jet black and polished to the hill. Jason thought, *He looks like a Wall Street executive.*

Dr. Han introduced Jason to the Secretary-General and he motioned them to sit down. He placed himself behind a huge desk and opened up a folder.

"Mr. Darvish, may I compliment you in rescuing Mr. Bada from some very bad people. They were out to kill him, no doubt at all in my mind." Mr. Domingo spoke English with a slight Hispanic accent.

"Thank you, sir. It is part of my job."

"And you do it with extraordinary skill. Mr. Bada told me all about it. He is safe now and has brought to us some very important information that will help us with world peace. I can guarantee that it is so."

Mr. Domingo stood up and went around his desk. Jason stood up and the Secretary- General shook his hand. The United Nations thanks you for your diligence, bravery and judgment."

Jason smiled, "World peace is a dream for all of us. Thank you for recognizing me." "Dr. Han has recommended you for a Section Chief's position. It is one step below our

executive levels and most of our administrators make chief in ten years. You have been here less

than one year and I have just signed off on it. It will be probationary for two years. Is this acceptable to you?"

"If Dr. Han has the confidence in me, then it would be my pleasure to serve."

Dr. Han shook Jason's hand. "I will work you very hard and I expect no complaints!"

Jason nodded, "Let's give it a go!"

Later in the day Dr. Han introduced Jason to his section. His section provided the security planning for conferences, seminars, and lectures by United Nation personnel that are held in the northeastern part of the United States. The nine states were: Connecticut, Maine, Massachusetts, New Hampshire, New Jersey, New York, Pennsylvania, Rhode Island and Vermont.

Jason learned that security had to be provided, even if a delegate went to an elementary school to talk to twenty-five sixth graders. It was protocol that all United Nation Ambassadors and their staff had to report their speaking engagements to security. Jason further found out that he was given the position because the former section chief was fired. Checking with his staff he realized that the former chief was incompetent.

Jason thought, *Well, I thought I wanted a safer job— now I have one.*

Chapter Twenty-one

Anna realized that Jason was moving up in the United Nations quickly. When she heard through the grapevine, which was actually her best friend Susan, that Jason was going to be a section chief she was thrilled. There was so much "star" quality about him; yet he was never a braggart, never an egotist, never exaggerated his situation and always modest. She called Jason and asked him over for dinner at her apartment.

"I have a new dish I want to try out. Are you game?"

Jason answered quckly, "Sure, I'll take a chance. What do I have to lose?" They both giggled as Anna said, "Make it at seven tonight."

Jason carried a bottle of champagne under his arm and knocked on the door. Anna rushed to the door and gave him a big kiss and hug. "Come on in handsome!"

Jason gave her the champagne, "I have some good news to share with you. Perhaps after dinner?"

"Okay with me. Sit down, you are going to have a Niçoise salad tonight followed by my own quiche. It's French night tonight!"

Her salad contained tuna fish in olive oil, olives, radishes, Boston lettuce, cherry tomatoes, small sliced potatoes, hard boiled eggs and thin green beans. Her dressing was well mixed and contained olive oil, minced shallots, fresh thyme, white wine vinegar, white wine, sea salt plus freshly ground pepper. It was a meal in itself.

They both wiped their plates with the garlic bread that Anna had prepared. Then she served her quiche. And keeping with the French theme it was Quiche Lorraine for the main course. Anna had bought Gruyère as well as Swiss cheese, heavy cream, eggs, thin bacon and baked a special pie crust that was as thin as a pastry tart. She finished it off with ground pepper and regular table salt.

Jason finished his second helping and said, "Le repas était exceptionnel! Which translated as 'The meal was outstanding!'—let's have some champagne."

Anna lifted her glass to Jason and they clinked glasses. "Tell me about it!"

He grinned and was very happy, "Dr. Han made me section chief today. I'll be in charge of a team of ten people working on security for the northeastern states. It will be a bit overwhelning at first, but I know I can meet the challenge!"

"Congratulations my dear. Susan told me about it today and I am thrilled for you!"

"This means more hours at work. I'll try to limit it to ten hours a day. I'm not sure about weekends as yet. It all depends on how well the team plans. We may see a bit less of each other."

"Well let's make the time we spend together quality time."

Jason went over to her and took her face in his hands and kissed her, "Exactly!"

Anna would have taken him into bed tonight except she had just gotton her period. She felt disapointed and thought of another way to satisfy him—then rejected everything. She wanted to have it on her terms and she wanted it to be memorable. She thought, *Perhaps another time when it seems right.*

The next few weeks were filled with long hours with Jason learning the protocols of the position as well as planning a number of security assignments. He was greatly helped by a woman named Sheila Harris. She was with the section for three years and had great insight into security for representatives of the United Nations.

Sheila Harris was twenty-seven years old with a Masters degree in Criminal Justice from New York University. She had been placed with the New York Police Department's Forensic Unit as an intern and was offered a positon immediatley after receiving her masters at the age of twenty- two. Ms. Harris worked for two years doing forensics, but decided to use her criminal justice education at the United Nations. Dr. Han stated to Jason that she was a rising star and will do very well moving up the ladder. After working with her for two weeks Jason agreed.

Jason made sure to have the team use first names as they worked together. He felt that he needed to develop complete trust among his section. The members of his team liked the idea. After two weeks of working together Sheila went into Jason's office.

"Jason, I really like what your doing wih the section. Everybody likes you and your quiet leadership. I do and am willing to share anything I know about the section and the job."

Jason loked at Susan and saw a woman who was tall, athletic, with auburn hair, a small well shaped nose and sensuous lips. She carried herself erect and had a marvelous figure. Sheila came into work with an eye on coordinating her outfits. This woman had a great sense of fashion and her best feature was a wonderful smile that lit up the room.

"Thank you Sheila. Your confidence in me makes me want to work harder in order to have our section really shine!"

"A few of us are going out Friday night after work to O'Shea's Tavern for a few drinks.

Can you make it?"

'Oh I wish I could, but this weekend Anna and I are going to Great Neck. It's a sleepover and my mother is making me a birthday party. The whole family is coming. May I have a rain check!"

She looked at him and grinned, "You bet. Happy birthday Jason."

When Sheila Harris left his office she thought, *Here is a man I could really go for. Anna better be good to him or I will.*

Penn Station is located between Thirty-first and Thirty-third Streets and Seventh and Eighth Avenues in Manhattan. It is located right under Madison Square Garden. The station is huge and has multiple connections from five different commuter lines including, Amtrack, The New York City subway system and the Long Island Railroad. During one day it services six- hundred-thousand riders. According to statistics it is one of the major transportation hubs in the world.

Anna and Jason carried small overnighters onto their Long Island train and thirty-five minutes later they were stepping off the train. It was the first stop in Nassau County, New York.

Waiting for them at the station was Mr. Darvish. Jason introduced him to Anna who smiled at him and said, "I've heard a great deal about you Mr. Darvish. Jason loves you very much and I am so happy to meet you."

She threw her arms around him and he hugged her. Jason's father said, "You are the first girl Jason has ever brought home, so I guess you are very special!"

Anna laughed, "Then I have to be perfect this weekend—after all I can't make Jason look foolish."

The drive back to the Darvish house took fifteen minutes and waiting at the door was Mrs. Darvish. Anna saw her smiling at them as they proceeded up the walkway. She kissed her husband on the cheek, hugged and kissed Jason and extended her hand to Anna. "Welcome to our home Anna."

Anna was a bit confused about Mrs. Darvish's formality, but she decided to be open and said, "Mrs. Darvish, you have raised a wonderful man. It is an honor to meet you."

Jason's mother smiled, turned around and said, "I'll take you to your rooms." Their upstairs rooms were adjacent to each other.

Mrs Darvich pointed to Anna's room, "This was our daughter's room. Melody will be coming in later in the day with her husband and twins."

"Oh, where will she be staying?"

"There is a wonderful motel with suites ten minutes from here. They have all the necessary things for the family. Thank heaven the three year olds are potty trained."

The Darvish family had a buffet dinner for the birthday party. Three of Jason's friends from the neighborhood came with their spouses and girl friends. Melody's husband was a sweet man who helped with the twins who were a handful. Later in the evening Mrs. Darvish brought out the birthday cake and every one sang "Happy Birthday" to Jason.

Later, Jason observed Anna playing with the children. She was a natural. They squealed and ran all over her and she laughed and played with them.

Melody came over and took Jason's arm. "She is a winner, do you love her?" Jason whispered into his sister's ear. "Head over heals— I'm in love with her!" It was a wonderful night and Anna helped Mrs. Darvish clean up.

Alone in the kitchen both women were putting the last of the dishes away when Mrs.

Darvish stopped and looked at Anna. "Do you love my son?"

"Yes, with all my heart! We are close to becoming a couple, but not yet."

"Let me tell you something young lady; my son is a jewel, his facets have been cut, but the jewel needs a special person to put a brilliant shine on this precious gem."

"I understand Mrs. Darvish, I truly understand."

Anna went to her room at midnight, tired but very happy. Jason's parents were articulate, intelligent and loving. She understood Jason's outstanding value system by meeting them.

Jason's room was adjacent to the guest room. He had waited for Anna in the hallway and kissed her goodnight. They both closed their doors. Anna showered, put on a nightgown and walked into Jason's room.

He sat up in bed, "Anna, what do you want?"

"You, all of you, body and soul — I want all of you now!" She slipped off her nightgown and quickly got into bed with Jason.

He kissed her passionately. "You are the best birthday present I ever had." Anna could not help herself, "I love you Jason, please I want you now!"

It was sweet and after the passionate first time they discovered each other as true lovers. They finally got to sleep at three in the morning.

Anna's final thoughts were, *I'm glad I waited. He is the one. I love him so much!*

Mr. and Mrs. Darvish were pleased with Anna. They liked her. It was about nine in the morning and they had finished breakfast when Anna and Jason appeared. Mrs. Darvish looked at both of them and instinctively knew they loved each other. Jason was holding Anna's hand and Anna was glowing.

"Mom & Dad, Anna and I are a couple, we're only going to see each other."

His parents smiled, nodded in the affirmative and Mrs. Darvish said, "Anna, take care of my boy."

"He will be my highest priority."

Mrs. Darvish stood up and approached Anna. "Welcome to the family Anna."

Anna understood and nodded as tears rolled down her eyes. She was truly touched by the approval of his parents.

The train ride back to the city was easy and enjoyable. The couple held hands yet did not say too much to each other. There was a feeling of total satisfaction for both of them.

Chapter Twenty-two

The following week Jason was placed in a very uncomfortable and serious diplomatic position. The situation developed because an Assistant to the Ambassador of Myanmar, Mr. Win Thaik, decided that he was going to speak at Brooklyn College without notifying security until the last day. Jason realized that Brooklyn College had many liberal students who would rally against the speaker since his country was run by a dictator and had numerous human rights violations. Jason called the individual and advised him that he could not provide security at such short notice.

Twenty minutes later Dr. Han called Jason. "Why can't you give Mr. Thaik security?" "Dr. Han, Brooklyn College is likely to have a riot if this man speaks. It would be

prudent not to have him speak until I am able to set up some major security."

"He has to speak, I promised his office that I would provide security."

"Well Dr. Han, I could strap on my gun and I would suggest you do the same, because all my personnel are on other jobs. He did not follow the rules."

"Don't bother Jason. I'll call in some favors and get the man some security. When you have a chance please see me later today."

It was six in the evening when Jason met with Dr. Han. "I guess the President of the United States knew what he was doing when he gave you a recommendation."

Jason looked surprised, "Thank you Dr. Han."

Dr. Han's next question was earth shattering as she said, "Do you report to the CIA, NSA, FBI or any United States organization about our activities?"

Jason was taken aback. Shaken, he stood up and looked directly into his superior's eyes. "I do not. If you think I am disloyal then I cannot work in this organization and I resign!" He turned around and left the office. Jason immediately left the building and went home.

Jason was in a dark place. He felt betrayed by Dr. Han's question and he felt depressed, dejected and anxious. He thought, I'll call Dr. Blackman tomorrow. I really have to see her. He took a xanax, yet could not get to sleep. He felt, despondent, defeated and frustrated. Jason thought, *Why, would she accuse me of being disloyal.*

Dr. Han was very upset. She just lost a valuable member of her team and decided to look deeply into Jason Darvish and his past. The Director called in many favors from people to learn about him. She was absolutely amazed about Jason's heroism in battle, his fantastic career in the Office of Naval Intelligence, his scholarship and honesty in everything he did. The fact that every source told her that he was a man of character with honesty as one of his finest traits made her feel that her questioning about his loyalty was a low blow. A very low and embarrassing blow! She pondered a strategy and decided to cool things down for a day or two. Two days later she called Jason and asked if she could come to his apartment to talk with him. He agreed.

Dr. Han apologized by taking Jason's hand and holding it as she said, "I am truly sorry that I even doubted your honor. Please come back to the team. I will never doubt you again. I need you, the U.N. needs you, perhaps right now the world needs you."

Jason did not accept. "I will think this over and let you know in a few days. I need time to process this and decide if working for you is the best thing for me."

Dr. Han understood. She reflected on her way out of his apartment, *Here is a man who will carefully consider his options. I wish I had more like him!*

Jason saw his therapist to vent his anger and feelings. Dr. Blackman let him curse, yell, cry, and shake. She used this as a cathartic strategy since there was no way she would be able to reason with him unless he let it all hang out.

"Okay Jason, I really don't want to go into problem solving with you—after all you are a big boy. However, I want you to think about all the options you have in terms of your position at the United Nations. It really is up to you and only you—God knows you have been in enough situations to work this problem through that skull of yours!"

"You missed calling my skull a 'thick skull' Dr. Blackman."

"No, but I never realized that you had thin skin when it came to your honor. Think about it Jason, you have handled situations far worse and far more dangerous than this. Why are you so upset?"

"My parents raised me honorably. We never lied to each other and always told the truth. I am Catholic and there is a certain nobility in the honesty. That's the way I am!"

"Have you spoken to Anna about this situation?" "No."

"The only advice I have for you is to speak to your soulmate and share your feelings and thoughts."

"Thank you, Caroline, I needed your counsel."

Later in the evening Jason told Anna the whole story. He shared his true feelings and told her about his session with Dr. Blackman. "What should I do?"

She held him tightly, "I can't give you any direction except to say — go with you heart. I know your logic is saying 'no', but what is your heart saying?"

"My heart says—go back and do your job. I'm going back to work for the United Nations."

"Sweetheart, I know you didn't plan to stay with me tonight, but I want you to—will you please?

"Of course."

When they went to bed Anna kissed him softly and said, "I want you to lay back and relax. You are to be passive and I promise to be gentle with you. I want to be in charge tonight. You have made too many decisions and for once I want you to just be a taker, not a giver."

Jason never experienced the type of sweet loving touch he received all over his body. He tried to get up once and Anna pushed him back. She kissed and made love to every part of his body. When he finally climaxed he fell asleep in Anna's arms. She held him tightly all night.

Jason woke up the next morning feeling refreshed and wonderful. He smelled bacon and walked into the kitchen to see Anna in her robe making breakfast.

She smiled at him, "Take a shower—breakfast will be ready in ten minutes—go!" "Yes Ma'am!" He felt marvelous as if everything was alright in the world!

Dr. Han was thrilled that Jason decided to come back to work. She resolved to made sure to acknowledge Jason's successes to his colleagues and to support his ideas at meetings.

Her first statement to Jason as he came back to work said it all, "I am sorry that I questioned your loyalty and values. I will never do that again!"

Dr. Han had a winner and had plans for him. He was an outstanding analyst, a fierce field operator, highly intelligence and exhibited outstanding values. His leadership skills exhibited themselves naturally and people gravitated to him. Dr. Han realized that he could easily handle the security section of her department. She thought, *I could see him replacing me at a certain time.*

Chapter Twenty-three

Anna wanted Jason to move in with her, but Jason declined.

He took her hand and explained, "When we finally want to become engaged and marry I will move in with you. It has been only three weeks since my birthday party and our decision to become an exclusive couple. I'm cautiously optimistic about our relationship, but I think it is too soon. Sweetheart, you always want the truth from me— and that's the whole truth."

She squeezed Jason's hand. "I've been disappointed in love and I don't think I could handle us breaking up. I feel that if we live together we could establish that loving base, that sense of togetherness that I really need."

Jason hugged Anna and gently kissed her lips, "I know you have been hurt and I recognize your needs. What we have to do is to work on our new togetherness for awhile and see if this is for our lifetime. Anna, I'm Catholic and when I marry it is for a lifetime!"

Anna thought, *Oh, my God, he is really thinking about marriage and having a life together. Back off, don't push so hard.*

She kissed him, "Okay, let's work on being a couple."

Jason nodded in the negative, "No, let's work on being partners." "Isn't that the same?"

"When we are partners we share everything. I don't think it is a fifty-fifty situation in all cases, but in our social relationships; our wants and needs; our desire to help each other; our unconditional love for each other; our understanding and support when we are moody; when we are hurting; when something horrible happens—that's what I mean."

Anna never heard any person describe the type of relationship Jason wanted. She was blown away by his sincerity, his depth of understanding and his need for a partner. Tears of joy ran down her face as she felt touched by his depth of feeling.

"Okay for now. Let's work on being partners!"

The next two months seemed to work out well for the couple. They were able to coordinate their work schedule and find time together. Weekdays were difficult because Jason had certain timeline and supervisory obligations that meant evening work. At times he had to work on the weekends, but not too many.

Anna and Jason loved to experiment with different food from all over the world. New York City was the place to be when it came to the greatest variety of menus from all over the world.

They loved to go to Chinatown and enjoy authentic Chinese and Vietnamese cuisine; East Harlem for Puerto Rican, Mexican and Dominican food; the Greenwich Village for terrific Italian food; the East Village for Japanese, Korean, Indian and surprisingly Ukrainian specialties.

Since Anna lived in Flushing she had discovered fantastic Korean and Chinese food just steps away from her apartment on Main Street. She loved taking Jason to undiscovered, small, "Mom and Pop" restaurants in Jackson Heights that had Bangladeshi food; Pakistani food; Filipino and Columbian cuisine. In the Glendale area they enjoyed German and Polish food as well as visiting one of their favorites, Forrest Hills, for Jewish and Russian food.

There were days that Jason invited Anna to stay over at his small apartment. He had a small balcony and barbequed steak, burgers, franks and tiger shrimp. Jason had become a decent cook when he lived in Maryland as a naval officer.

Anna for the most part seemed to be traditional in her cooking. She used her slow cooker since it was easy to set things up in the morning, go to work and have a meal ready when she came home. When Jason came over she served him well balanced meals and she enjoyed watching him eat. He ate with relish. Obviously, he enjoyed her food and ate with gusto and appreciation. That made Anna feel worthy. Thank heavens her mother taught her how to cook. At times Anna would call her mother to ask for recipes.

The couple double dated with Susan and a number of her dates. Susan was a free spirit and at times Jason and Anna would bet to see if Susan would bring a date along for a third time. Currently that was not happening.

Susan was sophisticated beyond her years because of her background in England and her work at the United Nations. She interviewed high level diplomats and their staff to get the essence of their needs. As a brochure and pamphlet writer she had the ability to crystalize main ideas into a few paragraphs. Her work was outstanding. As a writer Anna appreciated her work.

One Saturday evening in Jason's apartment the couple was watching the national news and a breaking news story came on the screen. It seemed that a group of Afghan terrorists went over the border to Pakistan and attacked a small convoy of Pakistani soldiers moving two atomic weapons. They killed all but one of the soldiers and stole the atomic bombs.

There was a full alert and the United States was asked by the Pakistan government to help in the search.

Jason and Anna prepared to go to bed at eleven-thirty that evening when the phone rang. "Lieutenant Darvish, this is Captain Duncan. Sorry to call so late, but we have a situation

and all personnel who speak Dari have been activated. It's about the stolen bombs. Report to

ONI no later than Monday at 0800. Got it!" "Yes sir."

Jason went into his closet and took out a small overnighter. He started to fill it with necessary items.

Anna looked at him, "What are you doing?

"I have to report to the Office of Naval Intelligence no later than Monday morning. They activated me because I speak Dari and there is a full alert to find those atomic bombs."

"Can they make you do it?"

"When I joined the Navy I had to commit to a minimum of an eight year service obligation. Every service man is obligated. It's called the Individual Ready Reserves. We really don't do anything, but we are obligated to go on active duty in case of an emergency. When 9-11 happened a lot of men were called up. It seems I have a skill that's needed. I know Dari and the Navy needs me. I have to call Dr. Han right now."

The flight took less then two hours flying Delta Airlines out of LaGuardia Airport. Jason arrived before ten in the morning to the ONI in Suitland Maryland. By noon time he had received his picture identification card and was on his way to Captain Duncan's office.

"Reporting to duty Captain Duncan."

"Thanks for coming in Jason. Here is the situation. This is a full court press. We have had the CIA as well as an FBI Forensic Unit fly to Pakistan to see if they might discover where the bomb is headed. Seal Team Four and Six have been ordered to be on a twenty-four hour alert and we need a Dari translator for Seal Team Four. You are flying out this evening at 1900. Go to the storekeeper and the armory to get your uniform and weapons. This is a national emergency. God forbid those thugs get to use the bomb where our troops are stationed and thousands of our men will die. Jason, find the bombs and get those dirty bastards!"

"Aye, aye sir!"

It was déjà vu. This time the plane was a Boeing C-17 Globemaster III. He sat in a reasonably fitted chair and was happy to hear less noise from the plane's engines. They refueled twice in the air and finally landed in Kandahar, Afghanistan. Due to some terrible headwinds the flight took over seventeen hours and Jason was starving when he got off. The best thing he ate on the plane was peanut butter crackers and coffee.

The duty officer read Jason's orders and said, "Okay Lieutenant, you are high priority and your copter will leave in ninety minutes. Get some chow and rest up—over there in Building Able. See you back real soon."

Jason flew out towards the Pakistan border and in two hours was deposited alongside three tents. When he landed a large man took Jason's gear and motioned him inside the first tent. All of a sudden he was slapped on his back.

"Nice to see you again, Lieutenant!"

Jason turned around and there was Chief Carson. "Hell Chief, you haven't aged at all!" "Chief Carson yelled at his men, "Loosen up guys—remember I told you the story of a dude

who saved my ass. Well here he is in the flesh. Jason Darvish!"

The men introduced themselves and it seemed to Jason that they looked very young. 'Hey Chief, are you running a kindergarten here?"

"No sir. Just you and I getting old."

"Look men, I'm a civilian and the CNO pulled my butt into service because I know Dari. I'm your translator and I promise I'll listen to all of you. No bullshit, I mean it!"

Chief Carson said, "Commander Casey will be coming in to take over the team. He's our logistic man and he's coming back from headquarters with the latest scoop."

Jason said, "Only one very important question Chief."

"Anything sir."

"Where the hell is the coffee."

All the men laughed. They realized that Jason was one of them. No bullshit—straight talk!

Jason enjoyed his large mug of coffee and prepared a MRE. The Meal, Ready-to-Eat is a ration packed in a sealed bag. It contained one precooked meal plus some supplements. Jason poured some water into the bag and his meal started cooking. In five minutes he opened up a can of chicken tetrazzini. It tasted like a feast for Jason since he hadn't eaten in twenty-one hours.

Chief Carson pointed to the left corner of the tent, "There's a folded cot over there. You can get some shuteye until we get some news."

Jason was asleep in five minutes.

Chapter Twenty-four

His shoulder was being pushed. Jason pushed back until he heard Chief Carson. "Wake up Lieutenant, the boss is here."

Commander Sean Casey came over to the cot as Jason was standing up. He gave Jason a hand and pulled him to his feet.

"Nice to meet you Lieutenant. I'm Sean Casey and I have the privilege to command Seal Team Four. My J.G. Williams is scouting up some night flares and then we're good to go."

"Where are we going Commander? Will you help me understand what really is happening."

"Okay Jason, here is the real skinny. The Pakistani government is in a possible state of collapse. When that happens the Pakistani military has a special protocol. It spreads out their nuclear weapons so no terrorist government or band of bad guys gets into the nuclear storage facilities. That's what happened three days ago. Now all of the weapons have been accounted for—except for the two bombs that were stolen and brought into Afghanistan. We know it wasn't the Taliban because the surviving soldier from the attack heard the bad guys speaking Dari. The Taliban speak Pashto. It's our mission to get the bombs back."

"Are there any leads?"

"Yes, the FBI forensic unit found some empty fig wrappers. They came from a small local factory in the city of Herat. We are concerned because the roads to Iran from Herat are strategic and it is really easy to get anything into or out of Iran. We fly out in fifty minutes."

The two helicopters were able to reach Herat in eighty-five minutes. They landed in a park just north of the Great Mosque of Herat and were met by two women and a man in civilian clothing. The Commander and his Lieutenant Junior Grade went to speak to the civilians. Jason thought they were probably CIA. Jason saw the Commander wave his hand at Jason. Jason sprinted over to them.

"What's up?"

The first woman never introduced herself as she verbalized, "Lieutenant, there is a coffee shop next block where we think we can get some intel. They speak Darsi. Go in there and see if you can get the lay of the land when it comes to them seeing any strangers. Here is some bribe money. You will probably have to use it."

"How do you know they have any information?" "That's for us to know—goddammit just do your job!"

Jason looked at her, put his hands on his hips and said, "Fuck you lady! You don't send anybody into any place without giving him a little heads up. I need some more information. Now you better shape up or this mission is blown. Do you understand?"

She was shaken to the core. It probably was the first time she was ever answered by a man who countered her. The woman stepped back and the male civilian stepped in.

"Now Lieutenant, I'm sorry for her behavior. We have been up for twenty hours trying to get leads on the bomb. Give her a break."

Look buddy, what's your name?" "Harry.'

"Look Harry. I'm a civilian who was just called back to do my duty. Give me some intel on the coffee shop."

"Okay. The owner seems to be at the cash register and he has two women working there.

One is middle aged and the other is a cute teenager. It probably is a shop run by the family. I think the best bet is the teenager. The older folks are usually weary of foreigners."

Jason looked at Harry and said, "Give me your sweater. I'm taking off my khaki fatigue shirt and I'm becoming a civilian."

The coffee shop was small. There were five tables and a small counter. On the counter there were some Afghanistan pastries. He sat down at the closest table and in perfect Darsi asked for black coffee and some Khatai cookies.

The teenaged girl answered, "We will brew a fresh cup for you." She smiled at him.

He ate his tasty pistachio topped cookies and while drinking his coffee he asked, "I am looking for my cousins, they were supposed to meet me here yesterday and I am late. Perhaps you saw some men, some strangers— as I am.?"

"No, but my mother said she saw three men who she thinks were Iranian driving a white van. They went into the hotel. She delivers Baklava to the hotel."

"What hotel?"

"Oh, it is down the street. It is a budget hotel and called The Star."

"No, they are not my cousins. They would go to a better hotel. Thank you for your service." He left a small tip."

Jason returned to his team. "They may be Iranian with a white van. Their staying at a hotel called The Star."

Commander Casey said, "Scottie take a sniper's position opposite the hotel; Johnny accompany Jason to the hotel to see if you can get a room number; Carl you and

J.G. Williams take the radiation device and see if you can find the white van. Chief, deploy the rest of the team to encircle the hotel so nobody can escape. Any questions?"

The CIA man called Harry asked, "What can we do?"

Commander Casey frowned, "Keep out of the way. In fact, get on your satellite phone and order a cargo plane to stand ready to land at the local airport."

Harry replied, "Done!"

Jason and Petty Officer Johnny approached the hotel. Jason looked at the youngster. He probably was no older than twenty-two. Johnny seemed nervous.

"Is this your first mission?"

"No sir, it's my second. The first was a dud. We flew in and ten minutes later we flew out. No positive results."

"Johnny, stay outside, at the door, and wait for my signal. I'll wave to you if I need you."

"Aye, aye sir."

Jason, still wearing his civilian sweater asked the clerk in perfect Dari. "My cousins came in yesterday. Their driving a white van. What room are they in so I can visit them?'

There was no hesitation at all. "Room two-twelve." "Thank you. I'll go outside and get my luggage."

Jason and the Petty Officer quickly walked to Commander Casey. "Room two-twelve," Jason quickly told Casey."

Let's wait until Williams and Carl get back from their search. They waited another ten minutes until around the corner came the white van with Carl driving it.

"What the hell," exclaimed Commander Casey.

J.G. Williams excitedly said, "Mission accomplished. We have the bombs. They were under a tarp. Carl hot wired the van and here we are!"

"Great work men!"

"Okay, let's round up those scum bags. I'm sure the Pakistani Army would like a word or two with them."

The rest of the operation was easy. A team of SEALs knocked on the terrorist's door and simply overpowered them. Among the group was one Afghan who spoke Dari. and two Iranians who spoke Farsi. They communicated in English.

The team waited for two hours until a military plane landed in the Herat Airport.

The bombs, prisoners, CIA and SEAL Team Four all went aboard. Jason was pleased with the outcome.

After depositing the bombs, prisoners and the CIA in Islamabad, Pakistan SEAL Team Four and Jason flew to Kabul in Afghanistan. From there they were ordered to give their report to Central Command in MacDill Air Force Base, in Tampa, Florida. They were told to remain silent about the mission since it was classified as top secret. The only saving grace was that they flew to Florida on a Boeing 747, chartered for them alone.

They were served real food and plenty of drinks. Jason had a New York strip steak and fries, a glass of red wine and went to sleep for nine hours.

Central Command for the Middle East, North Africa, Central Asia which includes Afghanistan and Iraq is located in Tampa Florida. It currently runs the major military operations in their responsible areas and is considered a "Theater-level Unified Combatant Command." In other words, they run the show! Sometimes they use the acronym CENTCOM.

The team was greeted as heroes by the officers who debriefed them. They all had to give their version of the mission separately. After that some of the team were recalled to go over some specifics of the mission. Jason was recalled by a Colonel who had some additional questions.

"Lieutenant Darvish, why did you speak to the teenager?"

"Harry from the CIA thought it would be best since the older folks would be cautious."

"Who suggested you put on the sweater?"

"I did. Nobody wants to talk to the military."

"I see here that you were called back to service for this mission. What do you do as a civilian?"

"I work for the United Nations in security. I'm a Section Chief doing security for delegates. It's sort of a middle managers position."

"May I congratulate you on your marvelous work in the field. To be quite honest with you, I think your talents are being wasted. I'd recommend you right now as a Senior Civilian Analyst for the Army. That would be equal to me as a full bird, or in the Navy a full four stripe Captain. Think about it. The weather in Florida is sunny most of the time."

"I'm flattered Colonel—I think I just want to go home."

Chapter Twenty-five

Jason called Anna, "Hi, I'm back." "Where are you?"

"Tampa Florida at CENTCOM. I mean at the big army base." "When will you be home. I miss you—oh Hon, I really miss you!"

"I've only been gone six days. I have tickets to fly out tomorrow morning. I just have to buy some civilian clothing. I don't think dirty fatigues would be proper on a plane."

"Can you talk about it?"

"Sorry, top secret. Cannot speak about it." "Were you successful?"

"Very successful!" "Were you an observer?"

"No, I was not an observer."

"Were you the anthesis of an observer?"

Jason started to laugh, "Anna, you are not going to get anything more out of me!" "Just one more question—would the mission you were on have been successful if you

weren't there?"

"Oh Sweetheart, please I really —" Anna cut him off. Please!"

"No."

"I love you Jason and I'm so proud of you. See you tomorrow."

Anna made dinner for Jason the next day. She set the table with brand new china, cloth napkins, a design tablecloth and new eating utensils. Her menu was a caesar salad, baby lamb chops, garlic mashed potatoes and candied carrots.

"This is a marvelous dinner. Are we celebrating anything?" Anna smiled, "You are back home safe and sound."

The meal ended with chocolate mousse. Anna went to the back of the kitchen and took out a small wrapped box. She placed it in front of Jason.

"This is a welcome home gift, welcome home sailor!"

Jason unwrapped the package and in it was a Rolex Oyster Perpetual Date watch. It was beautiful with an eighteen karet gold case and a combination gold and stainless steel band. It shone brilliantly and he immediately put it on his wrist.

"Oh Anna, it is beautiful—and so expensive." "I wanted something special for my boyfriend."

They gently kissed and continued kissing for the rest of the evening. Later, Anna and Jason made love quietly and it seemed differently. They were both making sure to gently pleasure each other. There was no rush, there was no urgency to achieve finality, there was pleasure in controlling their emotions as their passion continued to grow and grow.

Finally, Anna whispered to Jason, "Please baby, now—right now—oh my God!"

The next day Dr. Han walked into Jason's office. She was smiling and as Jason stood up she extended her hand and shook it.

"My sources have informed me that without you the bombs would not have been found." Jason said, "It's classified and—"

Dr. Han laughed, "Not only that, it's top secret and I know about it through my sources.

My compliments and respect to you."

She turned around and left the office before Jason had a chance to talk to her. He thought,

This woman has a huge reach!

Sheila Harris came into his office. She was dressed in a smart business suit with a colorful blouse.

"Welcome home Jason. Dr. Han had put me in charge when you were away. We had three security placements and there were no problems at all. The office was reasonably quiet. I'm glad you are okay."

Jason thought for a moment, "Sheila, what level are you?"

"I'm a P-3. Professional level with under seven years of experience."

"Well they made me a P-5 to be Section Chief. Perhaps I can get Dr. Han to recommend a bump up for you. I'm going to write a letter of recommendation for your file immediately.

Sheila, thank you so much for taking over."

"You're welcome, Jason. You are very kind to think of me." She left the office thinking, *Oh boy, I really like this guy!*

A week later Jason's mother called him at work.

"Son, we have just sold our business and our home. Your Dad and I will be moving to Florida next month after the house closing. Could you and Anna come over for an early dinner this Sunday? We would like to talk to you."

'I'll check with Anna, but I'm sure it will be okay. If you don't hear from me within the next hour it will be okay. Jason called Anna and it was okay with her.

Jason called Susan Han. She was Anna's best friend and confident. "Susan, will you be able to help me with a situation I have?"

"Sure Jason, what is it"

"What are you doing for lunch tomorrow?" "I'll be in the cafeteria as usual."

"Would you mind if you met me at Uncle Papa's for a slice of pizza. It's a five minute walk from here on Vanderbilt Avenue. How about twelve-thirty?"

"Okay, can you give me a hint?" "See you tomorrow."

Uncle Papa's was the typical pizza place in New York City. They had a menu for all sorts of Italian specialties although ninety percent of their business was pizza. The white and red checkered tablecloths were sparkling clean and the waitress who served them was the daughter of the owner. In the kitchen the owner and his son were making pizza and at the cash register was mama making sure that everyone paid.

When Jason and Susan finished their pizza and drank their diet drinks he was ready for some serious talk.

"Susan, I want you to help me pick out an engagement ring for Anna. Will you help me?" Susan stood up and went over to Jason, hugged him, kissed his cheek.

She said, "God, it's about time. She is so in love with you that I get sick and tired of hearing about how good a person you are—but goddammit, you are!"

Jason blushed, "I have no idea what to buy. My first thought was to have her come with me and then I thought I really want to surprise her."

"Okay, down to business. Do you have a budget? How much can you afford?" "I went on-line to sniff around. The best I can do is twelve thousand dollars."

"Oh, that's great. We are going to go to the Diamond District on Forty-seventh Street.

I'm positive you can get a good value and a superb ring for her. I know what she likes. The only thing is I really can't hold the secret for that long. When do you plan to give it to her?"

"We are gong to my folks house this Sunday. I'd like to give it to her there."

"Okay, then meet me tomorrow at noon in my office. We will go shopping. Make sure you have your money transferred into your checking account today."

"Thanks Susan, I never would have thought about it."

"Hurray, I finally found out something that you are dumb about." She giggled.

The Diamond District in New York City is world renown. There are over twenty-five hundred stores, and booths in diamond exchanges located on Forty-seventh Street between Fifth and Sixth Avenues. There is a hustle and bustle throughout the area with people rushing around carrying boxes and thin business suitcases.

"Jason, Anna likes a halo design. That's a round stone surrounded by smaller diamonds that are called pave set."

After looking at many rings, stones and settings Jason said, "I'm tired and confused.

Let's take a break."

Susan frowned, "Look Jason, this is for her lifetime so you have to get it right." "Okay, let's get a cup of coffee."

Later the right ring was found. It was beautiful. Susan did all the haggling and negotiations and finally said, "Okay Jason, we are now going to go to an independent Gemological Institute of America Graduate Gemologist to appraise the ring."

It took another hour but it was worth it. The appraisal was for nineteen thousand-seven hundred dollars and Jason paid eleven thousand two hundred dollars. The round stone itself was just under two carats with another sixty-six smaller diamonds set around it. Susan knew that Anna wore a size five and one hour later Jason walked out with the ring. He was pleased.

Jason kissed Susan on the cheek, "Thank you, Susan. You are terrific!"

"It was fun. I'll tell Anna all about our shopping, but only after you give her the ring. I'm so happy for both of you."

Jason was happy with his decision to give Anna the engagement ring. He knew that they were good for each other. Since his parents were moving to Florida next month he felt that they would be pleased to know that he would not be alone. The timing was good and he loved Anna so much. Perhaps her gift of the Rolex watch to him was a stimulus to move ahead with their relationship. Jason thought, *It's time to really be together and live together. I'm ready.*

Chapter Twenty-six

The family had early dinner at four in the afternoon. Mr. and Mrs. Darvish were full of plans and excited about their move to Florida.

"Son, I sold my business and made enough money for your mom and I to live comfortably for the rest of our lives. My financial advisor is conservative and has placed me in a good situation. Your mother and I will have a monthly income that is guaranteed."

Mrs. Darvish was thrilled, "This is the first time I feel relieved. Your father has worked very hard in his life time and he certainly earned the right to some comfort."

"Mom, you deserve it as well!"

Every one helped to clear the table and Mrs. Darvish pushed Anna and Jason out of the kitchen. "Out, your father and I will finish up."

Jason took Anna's hand and led her to the rear enclosed patio. He sat down next to her on a small couch and kissed her cheek. Then he took out the box.

"Anna, will you marry me?"

There was absolutely no hesitation to her answer. "Yes, my darling. I will marry you. She sweetly kissed him on his lips and opened the box."

"I hope you like it?"

"I love it. It's beautiful. How did you know I love this design?" "Thank Susan, she helped me out."

They held hands and went back into the house. Anna raised her left hand and Mrs.

Darvish yelled, "Oh my, oh my—that is fantastic—let me see it my dear!"

The rest of the evening was a discussion of plans; the timing of trying to meet Anna's parents; and of course the wedding.

Anna said, "Jason and I are in no rush to get married. We will work things out. The important thing is for you to get settled in Florida and when the timing is right we can plan it. My parents don't know about this as yet. I'm going to call them now."

The train trip back was a blur to the happy couple. They took an Uber from Penn Station and when Jason dropped off Anna at her apartment she kissed him for a long time.

"Don't forget, we will see my parents on Tuesday night. Jason, I want you to move in with me. Is that okay?

"Yes, it is okay!"

Jason walked the twelve blocks to his apartment He was happy and felt that this was the beginning of a wonderful part of his life's journey. Anna was perfect for him and he was not afraid to share his feelings with her. He thought, *Partners for life. Now that's great!*

Anna called Susan as soon as she got into her apartment.

"Oh Susan, the ring is beautiful. Jason told me you helped. Will you be my maid of honor?"

Susan started to cry for joy, "Oh Anna, I'm so happy for you. You are my dear friend and Jason is right for you. I will love to be your maid of honor. When is the wedding?"

"I have no idea. Jason will be moving in with me and we will have to work it out. We are not in any rush!"

"Great, I'm taking you out to lunch tomorrow. I'll meet you in the lobby at noon." Anna had trouble getting to sleep. There were so many plans to think about.

Dr. Han congratulated Jason. She was pleased that it was Anna.

"I have known Anna for a few years and she is perfect for you. Now the big question is— can you find a man for Susan? She is my only child and I am concerned about her future."

Jason shrugged his shoulders, "Perhaps Anna would be in a better position to help Susan.

I'll speak to her. On another subject, I'm moving in with Anna. Are there any United Nations protocols that would prevent it?"

Dr. Han shook her head in the negative, "I have something else to discuss with you. Jack Van, my Senior Supervisor of Field Operations, was in an automobile accident yesterday and he is in critical condition. I called the hospital in Vienna and they think he will pull through. The medical people think he will be laid up for at least six months to a year. I'm stuck because Jack's assistant left last month to get a job with Interpol. I called him this morning and he doesn't want to come back."

"Ouch, that puts you in a bind."

"Listen to my plan and then give me your honest opinion. I value your judgment. I am going to put my assistant, Charlie Rich into Jack's slot. Charlie is talented and he's single so there is no problem with him going all over the world putting out fires. Now that leaves me without an assistant."

"I'm sure you would have your pick of any professionals in your division." "I certainly have— and Mr. Darvish you are my new assistant."

Jason was shocked and did not say anything for a few seconds, "Dr. Han, am I up to the job?"

"I would not have nominated you if I didn't think you were the best choice." "Yes, I certainly would love to work with you."

"Who do you suggest take over your section?"

"Sheila Harris. She has great organizational skills, understands the role and is willing to put in the time. Perhaps she could be bumped up a grade?"

"Leave that to me. Okay Jason, you tell her. Your assignment starts tomorrow!"

Sheila Harris sat opposite Jason in his office. She was wearing a jersey dress that accentuated her fantastic figure. The woman never flirted or did anything improper, yet Jason felt that she was a dynamo.

"Sheila, I'm taking over the role of Dr. Han's assistant. It is temporary that could last from six months to a year. I recommended you to take over as Section Chief. Dr. Han will try to get you bumped up a grade. Are you willing to take over?"

Sheila jumped out of her chair and ran over to Jason. She planted a big kiss on his face, "Oh Jason, you are the best!"

He looked at her— her face turned beet red. "I'm excited for you Sheila."

"I'm so embarrassed Jason, I really got carried away. I really like you as a person and I would do anything for you—and I mean anything!"

"Then make me proud. You have outstanding qualities and if you need anything just call me."

The lunch between Anna and Susan lasted longer than the normal hour. Susan suggested they celebrate Anna's engagement by eating in an upscale restaurant. They selected "19 Madison Avenue" a very posh and expensive four star establishment. The wine flowed and both women were a bit giddy after consuming two bottles of wine.

Susan queried, "Does Jason have any special qualities. How is he as a lover?"

Anna, whose tongue was loosened by alcohol said, "Girl, when he does me he does me all over. He is such a considerate lover and he knows how to turn every part of me into a howling she wolf. Susan, I can't get enough of him I love him so. He walks in the door and I'm wet and ready to jump him. Oh God, I never felt like this before!"

They both started to laugh, then they broke into hysterics.

Chapter Twenty-seven

Dr. Han sat Jason down in her conference room and said, "Let me give you the big picture so you will understand what you are getting into. The countries that belong to the United Nations have spies. That is a given. Every country, no matter how small keeps a covert intelligence person or people who are always trying to get information to either protect, defend or attack other countries."

"I assumed that was the situation."

Dr. Han continued, "We at the United Nations Department of Safety and Security (UNDSS) protect all United Nations personnel in countries throughout the world. Jason there are many, many different programs throughout the world. My count is that there are over one- hundred and growing. We deal with many different situations. You have heard about armed attacks against our personnel, yet we also deal with problems as simple as petty theft. Our United Nations Management System has been developed throughout the years to deal with problems.

And trust me—there are plenty! Throughout the world dedicated personnel risk their lives to keep personnel safe. These committed people work all over the world in the areas of communication, armed defense, investigations and delegate security. This is a major league operation!"

"I realize the operation is big."

Dr. Han unrolled a chart and placed it on the conference table. "I want you to look at this chart. We are responsible for three million visitors, the heads of state and their delegations, thirty-six thousand staff members, fifty-eight thousand dependents, as well as lectures, symposiums, speeches, conferences and anything else named where any United Nations personnel are going. It is huge!"

"Where do you get the intelligence to keep up with this mass of responsibility?"

"Ah, we have the Threat and Risk Service of the United Nations (TRS) who has the task of analyzing threats, developing strategies to combat the threats, and of course keeping in sustained communication with us."

"What model do you use?"

"Jason, I knew you were bright, in fact brilliant—you are the first person who has ever asked me that. We use the military model—mission, objective, strategies, tactics, lists and schedules."

He laughed, "Sounds very familiar to me. Very!"

"Oh, I forgot to mention our Non-Government Agencies (NGO). Any peace-keeping movements—to tell you the truth any aspect involved with the safety of people.

"How do you keep up?"

'I read a lot and have assistants as you who will help."

Jason went back to his office and called his secretary. A woman of forty-five came into his office. She had been working at the United Nations for fifteen years and in her present assignment for five years. Dr. Han had spoken very highly about her abilities.

Her name was Ruth Goldman. She was wearing a blue business suit, simple white blouse, and her skirt came to the middle of her knee. Ruth had nice features, high cheekbones, dark brown hair and deep hazel eyes. She had a prominent nose and was short, about five feet one inches. Mrs. Goldman was married to her husband Martin for twenty-four years and they had one son who was a graduate student at John Hopkins in Baltimore.

"Mrs. Goldman, I haven't had time to tell you how appreciative I've been for all your tutoring about my duties. Please understand, your boss should be back to this office in six months to a year."

"Mr. Darvish, you are a quick study and your reputation precedes you. Dr. Han had mentioned you to other staff members. You are the first employee of the United Nations that has been made a section chief in less than a year. Outstanding!"

"Thank you. I was in the right place at the right time." "Did you need something sir?"

"Yes, I need the latest monthly business calendar for the World Health Organization." "It should be on your computer."

"I tried, but all I got was this month." "I'll check it out and get back to you."

Within five minutes Mrs. Goldman said, "I spoke to the secretary of the WHO and was told that they were tardy. The new monthly calendar will be posted in two days."

Jason thought, *I'm lucky to have her as my secretary.*

That evening Jason and Anna visited Anna's parents in Teaneck, New Jersey. They had dinner and moved into the family room to converse about the engagement.

Dr. Mason said, "It's important that you give us a date-certain time for the wedding. We have relatives all over the country who may want to come. The more lead time you give them the easier it will be for all of us."

Anna sat between her father and Jason. Her mother sat across from them in a comfortable chair. She was smiling and quite happy.

"Mom and Dad, we haven't talked about a date as yet. We don't even know if we want a big wedding. Jason's parents will be living in Florida by the end of the month and his sister lives in New Hampshire."

Mrs. Darvish asked, "When will we meet your parents Jason?" "I'm not sure. They are in the middle of moving."

"Jason, if its okay with you I'd like to have a dinner here, at your parents convenience, so we can get to know each other."

Anna spoke first, "Mom, I'll give you their number. I'm sure you can work something out."

During their train trip home Jason felt uncomfortable. He looked at Anna and she took his arm and squeezed.

"Hon, it will be okay. Let your folks and my folks work it out. I trust them!"

"Okay, I just am beginning to feel that the wedding is going to be an over powering event for both of us."

"Every little girl, as they grow up, plans and fantasizes for their own wedding. I really have some thoughts, but right now they are jumbled. Please give me some time and I promise I will lay it all out for you. Leave it to me and my mother."

Jason felt relieved, 'Okay, you have the ball. Let me know if I can help."

The family dinner was a great success. The Mason's and the Darvish's genuinely liked each other. There was a great deal of discussion about how they raised their children and it was decided that it would be up to Jason and Anna to state the type of wedding they wanted.

Dr. Mason was very witty, "Of course, the only advice I have for the couple is: 'Whenever you're wrong, admit it. Whenever you're right, shut up.' Not my advice, but Ogden Nash."

A week later Mr. and Mrs. Darvish moved to Florida and bought a condominium near their first cousin. They sent pictures of the club house, pool and social hall. There was no doubt in Jason's mind that they did the right thing. He felt relieved that they were happy. His sister Melody seemed upset since she wanted her children to have more time with their grandparents. Yet she understood and was happy for her parents.

Anna and her mother talked almost every day and Anna seemed to be in control. One evening after dinner she curled up next to Jason and hugged him.

"Hon, do you want a Catholic wedding?"

"I'm not sure. I know you are Christian, but pretty liberal."

"Would it hurt you too much if I told you I would prefer not to get married in church." He looked at her and realized she was afraid to hurt his feelings. Jason kissed her cheek. "Anna, I don't care if a priest marries us, a minister marries us, a rabbi marries us or a

basketball coach marries us—I want to marry you."

Anna jumped on him, pinned him down and kissed his face all over. "I love you, love you 'soooo' much!"

Chapter Twenty-eight

Jason got a call from Anna in his office. "Jason, may I come up and speak to you about a situation that just happened.?

"Sure, come on up."

Ten minutes later Anna appeared with a folder in her hands.

"I just had to change fourteen pages of a report that is being sent to the Security Council.

The Afghanistan Assistant to the Delegate came up and changed everything. The concept, wording and statistics are completely changed. I have the original and I have the final copy."

Jason looked up at her and smiled, "Isn't this normal policy?"

"Yes, but when you read both reports they are the antithesis to each other!" "Okay, the report may be the opposite, but that's what he wants."

"How do we know if it's what the Delegate wants? I've worked here for over three years and this is the first time this has happened in such a peculiar and severe manner!" Jason was pensive. He really had not seen Anna so concerned and he was befuddled. "Okay, leave the copies with me and follow through with the publishing. I'll check with my boss."

When Anna left Jason called his boss. He told her of the situation. Dr. Han seemed perturbed. "Jason, I just got news that the Afghanistan Delegate, Dr. Moradi, just died this morning of a possible heart attack. Please check this out, but quietly—very quietly."

Within an hour Jason found out that the deceased delegate was taken to Lenox Hill Hospital on East 77th Street. He had called the Mission and asked for Mrs. Moradi's cell number. Jason asked to see her as soon as possible. She was at the hospital making plans for her husband's removal.

Jason arrived in twenty-five minutes and flashed his United Nations credentials. He was taken to a small room where Mrs. Moradi was waiting.

"Mrs. Moradi, I'm Jason Darvish and I work in the UN. I'm so sorry for your loss. Your husband was so young."

"He was forty-five and in very good health. I don't understand how this could have happened,"

"Did he have any heart problems at all?" "No, he exercised and watched his sweets." "What happened?"

"We were having breakfast with Ari, his assistant at eight o'clock this morning.

All of a sudden my husband started to feel warm, then he collapsed. We called 911." Jason thought, *He was a healthy man, it doesn't make sense.*

"Mrs. Moradi, I think that it would be best to check with the authorities to see if it was really a heart attack."

"But Ari told me that my husband's body had to be immediately taken back to Afghanistan for a proper funeral."

"Mrs. Moradi, I am a security officer at the United Nations and I think it would be best if we have an autopsy performed."

"But we are Sunni, we don't do that!" "We must determine the cause of death." "No, I don't want to do that."

Jason left her and went outside. He called Dr. Han and told her what happened. He was suspicious.

Dr. Han instructed Jason, "Stay with Mrs. Moradi. I'll call the Police Commissioner and request that the body be held for an autopsy. It is suspicious. Don't speak to the press or anybody."

Twenty-five minutes later a NYC Police Captain, John Sparks, arrived and asked to speak to Mrs. Moradi. She was still located in the small waiting room when Captain Sparks came in. He was a tall distinguished looking man dressed in his New York Police department blue uniform. Captain Sparks looked at Mrs. Moradi and approached her. Sitting next to her he spoke gently.

"I'm so very sorry for your loss. We must transport your deceased husband to our medical facilities in order find out the cause of death. Do you understand?"

Mrs. Moradi started to wail and cry.

Captain Sparks placed a police officer at the door with the orders to wait for the Medical Examiner team to take the body for autopsy.

Jason left as soon as he got word that Captain Sparks put a guard in front of the room containing the deceased delegate. He decided to talk to Ari, Dr. Moradi's assistant. When he arrived at the Afghanistan Mission on Third Avenue between East 40th and East 411st Street he was denied entry by a guard.

"Why can't I speak to Ari Karem?"

The guard quickly told him, "Mr. Karem has put everyone on high alert. Nobody in or out!"

Jason was very suspicious, "Please tell Mr. Karem I am an investigator representing United Nations Security Operations."

Five minutes later the guard came back with a devilish grin on his face. "Too bad, get out of here!"

Jason returned to his office and called Anna.

"Anna, do not publish the changed Afghan report. I'll talk to you later."

"Should I tell my Supervisor?"

"Yes, tell her that Dr. Moradi's death is under investigation." "Oh my God, this is serious."

"More than serious, I was refused entry into the Mission to speak to Mr. Ari Karem."

Jason got a call from the Medical Examiner's Office.

"Mr. Darvish, this is Dr. Hammond. I have just been served with a temporary injunction that directs me to refrain from performing the autopsy that Captain Sparks requested. I'll keep the body on ice, I mean refrigerated and wait for further instructions."

A minute later Dr. Han called Jason with the news of the injunction plus other news. "We as well as Anna are to report to New York City Civil Court tomorrow at three in the afternoon. Make sure Anna brings copies of the two reports. Captain Sparks will be there as well.

It's on 111 Centre Street downtown. Let's try to fight this injunction."

At the end of the workday Jason called Anna.

"Let's eat out tonight. I have a lot to share with you."

They ate in a small mom and pop café located near the United Nations. The menu was eclectic. Jason munched on his fish and chips as Anna devoured her huge chef's salad.

"I'm really suspicious about the circumstances surrounding Mr. Moradi's death." "Perhaps refusing the autopsy is based strictly on religious beliefs."

"He was in excellent health—plus I don't like the way I was stonewalled by Ari Karem when I tried to see him at the Mission. The death and the complete one-hundred-eighty degree change in the position paper really smells. Something is wrong. It doesn't smell right!"

The couple finished their meal and as they were crossing the street to get to the subway entrance a large black speeding sedan rushed directly at them. Jason grabbed Anna and pulled her to safety as the car sped by careening off a parked car.

Jason yelled, "That car had its lights off. This wasn't an accident. That car was trying to run us down!"

Anna started to cry and Jason held her. She shivered in his arms. "Jason what are we going to do?"

"We are going to call Dr. Han and tell her what has happened."

Dr. Han said, "Take Anna to Susan's apartment. She is not to go into work tomorrow. I will arrange a car to pick her up for court. Jason, I want you to go back to your office and sleep there. I'll see you very early tomorrow morning."

Jason called a cab and escorted Anna to Susan's apartment. He took the same cab back to the United Nations. That evening he thought, *Someone did not want us to go to court tomorrow. And they were willing to kill us. You want to play hardball—okay I'm in the game!*

Chapter Twenty-nine

Jason slept in his outer office since it was bigger than his office. There were two chairs that had removable cushions, so he placed them on the floor and made himself a very uncomfortable bed. He had trouble getting to sleep because of the car attack, but finally exhaustion took over and he slept until six in the morning. He went into his bathroom and cleaned up to the best of his ability. As with most executives he had a clean white shirt hanging in his closet as well as a fully stocked toiletry kit.

Dr. Han met Jason at seven in the morning. She was carrying two paper cups of coffee and motioned him to sit down at his desk. She handed him a cup and sat down opposite him in his office and took a sip of her coffee.

"Look Jason, you are caught up in a very serious investigation. What do you think is happening?"

"It looks like the autopsy will let us know if there has been foul play. I don't think Mrs. Moradi has a clue, but I think we have a problem with Ari Karem. I think he is working against the Afghanistan government's positions. It could be that he may be trying to jeopardize the stability of the nation. Who knows, he may be working to establish a Califate and bring back Islamic Shariah law."

"Why do you say that?"

"I read both reports very carefully last night. The new report implies that all foreign influences get out of the country and let the political parties work it out. In other words, they don't want the United States and her allies going after the Taliban and other terrorists. I think this is a bold move by Ari Karem to get things going. The attempt on our lives, if successful, would have given the judge at the hearing no alternative but to release the body to go back to Afghanistan. I think Karem killed his boss!"

Dr. Han stood up and placed her hands on her hip, "That is quite an accusation. You don't have any proof at all."

"No, not yet Dr. Han, but let me tell you something—I will get the proof and make sure that Ari Karem will pay for his crime!"

"Be very careful young man! I have had great experience in Scotland Yard and Interpol and it is extremely difficult to make your case in front of a judge and jury."

"I will be careful, but I will get that bastard!"

Mrs. Goldman, Jason's secretary informed him later in the morning that the Judge granted a delay in the hearing due to Mrs. Moradi's grief and mental condition. The hearing was to take place in five days. Jason thought, *Sounds like a delaying tactic to me.*

Anna called him at noon. She sounded composed, yet her voice was soft and thin.

"Jason I am staying with Susan another day. Dr. Han suggested it. She felt that gong back to the apartment without surveying it first would be prudent."

"No problem. I'll go over there tonight and check it out."

"Please be careful."

"Love you Anna!"

Jason checked out the area and found no cars with men parked near the apartment. He made sure to survey the area thoroughly. Jason was wearing a hoodie and a baseball cap to make him as anonymous as possible. He checked the apartment very carefully and found everything in its place. He made himself some scrambled eggs for dinner and went to sleep early after watching the late evening news. There was no major change in Afghanistan that was reported.

The following day Anna reported back to work and was immediately called into her supervisor's office.

Thomas Edgerson looked at Anna sternly, "I don't know what is happening Anna, but the following things have happened since you have been away for two days. Mr. Karem demanded that we delete all the reports from our computers that were given to you to edit, as well as any hard copy reports. His explanation was that since Dr. Moradi was dead he would have to wait until his government replaced Dr. Moradi with a new delegate. He was concerned that any changes would not be authorized."

"What did you do?"

"Of course, I complied. Those were his reports—we are just functionaries. It does not belong to us. I'm surprised Anna that you didn't report any irregularities to me. I'm very upset with you!"

"I thought I did the right thing by bringing it up to Jason."

"That's the problem Ms. Mason, you did not follow protocol and I will write you up for this matter."

Anna became angry, "Just try to do that Thomas and I'll bring up the way you make eyes and harass the new girls when they start to work. You did it to me, but I didn't push it. If you want to start a war with me just try it!"

Edgerson turned white, "No—let's just forget about the whole thing. Deal?" Anna looked at him with distain, "Deal!"

Anna called Jason and in a shrill discordant voice said, "That son of a bitch is going to get away with his crime. The reports have been deleted and the hard copies are gone."

"Easy does it Anna, we're going to get to the bottom of this."

Later in the day Dr. Han called Jason. "I'm sending a messenger over to your office. Ari Karem has demanded the return of our hard copies of the reports — and he is justified. Please make sure you give back the reports."

"That sucks, the reports show the motivation and certainly it would have been easy for the judge to direct the medical examiner to do the autopsy."

"Will you be able to make a case without the reports?"

Jason reflected in an open manner, "Dr. Han, the geo-politics, notwithstanding, I really don't care— but when somebody goes after me and Anna to try to kill us I do care!

"Jason, I have read your service record and I fully realize what you can do. I do not tolerate nor does the United Nations tolerate any vigilante operation. Please do not put my office and your career in jeopardy. Do you understand me?"

"I promise you it will be legal in this country—and it will bring him down. I promise!"

A few days later the judge granted Mrs. Moradi's request to take her husband's body home without an autopsy. The aspect of the changed reports was considered hearsay, because there was no physical evidence. Even though Dr. Moradi was in excellent physical condition there was not enough evidence to approve an autopsy. Dr. Han, Anna and Jason swore they read the changed reports, but the judge needed physical evidence.

When they got back to the United Nation's they learned that Ari Karem was made Acting Ambassador to the United Nations by the Afghan government. They were shocked!

Ari Karem received the phone call from his attorney that the judge denied the United Nation's request for an autopsy. He was pleased and made sure to inform Mrs. Moradi that a plane would be ready by the end of the day to fly her and husband's body back to Afghanistan for burial. He smiled and thought, *Soon, we will have control of the country.*

Like many Afghanistan diplomats Karem went to college in the United Kingdom. His parents were very religious, true Sunni fundamentalist's. They owned a moderate sized bee farm. The honey they produced was marketed in and around a one-hundred-fifty mile radius. Many fundamental Sunni's bought from them.

As a young boy, Ari Karem's parents sent him to be educated in Pakistan during the Russian fights. During that time they lost their business and were helped by a local tribal leader. His parent's swore allegiance to the tribal leader because of his kindness to them.

Karem's education was in a Pakistan Maddrasa where he excelled in language skills and writing. After high school he was sponsored to go to the United Kingdom by his parent's local tribal leader. Ari was fortunate enough to see his parents twice a year. He swore allegiance to the leader as well.

By the time he received his Masters Degree Ari Karem was polished and ready for service. Since he excelled in communication and writing the Afghan government placed him in the diplomatic section of the government. He was advised by his Taliban Tribal Chief to work hard and do well. On occasion certain secrets and strategies of the Afghan government were reported to the Taliban by Karem. Ari Karem rose up the ranks quickly and after twelve years of service he became the Assistant to the United Nations Ambassador. He worked in that position for another five years until he was given orders to kill the diplomat and change the pro-United States position of the Afghan government. He truly was a sleeper agent for the Taliban.

The Afghan President called Karem and made him Acting United Nations Diplomat. He complimented Ari Karem and told him that he would talk to other members of the Government to see if he would be a candidate for the permanent position. Karem contacted his tribal leader who indicated that he would do everything in his power to influence the choice.

Anna and Jason went back to their apartment and talked about the situation they were in. "Anna, this isn't over for me. I'm positive that there was foul play in Dr. Moradi's death.

Dr. Han cautioned me about doing anything to embarrass the United Nations. I know she realizes that a murder has taken place although she is quite cautious."

Anna thought for a moment, "I think she is wise. We just can't go running around accusing Karem until we get hard evidence."

"I plan on doing that. Exactly!"

Chapter Thirty

Jason woke up from a dream that had him in the middle of violent storm twisting and turning. He could not get away from the storm and he seemed to be getting weaker and weaker as he battled to get away from the storm.

At breakfast he shared his dream with Anna who listened to him quietly. "Hon, I think you ought to call Dr. Blackman. You seem distressed."

"Good idea. It's been over a month—I've been so busy I didn't even think of it."

The session was more like a debriefing than a counseling period. Dr. Blackman asked one question.

"Jason, what's happening in your life right now?"

During the next twenty minutes she heard Jason unload in detail about his dream. He then talked about his United Nation's position and the changes that have taken place in his life because of his new position. Jason concentrated on his desire to punish Karem and how evil this man seemed to be.

Finally Dr. Blackman asked, "How is your love life Jason?"

"Great, I'm in love with Anna and we're going to get married," he replied in a completely different tone. "I love her so much!"

Dr. Blackman looked at Jason sternly and in all seriousness said, "You had better resolve your feelings in terms of Karem. I feel it is becoming an over-riding issue with you."

"I think it is."

"How will you resolve this?"

"I learned something in my Navy day's at ONI. I'm going to fight fire with fire." "Be careful Jason, we can't be judge and jury."

"Why should a man get away with murder? Isn't there a higher morality than diplomacy?"

"I don't know Jason, I'm just a psychiatrist who has questions—and no answers."

"Well, I'm a man who looks at Karem's actions as immoral, illegal and morally wrong."

When Jason got back to his office he had his secretary type out a formal request to meet with the Acting Delegate from Afghanistan to discuss security arrangemnents. This was standard protocol for all new positions.

Two days later he was escorted in Ari Karem's office. Karem's smile seemed as a grimace, but he said, "What may I do for you Mr. Darvish?"

"I'm here to discuss security for you. Do you need any additional personnel from our department?"

"No—I think it is best to use my security people." "Do you have a family here?"

"No. Is there anything else? I'm a busy man."

Jason got up & walked over to the side of Karem's desk. "I can assure you Ambassador that I will take a personal interest in you. After all, we don't want anything to happen to you in the UN. Unfortunately, New York City has some very tough people who would be willing to break your legs or take out your eyes for a price. You always have to worry about that."

Karem seemed disturbed, he started to sweat and with a shaky voice, "Why do you say that to me.?"

"Just protocol you know."

Jason pivoted in a military180 degree turn and left leaving Ari Karem upset.

Jason told his boss about the total conversation just before Dr. Han received a phone call from Ari Karem. She put the phone on speaker so Jason could hear the conversation.

"Dr. Han, I don't want your man Mr. Darvish to handle my security."

"What is the problem?"

"He threatened me!"

"What did he say?"

"He told me that New York City had bad people and I had to watch myself."

"We say that to all of our new delegates."

"Mr. Darvish sounded and looked menacing."

"I can't help it if you think that way, but my people are well trained in diplomacy."

"I demand that you remove him!"

"Read your book of regulations and follow the proper procedures. There has to be a legitimate formal complaint, then interviews by a third party, then I think a formal report. If I remember then— time for rebuttal from the aggrieved party or parties until a decision would be made by a panel of neutral representatives selected by a blind lottery. It would probably take about two months."

Karem yelled, "Forget about it. I'll handle it in a different manner!" He hung up.

Dr. Han looked directly at Jason, "You better watch your tail. He's going to sic the dogs on you." Jason smiled, "That's all I would want him to do. Can't wait to see how it turns out."

"The war cannot take place at the UN!"

"I doubt if it will. It will take place in some dark alley and very soon indeed."

When Jason went home. He called his former boss at ONI. His request was unique, but after going through his story he was told that something might be done.

After dinner Jason sat on the couch watching television. He shut the program off and kissed Anna ardently.

"Anna, I had a very tough meeting with Ari Karem today. He called Dr. Han. Karem was incensed about the meeting and requested that I have nothing to do with him. Dr. Han was all business and told him to do it in a formal manner. He told her, and I quote, 'I'll handle it in a different manner' close quote. Since I think he already tried to kill us once I'm expecting this bastard to try something very soon."

"Oh Jason, this is getting out of hand. What are we going to do?"

"You are going to take a two week leave of absence starting tomorrow. I want you to go to New Jersey and spend time with your folks. This situation is going to get worse."

"Do you need protection. I'm worried about your safety!"

"I've taken some measusures and I know how to take care of myself."

Anna started to sob, "Oh Jason, please don't do this. I don't want you hurt. I want you alive! Please!"

"Anna, please believe me that I know what I have to do and there is nothing you, Dr.

Han, or anyone can say to stop me from getting that killer."

"Anna threw her arms around Jason and whispered in his ear, "I trust your judgment, you are my soulmate and I will back you up in any manner I can. Okay, I'll go to my parent's."

That night Anna hugged and kissed Jason all night. She hung onto his body as if to shield him from harm. They finally fell asleep locked in each other's arms.

Chapter Thirty-one

When Anna returned to her parent's house in Teaneck New Jersey her mother greeted her with open arms. Anna quickly ran upstairs to her old room to unpack. She was feeling sad and dejected. Anna thought, *I am so concerned about Jason. He seems so intent on getting Ari Karem. I don't want him hurt or killed—our life together is just starting out!*

Jacki Mason knew her daughter well. Most of the time they were able to have in-depth conversations about anything. When Mrs. Mason observed Anna bolt upstairs she immediately knew that there was a huge problem and that it would be up to Anna to bring it up. There was no sense in trying to ask leading questions or being direct. Anna would not respond to that tactic.

She raised her voice from the bottom of the stairs. "Anna do you want some coffee?" "Thanks Mom, I'll be down in ten minutes."

They sat at the kitchen table drinking coffee from mugs that had the Columbia University logos on them. On the table were chocolate chip cookies, Anna's favorite. Nothing was said for a few minutes until Anna finished her second cookie.

"Mom, I'm here because Jason asked me to leave the apartment to be safe." "I don't understand. Are you in danger?"

"Yes. A little while ago there was trouble with the Afghan Delegate. Jason thinks he was poisoned by his assistant. We were involved in court to try to keep the body in New York for an autopsy and a car tried to run us down. Someone was trying to kill us."

"Oh my god!"

"Jason pulled me to safety and now has vowed to get the delegate, a man called Ari Karem. That man told Dr. Han, Jason's supervisor that he would take action against us."

"How long do you think you will have to stay here?" "Mom, I really don't know. Perhaps two weeks or longer."

"I knew that Jason worked in security, but I thought he is an administrator."

"He is—but he is much more. He never brags about his service in the navy, but between you and me he is a warrior. Jason was in combat and won the bronze star and silver star for gallantry. He saved the lives of men, actually SEALs. Oh Mom, I am so afraid that he will do something rash."

"But he's a civilian now."

"His job will always put him in some form of danger. That's what he signed up for when he joined the United Nations."

"And you still want to marry him? My god Anna, that's like living with a time bomb!"

"Mom, I take him as he is. Jason sees a therapist in the Veteran's Administration because he suffers from PTSD. He is getting better and he sees her only once a month."

Mrs. Mason stood up and cleared the table. She turned around with tears rolling down her face, "Anna, perhaps you should slow down and think about your relationship.

"I love him and want to make a life with him. He is kind and just and treats me as a partner. The fact is—we are partners! We are soulmates and I would never consider not marrying him."

"My god child, your life will be one of thinking that he may never come back to you. Is that the life you really want?"

"That's the life I choose as long as we can be together."

Mrs. Mason nodded and thought, *Perhaps Anna's father and I can convince her that her decision is a poor decision. I'll speak to him tonight.*

During the next three days Jason called Anna numerous times to reassure her that he was safe and that all was going along as planned.

"Oh Jason, I miss you so much and its been only three days. Are you eating enough, are you getting enough rest? Oh, sweetheart I want to come home and be with you!"

"I'm at work now and I'll go shopping later. I'm going to treat myself to a steak dinner.

Just try to relax Anna, things will work out."

"Jason, my folks are very upset with the situation. I really had to tell them about it."

"They're adults—you have to understand their concern about you."

"No, you don't understand. They're trying to convince me that because you are in security that it will be a poor marriage."

"Hon, they are you parents—try to convince them that you are not a little girl anymore and that your decisions should be supported."

"And what happens if they just don't agree."

"Too bad. Our life together as husband and wife will happen—whether they like it or not! Trust me Anna."

Anna started to sob, "Oh Jason, please let me come back now." "Anna, let's give it to the end of the week. Is that okay?"

"Okay, to the end of the week!"

"I'll call you tomorrow—love you!" "Right back at you!"

Dr. Han called Jason into her office in the late afternoon. Her wall television set was on and he recognized the 'Breaking News' headline.

"There has been a revolution in Afghanistan and we have serious problems!"

Jason saw on TV that there was a coup in the Afghan government and the hardliners took over. They wanted the U.S. out of the country. The background was that the Taliban supported the coup and arranged large financial rewards to the new government.

"Well Dr. Han, this supports the changes to the report by Karem. He is supported by the hardliners and will certainly be appointed their delegate to the United Nations.

"Jason, be very careful, they are now in power—and they are ruthless." "I'll be careful."

Jason went back to his office and received a vital phone call. He gave the caller his cell phone number and address.

"Hope to see you soon."

The supermarket had wonderful meats and Jason selected some New York strip steaks for dinner. He added a bottle of red wine, Idaho potatoes and fresh snap peas to complete the meal. There were fresh baguettes and he bought two of them with a pound of butter. Selecting some very fresh romaine lettuce and plum tomatoes Jason thought, *"Oh this will make a great meal!"*

Chapter Thirty-two

Jason approached his apartment house carrying two bags of groceries. As he started to move towards the outside steps three men attacked him. One man had a huge curved knife and approached him as two other men held him. Their hands felt like vise grips against his arms.

And then it changed! Out of the dark came three Navy SEALs, Jason's friends who decided to bust the attacker's arms, legs and heads. They brought havoc onto the would-be attackers. The SEALs made sure to punish the attackers. It was brutal and really was no contest. Jason got in a few punches although he left it to the professionals to do the job. Master Chief Jake Dugan, First Class Petty Officer Ken Bullett and Warrant Officer Jamie O'Keefe were part of the team that Jason saved on his first mission when he worked at ONI.

While dragging the men together in a pile Chief Dugan smiled, "Remember I told you that we owed you one. Well you collected tonight!"

Chief, I collected big time tonight. Thanks!"

Before deciding to call 911 Jason questioned one of the semi- conscious men.

"Who sent you?"

"Don't know."

"How was this set up?"

Jason took the man's upper arm and twisted it hard. "How?'

"Johnny's Bar on the lower east side. We get orders."

"What's your name?"

"Jorge Fernandez."

A neighbor hearing the commotion called the New York Police. The squad car pulled up and two NYPD officers approached the men.

One of the officers asked, "What the hell happened here?"

"My friends were visiting me and these men attacked me. My friends were waiting for me to come home and heard the commotion. They came over to help me. Those men were probably after my wallet."

"Okay let's get your name and all your information."

Jason gave the officer all the information that was required. "Now how about your friends?"

The SEALs corroborated Jason's story and flashed their identification.

The most senior police officer looked at the men, grinned as he looked at the damaged men and cynically said, Yeah, that story sounds just about right."

Jason smiled, "Yeah, let's leave it as that. Okay?"

"Yeah, let's keep it simple. I would not want any Navy SEALs involved in any hanky panky, would I?"

"Not really officer!"

The officer saluted the men and out of habit the SEALs saluted back.

The police officers dragged the semi-conscious men into their car and drove away.

Jason grinned, motioned with his arm, "I guess we have a little digging to do, but let's go to my apartment for some steaks and beer. I feel hungry.

All of the men laughed out loud!

At ten in the evening the men arrived at Johnny's Bar on East Broadway. The lower eastside had changed. It used to be a section of New York where artists and skateboarders hung out. Now it seemed to be upscale where sophisticated wine bars and clubs dominated. Yet, mixed in between were some old-fashioned bars. Johnny's was typical. When you entered you observed a long bar made of mahogany, backed by huge mirrors that needed redoing. In the rear of the establishment there were some booths and on the side there was a pool table and a shuffleboard table. Men wearing jeans and colorful t-shirts were scattered throughout the bar. There was a sign that indicated the special of the day was corned beef and cabbage.

Jason approached the bartender and took out his United Nations identification from his pocket. It indicated he was in security and investigations. "We are looking for information about Jorge Fernandez. Do you know him?"

"See that large man with the big mustache playing pool. That's his close buddy." Jason nodded and he and his companions went over to speak to the man.

"Excuse me sir," Jason said in a respectful tone, "may I speak to you about Jorge Fernandez?"

"Get the hell away from my game—or I'll club you with my cue stick."

Master Chief Dugan stepped in and grabbed the man's cue stick and broke it in half. "I'll stick this up your ass if you don't talk to us. Got it?"

It was easy from that point on. The man's name was Hector and he worked for Chili Hernandez, the manager of a local yogurt distributor. At times Chili Hernandez would ask a few of his workers to do some odd jobs for him. It may have included settling old bills, speaking with authority to some people or groups of people and on occasion settling a score with a few unworthy people. Knives and clubs were used, never guns and maiming was the order of the day, not killing. Hector gave Jason all the necessary information including phone numbers, addresses and the office of the yogurt company.

Jason strongly suggested, "Hector, I think you better leave New York State for a week or so. I suggest you do it now. Got it!"

Hector ran out of the bar as quickly as he could.

Since his SEAL friends had only one more day to help Jason he suggested they visit the yogurt factory the next morning. After a hearty breakfast they took their rented van to the factory located on Third Avenue near Fourteenth Street. The building was surrounded by a chain link fence and a uniformed security guard was at the gate. Jason told him they wanted to see Mr. Hernandez.

The guard nodded and called the main office, "No way. He says, make an appointment."

Master Chief Dugan, took his six foot four inch body out of the van and approached the guard booth. He opened up his wallet and the two men spoke for a minute.

Dugan came back, "He'll let us in. Looks like his younger brother is in training to be a frogman. He's really proud of him and of us!"

The gate lifted and the van drove to the factory.

When the men walked into the small office they saw Chili Hernandez holding a cup of coffee and leaning into a blonde woman with his arm around her.

He looked up, "What the hell do you want?"

Warrant Officer O'Keefe moved quickly and snatched the coffee cup away from Hernandez without spilling a drop.

Petty Officer Ken Bullet spun the blonde woman's chair around and winked at her as he said, "Hon, can you take a walk for about twenty minutes. I promise you that your boss will be okay.'

She whispered in his ear, "Kick the SOB for me," quickly got up and told Hernandez, "I'm going to the restroom."

Jason looked at Hernandez and pointed to him, "Do we make it easy or hard for you? Just answer a few questions."

"What the fuck do you want?"

"I'm the guy you sent your thugs to beat up last night. Looks like some of your men are in the hospital. Do you want to end up there today?"

"No."

"Who told you to get me?" Dugan moved to the left side of Hernandez and O'Keefe to the right side while Bullet stood next to Jason.

"Well?"

The man was terrorized, he shook and blurted out, "I take orders from my boss, Mr. Afsar Chanra. He lives on Park Avenue in one of those fancy condos. Once in a while he tells me to do a job for him or he'll fire me. I don't want to lose my job."

Jason looked at his men, "Okay guys, not much here. Let's go." Dugan looked at the terrified man, grabbed his hair and bent him over.

"Remember this the next time you order some thugs on a hit." Dugan kicked Hernandez in the knee, "It's not broken, but that bone bruise will be there for months. Remember that you piece of shit!"

They left the office and returned to Jason's apartment. Within the next hour the men left as Jason thanked them.

"Hooyah!" was the last thing they said.

Chapter Thirty-three

Dr. Han called Jason into her office the first thing in the morning. She looked tired and seemed to be in a very big hurry.

"I have been informed by the Under-Secretary General for Safety and Security that I must fly out to Geneva in less than two hours with most of the Executive Committee to discuss the possibility of negotiating a serious hostage crises in the Central African Republic. Some forty- five United Nations peacekeepers have been put into custody and our Response Team has struck out. This is critical."

"What can I do to help?"

"Jason, you have to take over for me. Don't make any critical policy decisions, but please make decisions on a day to day basis to keep the office running smoothly. It's is up to you.

Welcome to the world of being an executive at the United Nations."

"Ouch, I was going to ask for a week's leave of absence to hunt down some leads when it comes to Ari Karem."

"Sorry Jason. You are going to have to put in long hours and I'm afraid your investigation will just have to wait."

"Dr. Han, have a safe trip."

"Jason, move into my office. I want you to be right here behind my desk." "Why?"

"It makes it official. The staff will get my memo in fifteen minutes."

Jason called Anna to inform her of the news.

In a loud voice Anna said, "I'm coming back to the apartment right now and I'm going to work. I love my parents, but I want to go back to New York right now."

"Anna, please. There still is danger. There was an attempt on my life two days ago and thanks to some of my SEAL friends I wasn't hurt at all."

Anna started to cry and during her sobs she blurted out—"I'm coming back!" Jason raised his voice, "No you are not!"

"Don't tell me what to do!" "It's for your safety."

"I want to come back and I will!"

"Anna, I will be working very late in the evenings to keep up with my work as well as Dr. Han's. Please be logical!"

"I am not going to listen to you Jason. I'm coming back to my apartment." "I thought it was our apartment."

Anna snapped back in an angry tone, "Only if you cooperate!"

Jason felt conflicted, misunderstood and bewildered. He let out a deep breath through his mouth and tried to think logically.

"I'm gong to a hotel and hope that you calm down. This is our first fight and I don't like it!"

"Neither do I!"

Immediately after that she hung up.

The next two days seemed to be a whirlpool for Jason. He managed to keep the office running well making sure that all assignments were being handled and that all United Nations protocols were being followed. He was working twelve to fifteen hours a day.

Jason tried calling Anna on her cell phone and she never answered. He thought, *I wonder if this is the beginning of the end between us. God, I'm really stumped!*

It was eight in the evening when he lifted his head out of his paper work and saw Sheila Harris come into his office.

"Jason, you look like hell. You are overworked and I think undernourished. Isn't Anna taking care of you?"

"We sort of had a serious disagreement and I'm living at the Hampton Inn. It's two tenths of a mile from here and I can walk to it without any problems."

Sheila Harris walked to the side of his desk and held out her hand. He took it. "You are coming home with me for a home cooked meal. No strings at all." "No strings?"

"Exactly!"

One hour later Jason sat in Sheila Harris' kitchen. He was drinking a beer and eating a marvelous chili. He looked across at Sheila. She was a beautiful woman, a fantastic figure and humane.

"Thank you, Sheila, I really need this. Your chili is marvelous. Where did you get the recipe?"

"Oh, that was Fernando's recipe. He was a boyfriend of mine. It lasted six months." "I'm sorry."

"Don't, I have some great Tex-Mex recipes because of him!"

They both started to laugh and it turned into a belly laugh for both of them." Sheila went to the pantry and returned with two bottles.

"Are you a scotch man or a rye man?" "I'll take some rye if you please."

They drank and chatted about their experiences outside of the United Nations. The alcohol made them a bit silly and Jason felt light headed.

Finally, Jason looked at his watch and said, "It's late. I better get a cab and get back." "Jason, I have a guest room. You are in no condition to go to the motel. Stay."

"Okay, I guess I can use some shuteye."

One hour later Jason saw the door open and Sheila come to his bed. She was wearing a sheer short nightgown. The beautiful woman lifted Jason's blanket and crawled in beside him. He could feel her sensuous body against him and then she reached for him.

Jason said, "Please no."

She said, "I must!"

She trailed kisses down his chest, on to his belly and then she captured him. Sheila whispered, "This is all I want for now!"

Jason moaned and later moaned again.

The next morning Sheila woke Jason up with a tray of French toast and coffee.

He started to talk, but Sheila interrupted him. "I'm afraid we drank too much last night I really can't remember too much. Are you okay?"

Jason smiled, "I can't remember a thing."

Sheila said, "I guess you just needed some good sleep. I'm going in for a shower. Let's share a cab to work."

"No thanks, I have to go to the motel and change. I'll see you at work."

In the cab Jason thought, *I think I'll file last night as top secret. For my eyes only and no one else forever!*

The next two days were as hard the previous two days. Jason was able to clear most of his work and he decided to text Anna because she would not answer her phone.

It read, *Hey partner, miss you. Time to discuss our predicament.*

He immediately got a text back, *Meet me at Wo Hop in Chinatown at eight. You're paying!*

My pleasure!

Wo Hop is a landmark Chinese restaurant established in 1938. Located on Mott Street in New York City's Chinatown. It is subterranean and you must walk downstairs to get into it.

However, you don't have to worry about reservations. They are open twenty-four hours a day. If you want the old-fashioned type of Cantonese food Wo Hop is the best place to go. At times you will see the stars of Broadway or Hollywood munching on chow mein, egg roll, subgum- vegetables and egg drop soup with plenty of crispy noodles.

This was the restaurant that Anna and Jason loved to go to when they wanted to relax and enjoy each other's company. Most of the time it was on weekends and some holidays. Today was something different.

They both were quiet as they ate their food. There was tension between them and Anna's eyes were red from the tears she had shed.

"Jason, I thought we were partners."

"So did I."

"Then why did you tell me to stay with my parents?"

"Because I didn't want you hurt. I love you so much and I wanted to protect you."

"Thank you, but I'm a big girl and am mature enough to make decisions."

"The situation of me working very late every day and you alone in the apartment made me feel so frightened for your safety."

"But we are partners and you knew I needed to come back."

"Anna, what is your concept of being partners?"

"We share everything and make decisions together."

"And what happens if we cannot agree?"

"We don't do anything. There is no decision."

"Where were you when we argued?"

"In New Jersey."

"And if we didn't agree, what was the agreement we had as partners?"

"To do nothing. Oh my God, that means I had to stay in New Jersey!"

"Sounds logical to me, but since you are here I guess you are stuck with me."

Anna squeezed Jason's hand and said, "Hon, finish up. I want to go home with you—I'm aching for your touch!"

Chapter Thirty-four

The next day Jason received a call from Dr. Han. Her voice was penetrating, strident and to the point.

"Jason, I want you to find out where the Under-Secretary-General for Peacekeeping Operations is and request that he fly to Geneva as soon as possible. It seems that his delegates are not in sync with the Executive Committee and no one knows where the Under-Secretary is. Use all the investigative tools you have since time is of the essence. Some of the rebels are talking about executing some of our peacekeepers if we don't meet their demands. Do it now!"

"Yes Ma'am."

This was a serious matter. The United Nations Department of Peacekeeping Operations mission was the management and direction of all peacekeeping operations where peacekeepers would not take sides, involve themselves in politics, or discharge fire arms unless in self-defense. Jason thought, *Obviously the forty-five peacekeepers did not engage in combat when they were taken by the rebels.*

Jason decided that the best way to trace the whereabouts of the Under-Secretary was to interview his administrative assistant and secretary. He decided to walk across to an adjacent building to have a face to face conversation with the Under-Secretary's staff.

Monica LaPointe was the administrative assistant to the Under-Secretary. She was loyal to her boss and ran a tight office. The rest of the staff swore that she had larger "cajones" than her boss, but no one wanted to look under her skirt.

Her receptionist called, "A Mr. Darvish from security is here to see you."

"Tell him to make an appointment."

"He insists to see you now."

"Bon sang, *(good grief)* I'm coming out to scare him away."

Jason observed a large woman in her late forty's come barging out of her office. She had a scowl on her face.

In a French accent she said, "What do you want sir? We are busy here."

Jason decided to speak in French, perhaps it would quiet her down and he could get some information as to where the Under-Secretary is located.

"I'm looking for your boss because Dr. Han, a member of the Security Executive Committee is in Geneva. They are requesting your boss to fly to Geneva immediately before forty-five peacekeepers are executed!"

"Oh la vache *(holy cow)* please come into my office."

"Where is your boss? I must contact him!"

"He is on holiday." "Where?"

"I don't know."

"Does he have a cell phone?"

"Yes, but he turns it off when he is on holiday."

"How can I get to him?"

"You can't!"

Jason looked at her, pivoted and left the office. He took a chance and asked the receptionist, "Do you know where the Under-Secretary is?"

"No sir, but I know who he is with." "Who?"

"Janet Gorden, she works in our accounting department. They are taking a holiday together."

Jason walked down the hall to the administrative offices and immediately showed his security credentials to the supervisor. He explained the situation to the man and requested Janet Gorden's cell phone number. After fifteen minutes the supervisor came back.

"It took some arm twisting, but here is the number," he gave Jason a slip of paper. "Is there an office I can use for a moment to make a private phone call?

Jason was ushered into a small office that looked more like a closet. He punched in Janet Gorden's cell number.

"Hello."

"Ms. Gorden, this is Jason Darvish from UN security. I must speak to the Under- Secretary right now. It is a matter of life and death."

Jason explained the situation and was guaranteed by the Under-Secretary that he would be on a plane to Geneva within the next two hours.

"Thank you, Mr. Darvish, I will take the fastest jet to Geneva."

When Jason got back to his office there was a message waiting for him. It read, *'Well done! Dr. H.'*

Jason smiled he thought, *Perhaps, there will be no executions today.*

Anna felt much better this morning. It was a combination of last night's make-up-sex and her comfort level of being back on the job that she enjoyed. She was greeted by many of her colleagues including her supervisor. Anna was ready to get back to a normal life. She called Jason to tell him about her feelings and to discuss the evenings dinner menu.

'Hon, I feel great. I put up a slow cooker for pot roast tonight. Is that okay with you?" "If you made it—I'll eat it. You are a great cook!"

Anna heard the joy in his voice and felt that they were back on track. "See you tonight."

"Okay, about eight tonight. Love you!"

At lunch with her best friend Susan Han, Anna explained the total situation to her.

"Holy shit Anna!" Susan exclaimed, "you nearly blew your whole relationship because of your thick head."

"I really understand now— how partnerships work. It takes a lot of work to get it right." "Look girl, your man has the intellect, the tools, the looks, the drive to have any girl

swoon over him. If you threw him out I'd be on line with twenty other women going after him." They both started to giggle, because they both knew that she was right.

Late in the afternoon Sheila Harris popped into Jason's office.

"How is it going Jason?"

"Good enough to have Anna make me a pot roast tonight."

"That's great, have a good night."

Sheila left and thought, *Well, I struck out again, but what a night I had. Wow!*

Jason called Monica LaPointe, the Under-Secretary-General for Peacekeeping's administrative assistant. He spoke in French since it was an easier method to communicate with her. He learned at the Office of Naval Intelligence that almost all of the time, speaking in one's home language makes them feel comfortable.

"I assume your boss has spoken to you. Has he?"

"Yes, he told me that from now on he would keep his cell phone on for me to contact him. I actually scolded him."

"Let's pray that he and the Executive Committee will be able to get our peacekeepers back."

"Sir, that is my prayer as well."

"Please thank your accounting supervisor for his help."

"And Mr. Darvish, when our troops are safe they will have to thank you for saving them. Without your persistence it would have been a blood bath."

"We will see. Let's hope that the negotiations will pay off!"

Jason came home to see Anna dressed in a pink silk shorty robe with an apron over it. It was the first time he saw her with an apron. He approached her and kissed her firmly.

"Oh Jason, I think you will enjoy the pot roast." "I know I will."

Anna took Jason's hands and placed them around her buttocks. She was naked under her robe.

"Wow, what is up?"

"I hope you are. Oh Jason, I love you so much and I will do anything for you."

She took off her apron, took his hand and led him into the bedroom.

"What about the pot roast?"

"Later sweetheart, much later.

They ate two hours later.

Chapter Thirty-five

Jason came into his office an hour later than usual. He and Anna had talked and made love well into the early hours of the morning. Things between them were back to an even keel. He started to catch up with the paper work and finally looked up at the time. It was noon.

Jason yawned and picked up his phone. Dr. Han's voice was loud and excited.

"We have an agreement. The peacekeepers will be returned within two hours of this conversation."

"That's great. At least no one was killed."

"The Under-Secretary requested I compliment you on your investigative skills. I told him that this is what we do. I'm really proud of you Jason. You saved us a great deal of grief. Geneva is six hours ahead of you so I'm going to have dinner and sleep for twelve hours. I'll see you back at the office in two days."

"Safe trip home Dr. Han."

True to her word Dr. Han arrived in two days and took over her office. She discussed his decisions while she was away.

"For the most part you made the right decisions although I think you are too aggressive in your overall thinking when it comes to United Nation's security."

"I don't understand."

"Jason, your experiences at the Office of Naval Intelligence gave you a military point of view. In fact, you became a warrior because of that premise."

"The missions had to be accomplished."

"Correct, but at the United Nations we try to use diplomacy as our weapon of choice, not the gun."

"I have a lot to learn. Sometimes diplomacy doesn't work."

Dr. Han nodded, "Yes, at times we have to use force, but that is the last option."

'I'll make sure to use your words as a basis to my decision making when it comes to our unit. It is a learning process."

"Again Jason—nice job in covering for me."

Jason was happy to get back to his work as well. He was amazed about the critical decisions that had to be made on a daily basis to keep United Nation's personnel safe and secure. Jason thought, *I admire Dr. Han and the manner she handles her work although it is difficult to think that diplomacy will work in certain situations.*

Anna and Jason decided to spend their weekend in the Pocono mountains. They booked a romantic hotel located at Lake Wallenpaupack. There were three great restaurants, two bars, a night club with entertainment, massages, a wonderful indoor Olympic sized swimming pool and a jacuzzi in their suite. The best thing about the resort was that it was less than a three hour drive in moderate traffic from their apartment in New York City.

They got home late Sunday night and were thrilled with the time they spent together. If all went well in their lives they wanted to get married in ten months. That would give Anna and her mother plenty of time to plan the wedding. Jason agreed to help, although he thought, *I have absolutely no idea what I would have to do to plan a wedding—but I'm game!*

The bad news came on Monday morning when he got a call from Dr. Han.

"Jason, I have some bad news for you. Our new Ambassador from Afghanistan, Ari Karem has claimed prejudice against him."

"Why is this bad news?"

"Charges have been filed against me, Anna and you. The charges are based on us trying to keep the former delegate for autopsy which is against their beliefs; further he felt it was a slap in the face against his religion."

"What happens now?"

"We have been placed on administrative leave until a hearing takes place." "When will that happen?"

"Probably next week. The hearing will take place next week at the Office of Human Resource Management. At that time hearing officers will take testimony, interview all parties and make a judgment. If a party feels that the decision is unfair an appeal can be sent to the Secretary General of the UN."

"That is a blessing-in-disguise. I have to research a man called Afsar Chanra. He's the bastard who tried to get me killed. Luckily some of my SEAL friends took care of the thugs."

Jason asked for guidance from Dr. Han. "Do I go after him in an oblique manner or do I do it directly?"

"Diplomacy is the best answer for you. Later you can put on your boxing gloves." Jason quickly responded, "Oh, it's not going to be gloves, more than likely bare fists!" Dr. Han whispered, "Remember, the goal is to get Ari Karem!"

Jason and Anna talked about the administrative leave with Anna. She really was angry. "Jason, I had a great deal of experience with some low-lifes and politicians when I worked in the Bronx many years ago. In my experience it took time to get them, but most of the time they tripped up on their own mistakes and were taken down. That's going to happen to Ari Karem!"

"Meanwhile will you help me research and find Afsar Chanra?"

Anna came up close to Jason and kissed him on his lips, 'It may cost you."

"I'll pay the price."

Anna pulled away from him and giggled like a teenager.

Jason pulled her back and embraced her. She willingly responded!

It was relatively easy since Afsar Chanra was registered with the local Chamber of Commerce, the Afghan Community Support League, The National Yogurt Manufacture Association, and a host of smaller organizations. He owned or was in a partnership with a few laundromats, rug cleaning companies, and two real estate companies. Chanra was a nationalized citizen having become one some five years ago

Jason called the offices of Mr. Chanra. He identified himself as an officer of the UN and requested an appointment. The secretary told Jason she would get back to him. One day later Jason got his message.

"Mr. Chanra does not wish to meet with you."

Jason thought, *I'll get to you—you slimy bastard!*

Jason started to dig around the places where he might be able to meet up with Afsar Chanra. He lucked out while reading Chanra's Facebook page. It seemed that Chanra belonged to The Afghan Support League. The next meeting of The Afghan Community Support League was to take place this coming Friday in a private high school located on Avenue A in downtown Manhattan. Jason resolved to attend the meeting so he could get a fix on Chanra and perhaps speak to him.

The school was in red brick and old. Probably built during the 1930's. The neighborhood was considered in the East Village. Avenue A runs north to south and has a variety of furniture stores, bars and small discount stores. When Jason arrived there were people sitting on chairs, outside their apartment houses and chatting. He observed that about twenty percent of the women wore head scarves.

Since Jason had a great grasp of the language he was greeted warmly by many of the people inside the meeting. They had nothing to hide and talked to him freely. After the formal meeting he was drinking his tea and spotted a young man who motioned him to come over.

"I am working on my English. Will you speak to me in English?"

"Oh, most certainly. I am Jason Darvish. What is your name?"

"I am Armin Alam."

"How long are you here?"

"Just one year. I was the last to receive a visa from your country. I worked as a courier for your army."

"I understand that the visa program for Afghans have stopped. I'm sorry."

"My brother has been in the United States for a year and I will see him very soon."

"Where is he?"

"He works in a ranch in Montana."

"Armin, do you know Afsar Chanra?"

"Oh yes. A very good man who has helped many Afghans who have come to your country."

"Does he come to these meetings often?"

"No, he usually sends money through our Chairman."

Jason thanked the young man and turned around to see if he could see the chairman of the meeting.

He spoke in Dari, "Excuse me sir. I am looking for Mr. Chanra. Do you know where he might be?'

"Do you have business with him?"

"I have a yogurt situation and I must talk to him about production."

"He told me he will be in Boston at the yogurt convention next week. Are you going?"

Jason smiled, "Oh yes, I would not miss it in the world!"

Chapter Thirty-six

Dr. Han called Jason and Anna to inform them that the hearing for Ari Karem's complaint would take place this coming Friday.

"Dr. Han, that's very fast. What does this mean?"

"It probably means that the Office of Human Resource Management has conducted their own quick look into the charges and they are ready to hear our testimony. This isn't their first time to handle charges of prejudice."

"Oh, I just don't what they can really find out in such a short period of time." "There are police reports, interviews with hospital employees, interviews with the

lawyers, and perhaps an interview with the judge who handled the case."

"Do you think they interviewed Captain Sparks. He is a really good officer!"

"Jason, there is no sense getting yourself worked up over the charges. When the panel asks you questions, answer them as truthful as you can. Tell Anna to do the same. The truth is the greatest cleanser in the world."

"Okay. We will see you Friday at the hearing."

"Listen to me Jason—I will take the lead in terms of the overall responsibility of the complaint. I am the Director and it was my decision to move forward on the autopsy. Do you understand?"

"Yes Ma'am!"

The United Nations employs over forty-four thousand people throughout the world.

Many of the employees come from the one-hundred-ninety-three member states who belong to the organization. Over sixty percent of the staff work in field offices all over the world. Over ten thousand UN employees work in New York City.

There are many departments to register complaints in the United Nations. The simplest and easiest is to go through Human Resources. Usually the resolvement can be handled without difficulty. Ari Karem decided to complain through Human Resources because he wanted to quickly take any pressure off him in terms of the death of his superior. Karem thought, *They are like little insects. I will swipe them away.*

The hearing took place in a moderate sized room at the Human Resources Offices. Anna looked around and was struck with the richness of the wood panels that covered three walls of the office. There were sheer drapes covering some twenty feet of windows overlooking the East River of New York City. In the center of the room a huge conference table made of teak was surrounded by comfortable brown vinyl covered chairs. Anna felt that the room was designed to keep people calm and comfortable as they conducted business.

At nine-forty-five in the morning Dr. Han, Anna and Jason were ushered into the conference room by a receptionist. She pointed to their names on the left side of the table. They settled in.

Five minutes later Ari Karem came in with a man by his side. They sat opposite Dr.

Han's group. The receptionist quickly opened the door and five people came into the room. Two sat by Ari Karem and two sat by Dr. Han. The Hearing Officer sat at the head of the table.

Dr. Juanita Gonzales introduced the panel. One member was a human resource investigator from Norway, another a mid-level administrator from Ireland, another an attorney from Canada and the last an administrative assistant from Egypt,

She said, "I am an attorney who has been assigned as a liaison between the General Assembly Delegates and our United Nation's staff. My country of origin is Bolivia. I am this panel's chairperson. Our goals are the same in all cases: we are to ensure that our work at the United Nations run smoothly and effectively with superior efficiency. We try to maintain the highest level of competency and we pride ourselves on our integrity. We respond to keep this culture within all of our departments. We manage careers, movement of personnel, performance, and conditions of service. We are tasked to recommend and take corrective measures or sanctions to improve our overall operations at the United Nations. Are there any questions?"

The man sitting next to Ari Karem stood up. He wore a black pinstripe suit, starched white shirt and power grey-blue tie.

"I am Mohammad Kakar, a member of the New York State Bar Association representing Ambassador Ari Karem. Have you read our complaint?"

Dr. Gonzales said, "We all have read the complaint."

"It seems to me that it is a simple case of prejudice. Ambassador Karem has written his completely honest statement."

"Mr. Kakar, have you ever been involved in any United Nation cases?"

"No, I am a trial attorney."

"We investigate the claims, get both sides of the stories and then make a determination. If the parties are not satisfied there is an appeal process. Are you familiar with that process?"

"No."

"Well, let's get started. Ambassador Karem will you please tell us why you made the complaint of prejudice? "

He stood up and pointed his finger at Jason. "That man over there—he treated me poorly.

I was in shock over Dr. Moradi's death. He showed me and Mrs. Moradi no kindness. He was brutal in his questions to me. He seemed to accuse me of killing my beloved superior."

Dr. Gonzales asked, "Did he accuse you?"

"No, but he just about did it. He called the police to prevent Mrs. Moradi to take her cherished husband home."

"Why have you claimed prejudice against Dr. Han and Anna Mason?"

'It was that Anna girl who started trouble—

Mr. Kakar, Karem's attorney, took hold of Ari Karem's arm and whispered something in his ear.

"What I meant to say was that Miss. Mason thought it was in her power to question a report that I had written."

"Yes, the court testimony indicated that she thought it was peculiar that the contents changed by one-hundred-eighty degrees," said the attorney from Canada.

Karem raised his voice, "She has no right to think. She is just an editor, not an Ambassador!"

"Why did you file charges against Dr. Han?"

"She is the person who approved of the investigation. She is at fault!"

The administrator from Ireland broke in, "What was specifically said to you to think that the accused parties are prejudiced? Please be specific."

"I don't have enough time to remember all that nonsense. I know that they treated me as an inferior and I want them ousted.' He yelled, "I demand it!"

Dr. Gonzales looked at Ambassador Karem and said, "Please conduct yourself in a civil manner. Mr. Kakar please counsel your client to conduct himself in a civil manner or at least use good manners. Let's take a fifteen minute break."

Everybody left the conference room except Dr. Han, Jason and Anna. Dr. Han smiled, "Just tell the truth. That is all that is necessary."

When they returned Mr. Kakar said, "you have our written report and that is all we have to say for now."

Dr. Gonzales looked at Dr. Han, "Will you start. Why did you think it was necessary to start an investigation?"

"Thank you, Dr. Gonzales. It is the function of my office to investigate any possible breach of security. Dr. Moradi was in excellent health as reported by his wife. He was forty-five years old and Mr. Darvish called me because he thought that Mr. Karem and Mrs. Moradi were in a great hurry to get the body out of the country. I called the New York City Police Commissioner who advised me that it would be best if an autopsy take place to determine the cause of death. Even though Dr. Moradi was a diplomat, if we suspect foul play the rule is to investigate. I told Mr. Darvish to continue on the case."

Mr. Kakar interrupted, "We stipulate that Captain Sparks report and the rest of the reports are accurate. The point is that my client was treated as an inferior person because he is an Afghan citizen. We think Mr. Darvish is the person who should be punished!"

The human resource investigator from Norway said, "I don't think we have to hear from Mr. Darvish or Ms. Mason since Mr. Kakar has stipulated to the rest of the reports."

Dr. Gonzales quickly responded, "All in favor of adjournment raise their hands." All the members of the panel raised their hands.

"The decision of this panel will be made and we will report it to you by Tuesday of next week. Thank you. This meeting is closed."

On Monday morning Jason received a call from Dr. Han. I'll read you the decision that just came in. "It is our unanimous opinion that there was nothing done incorrectly by the UN Investigative Unit and that the Ambassador's charges cannot be substantiated."

"That's great. I'll tell Anna so we can get back to work. I have one request. May I take off Thursday and Friday. I have to go to Boston?"

"Of course, you can. I will see you back to work after lunch today. Tell Anna to report to work as well."

"Thank you, Dr. Han." "No Jason—thank you."

Chapter Thirty-seven

Anna called her mother and asked if she could spend Friday night and Saturday with her since Jason would be in Boston..

"Mom, it's really time to discuss my wedding. I need your help in thinking this through. We want to get married in ten months or so. That will be in either May or June. Will you help me?"

"Oh, sweetheart, this will be one of my greatest pleasures. I'll see you about seven in the evening on Friday and I'll take the late train out on Saturday night to go home. Your Dad really wants me home on Sunday in order to go to Church. He's giving the guest sermon."

Anna had read about Millennial females who grew up from the nineteen-nineties into the first decade of the twenty first century. The stimuli of television, social media and how females handled themselves in relationships were part of the delay pattern in terms of getting married early. Many Millennials wanted to live together and try it out before deciding on marriage.

Another factor was the attitudes of their friends who supported the concepts of independence, self-reliance and reality-based perceptions. She thought, *Well, that's me. I would like a wedding that's elegant and smart. I'm not a girly-girl, but I would love to have a church wedding, beautiful gown and all the trendy extras!*

Jacki Mason really felt good. She gave the cab driver a big tip and went up to Anna's apartment carrying a small overnighter. When Anna called her and asked for help to plan for the wedding it was a mother's dream. She was thrilled and promised herself that whatever Anna wanted, she would make it happen.

They ate a light dinner and immediately started talking about dates for the wedding.

Jacki Mason said, "Look Anna, we have to decide on a date as soon as possible because it will be hard enough to get a venue. Most of the time it takes a year or even more to get a decent place."

"Mom, Jason told me that I should control the wedding. He has given me carte blanche and I'm thrilled that he has so much confidence in me."

"Okay, let's determine a date and a backup date so we have something specific to tell the venue managers tomorrow.

They selected the last two Saturday's in May and all Saturdays in June. "Where would you like to have the wedding?"

"Let's start by calling the Plaza and perhaps Essex House." "Where else?"

"The Four Seasons and the Ritz Carlton."

Okay Anna, we start our calling tomorrow. I'm tired and I'm going to bed."

While lying in bed Jacki Mason thought, *I hope Anna can handle disappointment. I doubt that any of the premium hotels will have openings.*

The next morning and into the afternoon Anna and her mother kept on getting the same answer from the hotels. Plan for the venue in about two years. They are booked solidly with wait lists.

Anna said, "Let's be creative and move out of New York. How about some of our venues in Teaneck?"

They struck out at The Marriott, The Graycliff, The Royal Manor and six other venues.

At four in the afternoon both woman looked at each other. They were dejected.

Anna said, "Mom, perhaps I should change the date?"

'I agree. Perhaps you should. Let's open up a bottle of wine and just relax." Anna giggled, "That's a plan!"

Mrs. Mason's phone rang. She picked up and mouthed to Anna, *It's your father.*

"We are really finding it a problem. All the good venues are taken.

"No, I never thought of that. Okay, any Saturday last two weeks in May or any Saturday in June. Okay. Call me back."

"What's going on Mom?"

"Your father has suggested the Columbia University Faculty House."

"Oh, it's beautiful there and so historic. They serve great food. I've been there a few times."

Forty-five minutes later Dr. Mason called and excitedly said, "We are booked for the second Saturday in June. They just got a cancellation and I got preference because I'm a professor. Do you want me to book St. Paul's Chapel on campus? It's non-denominational."

Mrs. Mason gave her phone to Anna, "Speak to your father. It's your wedding."

"Daddy, I'd love to get married at Columbia University."

"What time for the ceremony at St. Paul and what time for the reception?"

"Make it for one in the afternoon for the ceremony and the wedding reception to immediately follow."

"You've got it Anna.!'

"Daddy, I love you!"

Both women hugged and Anna started to cry for joy.

Finally, Mrs. Mason said, "We have to set up an appointment with the Catering Manager and plan for the place settings, your colors, the cocktail hour, the reception, the music —oh my god—it sounds like a full-time job!"

"Mom, we have to plan for the ceremony at St. Paul's. Jason is Catholic and I'm liberal.

We have to decide on a clergy person, the type of service, transportation to The Columbia Faculty House, hotel reservations for guests, oh—and Jason's parent's, they live in Florida. Oh, Mom, I really need you!"

"Anna, this is my greatest joy—to help you."

"Mom, what about bridesmaids, gowns, maid of honor, summer tuxedos for the men, I forgot limousines —oh my, oh my—this is like a full-time job!"

"I'm working part time so I'll be able to handle a lot of the details. Even though Jason doesn't want any part of the planning you must make sure he is okay for the decisions. This is what partners do!"

"Mom, maybe Jason and I should just elope?"

Anna's Mom hugged her and whispered, "Sweetie, this will be a beautiful wedding. I will treat you to a wedding planner who is a good friend of mine. It becomes so much easier."

"I feel overwhelmed —there's a mom and pop Italian restaurant down the street. I feel like eating a mountain of spaghetti and meatballs."

"Okay, let's do it now. The last train to Teaneck leaves at nine-thirty tonight."

Later in the evening Anna called Jason. She started to tell him about the weekend accomplishments. Jason listened intently.

"Hon, the best news is that we will have a wedding planner."

"Oh Jason—you said 'we' and that is the best a girl can hear. I love you so much."

"I have to think about a best man and Anna, my sister Melody has to be in the wedding party and my brother-in-law can be an usher and—"

Anna cut him off, "We will speak to the wedding planner. Okay?" "Sounds like a plan, partner!"

Right before Jason went to sleep he remembered his friend Gary. They grew up together in Great Neck, Long Island. Jason was Gary's best man three years ago. Both boys were on their high school's Cross Country Track Team and Gary's father taught him seamanship. He visualized sailing with Gary on Long Island Sound and a big smile appeared on Jason's face.

He thought, *I'll call Gary tomorrow. He'll be pleased.*

On Sunday afternoon Anna received a call from Fran Hopkins. She was her mother's friend and a wedding planner. They made a tentative appointment to meet Fran at her office, downtown in the Village next Wednesday at eight in the evening. Anna texted Jason with the information and ended it with, *I'll treat you to Wo Hop if you are a good boy.*

She got a smile emoji ten seconds later.

Chapter Thirty-eight

Jason took a budget airline to Boston from JFK on Thursday night. It arrived in less than three hours and he checked into a moderate priced hotel three blocks away from the Boston Convention and Exhibition Center on Summer Street. He settled in and went out to eat some pizza before going to sleep. The convention started at ten in the morning on Friday.

At Jason's request Dr. Han set him up with a press pass from the magazine called "Making It." It is published quarterly by the United Nations and provides articles of interest in the fields of industrialization. Jason read a few articles on the plane trip to Boston. The articles were impressive with a great deal of information in terms of start-ups for small companies in third world countries. He familiarized himself with some of the terms used in the magazine.

The annual meeting of The National Yogurt Manufactures Association had over two thousand visitors a day. There were key note speakers, workshops and a huge hall with all sorts of the newest equipment and products all focused on yogurt. Close to half of the displays were spotlighted on frozen yogurt— and they gave away samples. Jason walked along and enjoyed his frozen chocolate cone as he became familiar with the layout of the conference. He had a fictitious name on his credentials and had used his printer at home to make business cards as well. Jason sat down in a rest area and leafed through the convention program looking for Afsar Chanra's name. Jason finally found it. Chanra was giving a workshop entitled "Good

Personnel—Green Cards Only." The workshop was gong to take place on Saturday at one in the afternoon. Jason decided that it would be good strategy to attend the workshop and interview Afsa Chanra after the workshop. He thought, *One's ego is always puffed up after being applauded.*

Afsa Chanra was born in Afghanistan, fifty-two years ago in the northern plains region which extended eastward from the Iranian border to the foothills near Tajikistan. His home was north of the central highlands. The good news was that the area had fertile foothills with excellent irrigation from a large river called Amu Darya. The land never exceeded two-thousand feet and contained in addition to fertile soil a plethora of natural gas. His mother and father were well off owning a large farm producing Gonzo beans, chickpeas, and corn.

In nineteen-seventy-nine the Soviet Union invaded the country to help support the Communist government. They ran roughshod over the area and Afsa's parents sent him, at the age of thirteen, to go fight with the Mujahideen. It was a jihad against the Communists. The war lasted twenty-three years and Afsa rose up the ranks to become one of the top leaders. He was a fearless fighter and killed many Soviet soldiers. When the Soviets left in nineteen-eighty-nine Afsa was twenty-three years old. He immediately took a position as a political administrator in the foothills and made a fortune selling his influence to new business operators and start up mining companies.

When he was forty-one he was asked by the ruling General's to eliminate three members of a rival political party. Things got really bad and there was a coup. Afsa Chanra escaped with his family to the United States where he became a United States citizen. He had a large Swiss bank account and was considered a successful business man who gave greatly to Afghan refugees. Finally, the ruling party was overthrown and he was back with the new conservative ruling class. He had no allegiance to any party. His only allegiance was to himself.

On Saturday Jason sat in he back of a large room listening to Afsar Chanra verbalize about the benefits of only hiring legal immigrants. He gave good suggestions in terms of how to sponsor newly arrived Afghan people and provided handouts to the thirty-five people listening to his lecture. After forty-five minutes of his presentation he answered questions and then the workshop ended with a good round of applause for the workshop leader.

Jason waited until the room was just about empty and introduced himself. He asked if he could interview Mr. Chanra for an article he was writing for the magazine "Making It."

Chanra was flattered and Jason started with asking questions about Chanra's early childhood, the war against the Soviet Union, the eventual victory of the anti-Communists and his war record. He flattered the man and Afsar Chanra loved it. Finally, Jason asked him about friends and contacts in New York City.

"Do you still have contacts with any important people in New York?"

"I am proud to say that a childhood friend of mine, Ari Karem has just been made the Ambassador to the United Nations. I am very proud of him."

Jason thought, *Bingo!*

When Jason asked more political questions, Chanra backed off.

"I really don't know too much about the current political situation. I am too busy running many businesses."

Jason thought again, *You, are a very cautious man.*

Jason took an early flight out of Logan Airport on Sunday. He was anxious to get home and tell Anna about the connection between Karem and Chanra. Further, he wanted to talk about some strategy with Dr. Han to get evidence on Chanra. He was the man who ordered the hit on Anna and himself; as well as the attempted attack thwarted by the Navy SEALs. There was a lot to think about and it would take some specific action to get things sorted out. The plane landed with a soft bump and Jason was home in less than an hour. Sunday morning was a good time to fly.

Anna heard the door open in the apartment and she ran to it. She kissed Jason and wrapped her legs around his waist. She kissed him again and again.

"Hey, I'll take this greeting every day!"

"Oh Jason, I'm so happy about the venue and my parents help. The wedding will be super!"

"I have no doubt that it will be; and I'm looking forward to meeting the wedding planner as well."

"Did you have breakfast?" "No, just coffee."

"Why don't you unpack and take a shower. I'll have a nice meal ready for you when you come out."

The waffles, bacon and eggs, over easy, were delicious. Jason was drinking his second cup of coffee and feeling that things will be coming together for them. He thought, *I still have a mission to get that bastard Afsar Chandra.*

Dr. Han was on three days personnel leave so Jason was stuck with a great deal of paper work for that period. He called Susan Han to find out what was happening to his boss.

"Susan, is your mom okay?"

"Jason, she is dead tired. When she was in Africa she hardly slept at all. The negotiations were intense and she's not a spring chicken anymore."

"Is there anything I can do for her?"

"Yes, don't bother her with any minor calls. She trusts you and you are a damn good decision maker."

"Will you see her soon?"

"No. She doesn't want any visitors at all. She just wants rest. I laughed when she used the sentence, 'I just want to chill out.' She doesn't usually use slang, especially that old."

Both Susan and Jason laughed.

"Okay. I won't bother her unless it's life or death.

"Jason, I'm changing the subject. It's about the wedding." "Make sure Anna uses me. She wants me to be Maid of Honor."

"We're seeing a wedding planner Wednesday night. More to come." "Okay. You make a beautiful couple and I'm so happy for both of you!"

On Wednesday night they met with Fran Hopkins, the wedding planner. She had a tiny office in the back of a bank building. Fran was about fifty-five years old with a girlish figure, dark brown hair and a smile that would light up a large room.

"Let me reassure both of you that the venue you picked could not be better. I've called the Catering Manager and he will be available for us Saturday morning at eleven. Is that okay with you?"

Anna nodded and Jason said, "You are a fast worker."

"Here is a print out of what I can to do for you. It covers almost everything. Anna and Jason, please go over it at your leisure and check anything you want me to do for you. I promise you that the prices on all services are competitive. I make my money on the fee I'm charging Anna's parents and the industry standard kickback I get from the vendors. Kids, I'm your wholesaler and I know where all the bargains are! Any questions?"

"I'm concerned about my parents. They are coming in from Florida and may be a little fragile."

"I will make sure that they will be picked up by my best limo driver and I will give them a nice suite in a hotel near the venue."

Anna looked confused, "Perhaps my parents would want to house them in Teaneck.

Should they?"

"Absolutely not! Your mom will be very busy and we have to make sure Jason's mom gets her hair and nails done in the morning before going to church. Jason, will you give me their Florida phone number. I need to get information in order to order your dad's tuxedo."

"How does that work?"

'I will have a tailor measure your dad in Florida and he will send the information to my man who will have the tuxedo ready. As for your mother's gown. I'll talk to her about that."

On their way home Jason said, "That's one hell of a business—wedding planner I mean!"

Chapter Thirty-nine

Jason had to work well into the evenings from Monday through Wednesday to keep his work and Dr. Han's work up to speed. As in any large corporation there were budget constraints on security as well as the high demand for protection. He had to call various departments to check on the actual need for security for minor functionaries who interacted with the public.

An example of this was the request for two security guards for a UNICEF speaker who was going to an elementary school in Harlem. It was denied by the investigation agent and the UNICEF speaker challenged the decision. It was then bumped up to him. She was concerned about recent violence and felt the need for additional security. Jason investigated and denied the request since he found out that there was a New York Safety Officer assigned to the school. He received a call from the speaker.

The UNICEF speaker, Amelia Koenig was a young woman of twenty-two who was from Luxembourg. This was to be her first time out and she was anxious.

"Mr. Darvish, I am frightened to go to the school. If you don't give me protection I will cancel."

"Ms. Koenig are you going alone to the school?"

"No, Mr. David my supervisor will be with me."

"Well then—did you speak to Mr. David about your concerns?"

"No, the engagement is my responsibility."

"Tell you what I'm going to do for you. I'm going to call the school and have the officer meet you at the entrance of the school and escort you to the place you will speak. It will be your responsibility to talk to your supervisor about your fears."

"It will show I'm not prepared."

"No Ms. Koenig, it will show your supervisor that you are mature and willing to talk to him about your concerns."

"I don't know."

"Take it or leave it. That's the best I can do for you."

Later in the week Jason found out that Ms. Koenig did go to the school and made her presentation. A simple situation that took time to resolve. Certainly, there was more to do.

Jason called the Security Office that originally denied the request and bumped up Ms.

Koenig request to administration. He spoke to the woman, Rhea Coggins, who denied the security request.

"Did you offer any options to Ms. Koenig?"

"No, I told her that we have had no problems with any of our speakers going to Harlem and it would be a waste of time and personnel to approve her request."

"What else did you offer?"

"Nothing, I told her if she has a complaint call Dr. Han's office."

"How long have you been in the department?"

"Sixteen years. I know what I'm doing!'

Jason thought, *This woman sounds burned out and dejected.*

"Well Ms. Coggins, perhaps you should have considered the situation. We had a young woman of twenty-two, from a foreign country, frightened out of her gourd because of rumors, requesting protection. You could have been softer and more understanding."

"I've been doing this for sixteen years and I have had no complaints."

"Well Ms. Coggins, perhaps you have been doing it wrong for sixteen years. You will be getting a letter of reprimand from me because of your lack of flexibility. Further, I suggest you look for a less demanding job in another department!"

Late Wednesday evening Anna was massaging Jason's back with a funny looking roller gizmo. He sighed and just enjoyed the massage.

"Why the big sigh Hon?"

"I really don't know if administration is my cup of tea. I feel like I keep on putting out small little fires all over the place. I don't know if I'm really helping."

Anna hugged him, kissed the side of his face and whispered in his ear. "The buck has to stop some where or we would have chaos."

He rolled over and pinned Anna to the bed. "I'm going to have chaos with you right now!"

"Oh, it better take more than ten minutes because—

He cut her off with a passionate kiss. The "chaos" took thirty minutes.

On Thursday Dr. Han came back to her office. She called Jason and complimented him.

"Jason, thanks for covering my office. I really need to get away."

"I'm glad you're back. Let's try to do lunch today."

"Not today, I'm stuck with a luncheon with the big boys at the General Assembly."

"Okay, let's do a raincheck. You let me know."

Jason called Captain John Sparks, who was the police officer in charge when the body of the Dr. Moradi was being held by the New York City Medical examiner.

"Captain Sparks, do you remember me, I'm Jason Darvish, a UN investigator."

"Oh yeah, that Afghanistan delegate screwed us. I was told that the judge gave them the body without an autopsy. That's a travesty of justice."

Jason explained the total situation. He included the attack where Anna and he were nearly killed by a car right before the court case. Then Jason discussed what happened at his house where his friends, the Navy SEALs came to his rescue and the visit to the bar to get information. Further, his recent visit to Boston to get information on Afsar Chandra.

Captain Sparks said, "Jason, this is a life and death situation. We are talking about Anna's safety as well. I'm concerned about both of you."

"Look, Captain Sparks, there is a direct connection between Ambassador Karem and Chandra. They were childhood friends. I have no doubt that Chandra does the dirty work for Karem."

"We need more information."

"Is there a way to tap the phone of the Ambassador?"

"I'll talk to the Police Commissioner! I think you are being screwed, in fact we are all getting the shaft! I have no doubt that Dr. Moradi was assassinated."

'I think so as well, but without the autopsy we have to get the goods on them another way."

Two hours later Captain Sparks called Jason. "We got the tap on his home line and we are also tapping the yogurt guy. We can't tap the embassy or the United Nations."

"Hell, it's a beginning. Let's compare notes on Monday night. How about dinner out on Long Island? Let's get out of the city!"

They exchanged information and set up the meeting.

They met for dinner in a diner in western Nassau County. Captain Sparks was dressed in jeans and a New York Giant sweat shirt. Jason felt awkward as he was wearing a suit and tie.

Sparks laughed, "I didn't know this was a formal meeting."

"Sorry, I just am used to regulations. I served in the Navy for five years.

"What unit?"

"Office of Naval Intelligence"

"Wow, ONI—no wonder you're an investigator. If you ever get tired of working for the United Nations I'm sure I can get a placement for you in the NYPD."

"Any news from the wire taps?"

"Nothing yet, except for a strange call to the ambassador. It came to his home number from Afghanistan. It seems the caller wanted to tell him that the package he requested will be in the diplomatic briefcase coming to JFK in two days."

Jason placed his hand under his chin, "We can't open or search diplomatic briefcases, but perhaps the TSA bomb sniffing dogs can be nearby when the package comes in. They can sniff our all sorts of explosives."

Sparks finished his dessert, "I'll ask a supervisor I know at JFK to see that it will happen. I'll text you with any information. Why do you think it may be explosives?"

"There has been a massive crackdown on the sale of dynamite, plastique explosives, C-4 and nitrates in our country. I was told that the FBI, ATF and other agencies have tightened up security."

"Okay. I'll call the TSA tonight."

Jason and Anna were watching the eleven evening news when "Breaking News" came on the air. It seems that a TSA's explosive sniffing dog was nearby a diplomat arriving from Afghanistan and the dog detected explosives in a diplomatic pouch. The diplomat was being held in a detention room at JFK. That was the end of the news report.

Mohammed Poya is an Afghan courier. All he does is carry pouches to and from Afghanistan to countries around the world. He never gets involved in policy matters and is always on time.

When the bomb sniffing dog sat in front of him a group of TSA guards placed him in custody. Poya took out a card from his wallet and asked to make a call. He called the Washington DC Ambassador who was out of town. His second call was to the United Nations Ambassador.

Twenty-five minutes later Ambassador Ari Karem showed up. Ambassador Karem was incensed. He waived his arms at the TSA supervisor and started to yell, "How dare you stop my courier. What right do you have to do so? He is travelling under diplomatic security!"

Lieutenant Shawn O'Keefe, the TSA officer in charge quietly said, "We cannot permit this pouch to leave the airport until the New York Police Department Bomb Squad shows up as well as representatives from our State Department. Your courier may be carrying a bomb."

"Ridiculous, I want my man released immediately!"

"Sorry, I can't do that. This is for the safety for everyone."

Karem grabbed the couriers arm and started to leave the room. Lieutenant O'Keefe signaled to his men who blocked the passage of the two Afghan men.

"How dare you prevent us from leaving. I will have your job."

"Mister, sit down or I will personally knock you down—got it! Boys, please escort those gentlemen to the holding room. We will wait for the big guys to figure it out."

During the exchange between Lieutenant O'Keefe and Ari Karem the Bomb Squad placed the diplomatic pouch in a bomb cage. It was a large sealed container that would prevent shrapnel to fly out as well as minimize the blast radius of a bomb if it went off.

Forty-five minutes later a representative from the United States State Department showed up. He went into the holding room to talk to the Afghan men. It was decided that the pouch would not be opened but the courier and the pouch had to return to Afghanistan immediately.

The courier would be considered "persona non grata" and not be allowed to ever enter the United States again.

The newspapers and the television reporters were given the story by Lieutenant O'Keefe and the State Department representative. This was most embarrassing to the Afghan government and Ari Karem.

Jason and Anna felt elated that Ari Karem's face was plastered all over the news. The next twenty-four hours the news had this story as their top feature.

Captain Sparks texted Jason, *"One for our side!"* Jason responded, *"Hooyah!"*

Chapter Forty

Afsar Chandra owned a very expensive yacht. He named it "Taschakor" which in Dari means thank you. The reason for that was he thanked his God, he thanked his parents, he thanked his luck and he thanked his intelligence. After all his wheeling and dealings, at the age of fifty- two he had thirty-five million dollars in hard cash. The multi-millionaire spread out his money in off shore banks in Switzerland, Isle of Wright, Belize and Panama. Added to his cash position Chandra owned a chain of laundromats, check cashing stores, some rental apartments. The very rich Afghan owned a beautiful condominium on Park Avenue valued at fifteen million dollars.

The yacht was a beauty. It was built in Italy for a Spanish soccer star who defaulted on his payments. The Spanish bank took possession of it and offered it up on auction. A friend of Afsar happened to be at the auction and called Afsar to tell him that he could buy an eight- million dollar yacht for perhaps four million. The deal was closed at four-million-three-hundred-thousand dollars. Afsar Chandra never sailed in his life, but he was willing to take a chance.

The yacht was one-hundred-fifteen feet long and had three decks. It was considered a superyacht by some experts. The design was strictly Italian in motif as well. It offered a sleek look with many contemporary factors. It slept up to twelve people, had four cabins, two twin cabins, and two convertible cabins to be used if necessary. There were six bathrooms all done in Italian tile as well as a dining room that seated twelve people. Outdoor and indoor white upholstered benches and chairs added to the beauty of the yacht.

Afsar had an agent rent out the yacht to make it a profit-making venture. The crew and captain were sometimes different, but Assar never worried since the money for the rental was excellent. Once or twice a year he would cruise to the Bahamas or to Mexico with his wife. They had no children.

One of the most profitable ventures for Afsar was his hookup with Diego Lopez. At least that was the name given to Afsar. Diego would call him directly and request a certain crew during a certain week for triple the rental price. Diego paid with cash and Afsar loved that type of arrangement.

The yacht broker warned Afsar that Diego might be a drug smuggler and if the Coast Guard caught Diego or his men the yacht would be confiscated. Afsar didn't mind it.

He said in a contemptuous voice, "I have boat insurance that will protect me. I made sure that clause was in the policy. I know nothing, I'm just a small business man who was duped."

Then he laughed out loud.

"Okay Mr. Chandra, I'm just trying to warn you." "Never fear young man, I have it covered."

Ari Karem, the permanent Ambassador to the United Nations received a phone call from his childhood friend Afsar Chandra.

"Ari, you are invited to take a cruise on my yacht in four weeks. We will fly out to Miami and pick up my yacht. I have business to discuss with you."

"What business?"

"We have to remove the flea that has bothered us."

"Permanently?"

"Oh yes. We can discuss it privately on my yacht."

"I would be grateful if you could do that!"

"It would give me great pleasure to do that small favor for you."

Captain John Sparks had put a tap on Ari Karem's home phone and when he heard the recording of the conversation he called Jason.

"Jason, your boys are planning to get you—big time."

"Captain, what do you mean?"

'Call me John, please.'

"Okay John, what do you think?"

"They are going to discuss a plan in four weeks on his yacht."

"Thanks John."

"I'll get back to you—I'll make sure to cover your six." "Thanks John."

Jason thought, *John must have been in service to use the term cover your six—cover your back!*

John Sparks was twenty-four years old in nineteen-ninety-one and a United States Army First Lieutenant who was a tank commander of an Abrams M1 tank. He had just finished his Masters degree in Criminal Justice and was a New York City Police Officer. During Desert Storm his National Guard Unit was called up because the Army needed more tanks and tank commanders.

Lieutenant Sparks was recently divorced, by mutual agreement, to his childhood sweetheart. They were married at nineteen and it just went downhill from that point on. Luckily, there were no children.

He was six feet tall with sandy colored hair and a smile that was contagious. His parents were retired and living in Phoenix Arizona. John had been the last of four children. They grew up in the Bay Ridge section of Brooklyn, New York. John attended public school and went to Brooklyn College for his Bachelor's degree and New York University for his Masters.

He joined the National Guard because it gave him twenty-one-hundred dollars for his annual training pay and six-hundred dollars for his weekend drill pay. It helped him greatly for his tuition. In addition, he received four-thousand a year for tuition as an officer in the New York National Guard.

John's Platoon had four tanks and his Company had three Platoons. Beside the twelve tanks there were two additional tanks in the Headquarters Platoon. It was a mighty force to deal with in the battle that was coming up. His Captain informed all the members of the Company that they were the tip of the spear going into battle.

The battle was sheer destruction and a slaughter. The old Russian T-72 and T-55 tanks were no match for the American units. During the first day his company destroyed fifty-five tanks and the second day another thirty-two. They were ruthless leaving no one to surrender. The job was to break through and destroy the Iraqi Republican Guard. The war was over quickly.

Later, during John Sparks debriefing a field psychologist asked him, "How do you feel?" "Shitty, those Iraqi's never had a chance."

"That's war young man."

"I never said I wouldn't do it, I just think it was a blood bath."

Two months later he was released with a field commendation and a batch of medals for serving in the war. He took one week off and reported back to his Police Precinct where he was notified that he had passed the Sergeants exam and would be placed in one month. John Sparks became the Desk Sergeant at the Sixtieth Precinct in Coney Island, Brooklyn, New York.

The tourists who came to Coney Island loved the beach, loved the amusement parks, loved the frozen custard, loved the Nathan's hot dogs and just loved to drink beer and get drunk. His precinct had the most arrests, the most writeups, the most action then any in New York City from May through September. The rest of the months were quiet.

John had an excellent IQ and waited four years before taking the Lieutenant's test. He passed and was near the top of the list, but a sudden downturn in the City's tax revenue forced

the Police Department to freeze all positions. That lasted for nine years as the City was in terrible financial shape. Since many of the Lieutenants never wanted to take the Captains examination there really were no openings for the men and women who passed the test. Their only hope were retirements. It seemed that Captains were forced to go to many meetings and did no field work at all. For that reason men of action did not want to become a Captain.

Finally, at the age of forty-two John Sparks became a Lieutenant and he quickly established himself as a no-nonsense crime fighter. His name was in the newspapers often and at times the Police Commissioner called him, off the record, for information. John was awarded the highest medal, the Medal of Honor, from the NYPD when he led a small unit of undercover officers breaking up a large dope ring. He was pinned down in a fire fight, although wounded, he managed to lead his men to victory.

When he became a Captain at the age of forty-eight he felt he had accomplished his goal. The rest of the higher rankings were more in the realm of a political nature and he wasn't sure he wanted that. John was assigned to the Precinct that housed the United Nations. It was a large headache but he loved the challenge.

Mercedes Wright never wanted to marry John Sparks. She was burned by a bad divorce and had to take care of her twin daughters with no child support. Mercedes made a living by being a telephone travel agent for a large cruise line. She was a superior saleswoman. Ms.

Wright met John Sparks when he was forty-one years old and she was forty-three. Both of her daughters had finished college, with one living in San Diego as physical therapist and happily married. Her other daughter was in the United States Navy as Warrant Officer who flew helicopters. Mercedes and John were a very happy couple.

Jason had asked Anna if it would be okay to invite John and his sweetheart to dinner at their apartment.

"I really like John. He's the type of man who has the type of ethics I can relate to—and I really think you—"

Anna cut him off, "Okay!" Jason grinned, "I'll help."

The couples had caesar salad, lasagna, garlic bread, red wine and store-bought cannolis for dessert. They hit it off right away and Anna and Mercedes put their heads together in some bride magazines. Anna wanted her opinion of some bridal gowns she was interested in.

Jason said, "John, I really like Mercedes. She is really a sharp woman." "Sometimes sharper than me, although she still doesn't want to marry me." "Leave it up to her. When the time comes she will ask you!"

Both men finished their red wine and laughed.

Chapter Forty-one

Jason 's phone rang at two-thirty in the morning. It was Dr. Han.

"This is a red alert—we have good intelligence that a bomb is going to go off during the General Assembly's meeting tomorrow."

"Tell them to cancel it."

"I already did—they don't think it's as serious as I do. The meeting will take place at two in the afternoon. I need you Jason. Meet me in my office."

"Okay, I'll be there as soon as I can!"

Dr. Han had the following people in her office by three-forty-five in the morning: The NYPD Deputy Commissioner of Intelligence and Counterterrorism, Captain John Sparks, the Captain of the Precinct, Captains from the NYPD East River Patrol Boats, Airborne Units, Counter-sniper unit, Emergency Service Unit, the Supervisor of the United States Secret Service, and the Commander of the Uniformed United Nations Guards.

The Deputy Commissioner spoke first, "I have plain clothes officers and detectives working behind the scenes looking for bombs right now. We have on hand our bomb detection K-9 units as well as belt-worn radiation detectors, chemical and biological sensors and bomb and hazmat response teams."

Dr. Han replied, "This meeting will have the President of the United States as well as the foreign leaders of five members of the Security Council. I cannot get these people to cancel the meeting."

The Secret Service Supervisor spoke up, "Let's rip this place apart. We have about seven hours to find the bomb, if there is one."

Jason said, "We will have teams from our departments keep a vigil on our scanners. They are all over the building. I'll supervise that aspect and I intend to study the previous twenty-four hours to discover any irregularities."

Captain John Sparks stood up and looked around at the members of this meeting. "I'll have my guys continue their search and report anything that seems peculiar to your office Dr. Han. Then I want your uniformed guards to work with our men to get to those suspicious areas as soon as possible."

The Deputy Commissioner raised his voice, "I'll coordinate our special units and report back to Dr Han as well."

Dr. Han said in an intense voice, "Have we forgotten any resource?"

Jason quickly answered, "Commissioner, did you notify the Joint Terrorism Task Force?" "No—good point. They have the FBI and perhaps we can pick up some intelligence or at

least a rumor or so from that area. I'll call them immediately."

Dr. Han said, "Go and find the bomb."

Almost all the men took out their cell phones and started giving orders.

Jason went to a room on the second floor filled with television monitors and digital video machines. The total floors of the General Assembly were constantly being scanned. A number of years ago some delegates thought it was an intrusion of their privacy, but the Secretary-General just told everybody that it was for their own safety and security. No one complained after that.

He met the supervisor of the unit and told her, "We have a bomb threat. Call your people to come in to work right now. I want your staff to tell me if they see anything irregular. We are going to go back twenty-four hours."

Julia Montgomery, the supervisor looked startled, "Who are you? Do you have any clearance to be here?"

"I'm sorry—" he flashed his security card and made sure she read it carefully. "Are we clear!"

"Yes sir!" She got on her phone and started to make calls.

After viewing four hours of the tapes, Jason and five other people did not see anything unusual. He stopped and went to the coffee urn to get some coffee the janitors set up for the unit. Jason observed one of the janitors taking out the trash and he thought, *Janitors have the run of the building, and no one pays any attention to them.*

Jason called Dr. Han. "I need to know if we have had any new janitors or substitutes in the General Assembly during the last twenty-four hours."

'I'll get back to you as soon as I can."

Fifteen minutes later Jason answered his cell phone. It was Dr. Han.

"We had four regular substitutes that have worked here for three plus years and one new man who started ten days ago."

"Let's work on the new guy. Is he in today? What's his name?"

"I'll check."

Five minutes later Dr. Han said, "He called in sick today and his name is Thomas Riggio."

"Okay text me his address—I'm going out to interview him."

"Take someone with you."

"I'll text Captain Sparks to be with me and I want to use his car to get through traffic."

"Okay."

"Ms. Montgomery, I want you to speak to the Supervisor of Janitors and find out where this new man, Thomas Riggio worked. Then I want your total team to trace every move of his on his eight hour shift. He may have hidden a bomb somewhere. This is really important."

"Yes, sir" she raised he hand and saluted.

John Sparks texted Jason to meet him on the west side of the building. Jason had to show his credentials three times in order to get by. It was good police work and he did not mind it in the least. Finally, he saw John waiting by his car.

"I'll give you the address as soon as we get in."

John Sparks punched the address into his car's navigator unit and put on his siren and lights. They were off in a flash headed to Brooklyn. John was an excellent driver although he nearly got into three accidents. They were headed to East New York.

Captain John Sparks called the Seventy Fifth Precinct to inform them that a person of interest was to be interviewed by him and that backup was requested. He was informed that the address he gave was really part of a New

York City Housing Project located in the eastern part of Brooklyn close to Jamaica Bay.

Jason heard the Desk Sergeant say, "The residents are predominately Latinos and African Americans—just watch your back!"

Jason frowned as John looked at him.

"Jason, that Sergeant was trying to protect us. He knows his crime statistics— I can assure you, that's all he meant!"

When they arrived, there were two squad cars waiting for them. A Lieutenant saluted Captain Sparks and they talked for a moment. Sparks came back to Jason.

"We will have a police escort right up to this guys apartment. Do you carry?"

"No, I don't even have a license."

"Then Jason, you stay behind me. Got it."

Jason nodded and they took a urine smelling elevator up to the fifth floor. The hallway walls were painted in dark green, quite dirty and there was some graffiti on the walls as well. They got to "Five A" and John Sparks knocked on the door.

The peep hole was opened on the other side and Thomas Riggio said, "If you don't have a warrant get the hell away from here!"

Captain Sparks said, "This is a national emergency and this involves terrorism. If you don't open the door we will knock it down!"

They heard movement from the apartment and John motioned everyone to move away from the door. A moment later the door opened and a large bearded man came out of the apartment shooting a shotgun.

Two police officers shot him dead in five seconds. It seemed that the man knew he was going to die.

"Let's go into the apartment to see if we can get some intelligence," Jason said intently.

There was a prayer mat on the floor and an opened Koran on the kitchen table. It was obvious that this man planted the bomb, but where?

John Sparks and Jason Darvish tore apart the apartment looking for any clues that might help. They found nothing except a quart sized bottle of hydron peroxide.

Jason said, "Oh my god, that's a component for a deadly bomb. I learned about it from my time at ONI. Its mixed with chemicals and usually contained in some sort of knapsack or carry-on luggage. That bomb has to be somewhere in the hall of the General Assembly. It could be deadly indoors.

He quickly called Dr. Han. and said, "The bomb is in the main hall of the General Assembly hidden somewhere. It probably is in a knapsack, or small suitcase, or sports bag, or box. I'm sure there is a timer set for the meeting. Tear up the place and find it. Transfer me to Ms. Montgomery."

"Yes."

"This is Jason Darvish, concentrate on the main hall of the General Assembly only. Find out where that bomb was planted. It probably is no bigger than a back pack!"

John Sparks was on his phone directing his bomb crew to search the main hall as well.

He finished talking to the Lieutenant and left with Jason to go back to the United Nations.

In the car Jason said, "Let's pray we can find the bomb."

Julia Montgomery's team viewed Thomas Riggio cleaning behind the large video screens set up high on the wall of the General Assembly hall. The bomb squad found two bombs that would have decimated the first half of the auditorium. It was safe to have the meeting.

Jason and John were notified by Dr. Han.

"We found it. Thank God! Nice work guys."

John and Jason decided to have a victory cup of coffee in a small diner somewhere between East New York, Brooklyn and First Avenue and Forty-fifth Street in Manhattan. It was a hell of a morning!

Chapter Forty-two

Anna and Jason as well as Mercedes and John sat in the rear of Wo Hop munching on egg rolls and drinking Chinese oolong tea. It was sort of a victory dinner after the intense hunt for the bomb at the General Assembly. Mercedes Wright looked at Anna and then gave John Sparks a kiss on the cheek.

"Anna, when Jason is on assignment do you ever get that queasiness in your stomach?" "All the time. I worry about him and I have absolutely no control over the situation."

"I have been living with this every time John goes out in the field. I would have hoped all the administrative and personnel work would keep him in his office."

Captain John Sparks, dressed in his favorite New York Giant sweatshirt, took a swig of tea and said, "Would you marry me if I promised you I would go out in the field only when ordered?"

Mercedes looked around the table, placed her tea cup gently on the table, looked with adoring eyes at her man, "If you promise me that I will marry you tomorrow!"

"My sweet Mercedes, then I will have to demote myself because my responsibilities must include critical decision making which keeps me in my office and at times in the field. It is situational."

A tear ran down Mercedes face, "I love you because you are so dedicated, but I am still scared."

Jason realized that the situation was getting intense and he decided to break it up with a joke.

"Look folks, when it comes to relationships couples handle things differently. Here's a story of a couple who has had a very successful marriage. Remember the story of a new married couple coming home using a horse drawn buggy. Well after a mile the horse started giving them trouble and the husband gave the horse a little whip. His wife said in a low voice, 'That's strike one.' A little while later the horse stopped again and she said, 'That's strike two.' The third time the horse stopped she grabbed the shotgun from its rack and shot the horse in the head. The husband was in shock and said, 'What in the world was that all about?' she looked at her newly married husband and said, 'That's strike one.' They have been married for forty years and the marriage has been a great success!"

Everyone laughed and started to roar from the old joke they must have been heard over and over again. Finally, Anna wiped her mouth and kissed Jason fully on his mouth.

"That's strike one."

"I want to know what strike two brings?"

"Wait until you get home and I will demonstrate it to you!"

Mercedes said, "Okay. Okay I get it. I'll think about marrying John. You are too persuasive."

John Sparks sat at the table in amazement. He never heard his sweetheart contemplate marriage. He thought, *Maybe, we have a chance!*

The next day at work Dr. Han walked into Jason's office and said, "Let's go. We have to see the Secretary-General right now."

"What's all this about?"

"I have no idea, but he's a very busy man so we are to move quickly."

Secretary-General Som Phon Montri from Thailand was a small man dressed in a well tailored black business suit. He was sixty-two years old and was revered by many people as a pacifist. He motioned to Dr. Han and Jason to sit down in front of his desk.

In a superior and well exercised English accent he said, "On behalf of all the members of the United Nations we wish to thank you for all your efforts to find the bomb. As I understand it, Mr. Darvish, it was your thoughts and plan that finally found the bomb."

"Sir, thank you—it was a team effort."

"Dr. Han interjected, "Mr. Secretary-General, although it was a team effort, without Mr. Darvish's insights we could have had a disaster."

The Secretary-General stood up and shook Jason's hand and Dr. Han's hand.

"What can I do to help your department?"

"Dr. Han replied, "If we could hire one more middle manager to handle our United States security for delegates I would be grateful."

"Done. I will tell my administrator to transfer funds from my budget to yours!"

Jason verbalized, "Sir, that would be a great help to us. Thank you."

"No, young man. We thank you."

Dr. Han was jubilant. She and Jason were in the cafeteria drinking some coffee and going over the wonderful meeting that just happened with the Secretary-General.

"I am thrilled that we were rewarded. Jason, that almost never happens at the United Nations. I have been struggling with budgets since I have been here."

"I'm happy for our department, but right now I would like to get back to work because I am really backed up."

They both laughed and returned to their offices.

Jason made sure to write letters of commendation to Julia Montgomery and her team. They were the people who came through with their dedication to duty and their persistence viewing the video's. He thought, *I have met many dedicated staff members who are committed to the mission of the United Nations. It's a good place to work!*

Mercedes Wright called Anna late in the afternoon.

"Anna, can we meet together. I really haven't any friends who are women, but I like you, trust you so I need to talk to you."

"Of course, Mercedes, when do you want to meet?"

"How about this afternoon or later in the day?"

"I'll tell you what we can do. I'll get out of work earlier today, say at four-thirty. Meet me at Oren's Daily Roast on First Avenue Ave. We can have some coffee and talk."

"Great, I'll see you there!"

The coffee house was a fixture on First Avenue for over thirty years. Their coffee was superb and they sold quantities in bulk as well. As Anna entered the store she spotted Mercedes on a side table waving at her. Mercedes was wearing a smart warmup jacket and matching pants. Her hair was in a bun and she hardly had any makeup on.

"I decided to walk here. It was only seven miles."

"You're in much better shape than I am. I just don't seem to have the time to work out."

"I find it important for my sense of well-being. Anna, I am truly conflicted and after our get together at Wo Hop I had to speak to you."

Anna looked at Mercedes and recognized a person who was in distress.

"Mercedes, perhaps speaking to a therapist is better than speaking to me."

"No. I see your relationship to Jason. You are partners and you respect each other so much. I think it is great."

"Okay girl, lay it out for me!"

"In a torrent of words Mercedes said, "I love John. I am worried every day that I will lose him to some crazy shooter. I live in fear every day and feel blessed when he comes home safe every day. Do you think I'm crazy?"

"Hell, no Mercedes. What you are feeling is what every law enforcement wife, girlfriend, lover or companion feels when their loved one leaves."

"It's overwhelming! That's why I won't marry him!"

"Would it be the same overwhelming feeling whether you married him or not?"

"I don't understand the question?"

"Let's say you are married. Would it change your feelings about worry?"

"No."

"Then what decisions might you make to change your feelings?"

"I don't know. I love him and I'm not going to leave him. What should I do?"

"Mercedes, perhaps you and John should see a family counselor together to work it out. I understand that it really can help a couple decide on where they are going and what they want to do!"

"I'll speak to John about it."

"No Mercedes, make the appointment and tell John about it! Make sure he realizes that this could be a seminal moment in your relationship."

Mercedes looked at Anna, "Wow, how can somebody be so young and be so wise?" Anna responded, "Hon, I bump into walls like every person."

Both women laughed and Anna saw the worry lines disappear from Mercedes face. She thought, *I pray that John and she go to see a counselor.*

That evening before going to sleep Anna told Jason about her meeting with Mercedes.

She hugged Jason and whispered in his ear, "I still worry about you when you are away on assignment, but I'm thrilled when you come back to me."

Jason whispered back, "I'll always come back to you."

"I love you Jason."

"I love you Anna."

They slept pressed together for the night. The couple had truly become partners.

Chapter Forty-three

Captain John Sparks called Jason the following week. His voice sounded edgy.

"Hi Jason. I just wanted to keep you informed that the tap on Ari Karem's home phone is still on. The Commissioner wanted to take it off, but when I told him about the yacht trip and their plans he acquiesced. They will be taking that trip in two weeks. As soon as they come back I'm going to put a detail on you and Anna. You may not see them, but my men will be there for you."

"It sounds like I'm going to be the bait."

"Yeah, sorry about that."

"As long as we get those bastards—it's okay with me."

"Let me bring up another issue. Mercedes and I are seeing a couple counselor to work things out. It was Anna's idea."

"Well, I didn't do it."

"Hell man. We already have had two sessions. I think it's great!"

"How about you and Anna coming over to my place on Saturday night? I cook a mean steak."

"John, when you learn to say 'our place' then you will get it."

"Oh shit—will you come over to our place?"

"Sure, attaboy!"

John and Mercedes lived in the So Ho district of New York City. The area is in Manhattan and So Ho has as its boundaries set as south of Houston

Street and north of Canal Street. Condominiams and Coops start at one million dollars and go up to fifteen to twenty million. It was an expensive place to live. They lived on Prince Street.

John and Mercedes apartment was a two bedroom, one bath apartment that had an eat in kitchen and dinette. It was well decorated with lovely paintings and comfortable classic furniture.

Jason said, "Wow John this is a very expensive neighborhood."

John said, "This building was built in nineteen fifteen and has been refurbished a number of times. My parents lived here for forty years before they retired to Phoenix. They gave me the condominium. Believe me, it wasn't so rich when they lived here. It took a lot of real estate developers and inflation to make this apartment worth big money. The good news is that my taxes are less than a thousand and my maintenance is less then seven-hundred dollars. I can't afford to move out. Trust me Jason, I have been offered two million bucks for this place. As long as I'm working we are going to stay here."

Mercedes joyfully said, "the shopping is fantastic, the area is alive with people and places and great entertainment venues. It's a great place to live."

The New York strip steak was one of the best Jason had ever eaten.

"My word John, where did you get this steak? It's the best I've had!"

"I can't tell you a lie. It's from one of the best steakhouses in New York. The owner owed me a favor and just insisted I take his thanks in steak. Mercedes made the mushroom gravy from scratch."

The meal was delicious and the couple finished a bottle of red wine as well.

Later they sat in the living room and Anna asked, "How are things going?"

Mercedes smiled at John. "We have had two sessions with the counselor— but do homework every night."

Anna queried, 'I don't understand. Homework?"

"Yes, we have to answer a question a night by writing about our feelings. Then we exchange our letters, but we are not supposed to make a value judgment about any of it. This process is designed to get to know us better."

"It really is working. We were told we cannot judge feelings. That's important!" piped John, "Really important!"

"Can you give us an example of the questions?"

"Sure Jason."

John went over to a corner desk and took out a sheet of paper.

"Here are a few that we have to work on. What are my feelings when you tell me you need me? What are my feelings when I am aware that you had a bad day? How do I feel when I see you after a long day? What are my feelings when I know I have hurt you? How do I feel when I listen to you with all my heart?"

Anna started to cry, "They are wonderful, beautiful, oh I am so touched."

Mercedes gave Anna a tissue as she said, "We are discovering feelings about each other that are really deep. The counselor guided us through some questions in terms of explaining feelings through happenings."

John said, "Yeah, like how I felt when I struck out and my team lost. I can relate things that have happened in my life so Mercedes can understand my feelings."

"It took a little doing, but John writes beautifully and shares everything with me."

Jason and Anna took an Uber back to their apartment. When they were in bed Anna looked at Jason and gently kissed his lips.

Jason gently kissed her back and said, "Thank you."

"Oh Jason, I think Mercedes will marry John. I can feel it. The way she looked at him when he was reading the questions, with so much love in her eyes. Yes, they are certainly going to tie the knot."

"I drank too much wine—love you."

He was asleep in ten seconds. Anna looked at him and thought, *When we are married I want to have a baby as soon as possible. Wow, I never felt this way before.*

Sheila Harris was making a name for herself as Section Chief. She had reorganized the section and made it run smoother and better. Her decision making was superior and Jason heard nothing but good things about her work. He thought, *I really don't want to go back to that position. I'm going to talk to Dr. Han about it.*

Jason called Sheila Harris to his office. She came in smiling and wearing a colorful dress that accented her wonderful coloring.

"Yes sir, boss man. What can I do for you?"

"Call me Jason, okay Sheila?"

Her smile dropped, "Did I screw up?"

"Hell no. I'm advising you that I have just written a position paper recommending you to be permanent Section Chief. You are doing a great job! Sheila, you deserve a bump up in pay grade and I'm trying to get it for you."

"Thank you, Jason. I have only one regret."

"What is that Sheila?"

"That Anna got to you first. I admire you and wish both of you the best, but between me and you Jason— I really care for you a lot!"

"Well then, let's keep it professional because I care for you a lot as well."

Sheila stood up and left the office as Jason thought, *My God, she is one hell of a woman!*

Later in the day Dr. Han called and told him that she hired a very experienced middle manager who would be able to work with her. She stated that she needed a bureaucrat to be her assistant and that Jason was more of a field person.

"Dr. Han, if so— what will be my role?"

"Human resources is in the process of approving my recommendation for an executive position called 'Section Chief Manager' who will supervise all the Section Chiefs of the United States where we have to provide security. That means that on occasion you will have to travel. Is that okay with you?"

"Sure, but with facetime, texting, computers and cell phones we can communicate quite a bit. I'll travel if any of the Section Chiefs have major problems. Is that okay with you?"

"Jason, I have never doubted your judgment. Obviously, you have great leadership skills and I can only say it was ONI's loss and our gain to have you working here. If all goes well you will be on the top level of our professional staff. Your next step would be to replace me as Director. That may be sooner than you think."

"Thanks for the opportunity, I won't let you down."

"You never have Jason!"

That evening Anna and Jason discussed their wedding plans and the aspect of perhaps buying a condominium or home in the city or near the near the city. They discussed Jason's new position as well. His new position gave him a hefty raise in salary.

"I know that a house is a great deal of work, but it probably would be best to raise a family in the suburbs," Anna said in a pensive tone.

"Well we both were raised in single family homes so that's all we know. We have to consider our finances and what we can contribute to make it work. Most banks want at least twenty percent down for a mortgage. I used half of my savings for your engagement ring, and I'm happy about it."

"I have been saving a lot since I'm not paying income tax because I work for the United Nations. The same for you. Perhaps we should see a financial consultant."

"Anna, I really like the way you think. Perhaps we could start a special savings plan for a house."

Anna smiled, kissed Jason and said, "Perhaps."

She was sleeping in thirty seconds and Jason followed quickly, but before he fell asleep he thought, *I wonder how many kids Anna would like to have.*

Chapter Forty-four

One week later Jason received a phone call from Captain John Sparks.

"Jason, our tap on Ari Karem has paid off. He got a call from Afra Chandra who said, 'our problem will go away this week.' I assume they have hatched a plan to get you."

"Okay John. I'm the bait. Should I send Anna back to her parents?"

"No, that would look too suspicious. You won't see us, but Jason, I've got your six.

Believe me I placed my best men on this detail!"

"Okay John. We are in the hands of the New York City Police Department." John quickly replied, "The best in the world!"

That evening at dinner Jason and Anna talked about their position of being the bait to catch Ari Karem and Afra Chandra.

"Jason, I'm frightened, but I trust John Sparks."

"Let's make sure to be together during this time. I'm anxious about what might happen, yet I'm hoping we catch those bastards."

The next two days were anxious days. They were worried, troubled and distressed.

Anytime they heard a noise that was out of the ordinary they almost jumped out of their skins. It was so bad that Anna complained to Jason that she was having trouble eating and doing her work.

Jason said, "It has to happen soon Anna. Please hang in there."

On Friday night, after work, Jason and Anna took an Uber to their apartment. As the Uber car pulled away three men pulled up in a panel truck and jumped out. Jason shielded Anna when one of the men tried to club her, but before anything else happened six NYPD plain clothes men jumped out of the shadows and took care of the attackers.

The under-cover police officers were not too kind to the perpetrators. They used their clubs to break a few knee caps and smash a few skulls in defending the couple. Jason was so incensed that he got a few punches in as well. It took less than three minutes, but the three men sent to kill Jason and Anna were cuffed and placed on the ground.

Five minutes later two police cars rolled up. They placed the thugs in their cars and swiftly drove away. Ten minutes later Captain Sparks showed up.

"Okay, we need you to file a complaint, but better yet, we're going to have a little Q&A with these men tonight. Please show up at my precinct tomorrow about ten in the morning to file your complaints."

Anna was in a state of shock. Jason held her tightly as she shivered and cried. "When will this end? Oh, I am so tired."

"Soon Anna, very soon. Let's try to get some sleep. We have to go to the station house tomorrow to file the complaint against those men."

"Hold me Jason, please hold me."

The couple finally fell asleep at three in the morning.

Between 1938 and 1939 the WPA built the station house for the New York Police Department. It was an old building that had been refurbished a number of times. There were two floors of cells with a definitive group of cells dedicated to females. The Captain's office was large and had a private bathroom and shower. There were four Lieutenant rooms; six Sergeant rooms; three Detective rooms; three bathrooms; three holding rooms; a conference room; the Desk Sergeant's reporting station and citizen area; a matron's room; an armory; a communications room; two civil service dedicated private rooms; and a working kitchen with many tables and chairs. It was a self-contained unit. Although it may have been old— it was a most effective precinct house.

The next morning Jason and Anna arrived at the huge precinct house in downtown Manhattan. Anna and Jason were escorted into a large office where Captain Sparks was sitting at his desk. He looked tired yet wore a smile on his face.

"Hey, don't look so gloomy. We've arrested Afsar Chanra, the yogurt bigshot, and have spoken to the State Department and the Secretary General's Office about Ari Karem. We are waiting for answers. The other scum bags are going away for a long time. I guarantee that!"

"How did you get those men to talk?"

"That's easy. The District Attorney's office promised them that she would change their charges from attempted murder and kidnapping to assault with a deadly weapon. In the long run they're going to be put away for a long, long time."

"What about Chanra?"

"He's already lawyered up, but the DA is requesting no bond because he would be a flight risk."

"What will the judge do?"

"We'll see. It doesn't matter. If the judge let's Chanra go I'll have a team follow him where ever he goes. He's not getting away. Okay, one of my men will escort you to an office to write down your observations of last night's attack and then you will sign the complaints. We will do everything by the book."

Jason turned around to go to the door, but Anna started to cry. John got out of his chair and went over to hold Anna. He whispered in her ear, "You are like a sister to me and I will make sure they get what they deserve. Anna, you are safe now!"

The paper work took two hours and by one in the afternoon they stepped out of the precinct house and into a lovely sunny day.

"Anna, let's go to Central Park and rent a paddle boat. It's warm enough and I need the sunlight"

Anna laughed and hugged Jason. She was thrilled with the idea.

"Okay, but first I'm going to buy you lunch at Tavern on the Green.

Tavern on the Green is located on the west side of Manhattan in the middle of Central Park at sixty-ninth street. It over looks an area called "Sheeps Meadow" because in the 1800's sheep actually used it to graze there. It is surrounded by marvelous green grass and very near a lake where paddle boats and row boats meander. The tour books describe it as a "modern tavern", but it is much more. It has a pastoral feeling to it and during the spring and summer there are many first-time visitors who as tourists are amazed that such a beautiful setting can happen in New York City. The Tavern has been in operation since 1934 and have had visitors ranging from presidents, royalty, artists, actors and New Yorkers who call it their own.

They both ordered the Eggs Benedict Florentine, a specialty of the house. It was delicious with grilled Canadian bacon, creamed spinach and the best hollandaise sauce in the city. Jason ordered the Honey Cinnamon Crème Brulee and Anna ordered a Sticky Pecan Tart for dessert.

They finished their coffee and right before Anna paid the bill Jason received a phone call from Captain John Sparks.

"Jason, Ari Karem was instructed by his government to leave the United States immediately. He's on a plane right now. As you know, we could not stop him because he has diplomatic immunity"

"Shit, I know that."

"The good news is that the judge denied bail for Chanra. Wait until the inmates at Riker's Island get ahold of that Arab. His ass will be in a sling for a month."

"Thanks for everything John. I'll call you on Monday."

Jason remembered the workshops he attended when he first started working for security at the United Nations. The instructors were quite clear on arresting diplomats. The rules concerning diplomatic immunity were established in 1961. It was called "The Vienna Convention on Diplomatic Relations." At that time one-hundred-eighty-seven countries, including the United States, promised to treat diplomatic agents including "the members of the diplomatic staff, and of the administrative and technical staff and of the service staff of the mission" to enjoy "immunity from the criminal jurisdiction of the receiving States."

He looked at Anna and quietly said, "Ari Karem is on his way to Afghanistan. We can't hold him because he is a diplomat."

"I guess nothing else can be done. At least we are finished with that horrible man."

"I guess so. Anyway, I'm going to get a paddle boat and row you around the lake."

"Hon, I'd rather go home, take a shower and take a nap. I'm exhausted."

"Sounds like a plan. Let's go home."

The couple slept three hours and when they got up they discussed their situation. Anna said, "I'll have to get used to feeling safe. It's been awful."

"I'll have to get used to knowing that a murderer is free and I can't do anything about it." Yet Jason thought, *Perhaps, there is a way to get that murdering son of a bitch!*

"Jason, I want to concentrate on our wedding. We have a lot to do!"

Jason hugged Anna, "Okay my dear, we concentrate on the good times to come!" "I love you partner—oh so much!"

And Jason kept on thinking, *I've got get that murderer. Justice has to happen!*

Chapter Forty-five

Jason looked at his calendar on his computer screen and realized that he only had two months until his wedding on the second Saturday in June. Anna and her mother had sent out "save the date" cards to over one-hundred families. He started a time line for a mission he thought about and realized he had to move quickly.

That afternoon he received a phone call from John Sparks.

"Jason, will you please stand up for me. I want you to be my best man."

"It would be an honor. When, where —give me the details?"

"Mercedes and I will get married at City Hall the last Friday in May, at one in the afternoon. Just wear a jacket and tie, nothing too fancy. My parents' are coming in from Phoenix and Mercedes kids will be able to make the ceremony as well. That's the whole wedding party. After the ceremony we all will go to my favorite steak house in Brooklyn, 'Peter Luger'."

"Sounds good to me."

"We got your 'save the date' for the second Saturday in June. We will be there!"

"John, will you be my best man. I have many acquaintances, but you are my friend?"

"My pleasure. Tell me when I have to go to your tuxedo place with you?"

"Huh?"

"Jesus Jason, get with the program." *I've got to get that murderer.*

"To tell you the truth John, I've left the whole wedding thing to Anna and her mother."

"Okay John, Mercedes and I will see you next Saturday night. We're going to see some Off-Broadway show."

"See you there."

Jason looked at his time line and it seemed to him he had to move quickly in order to complete his mission. He picked up his phone and called Captain James Duncan at the Office of Naval intelligence. The civilian administrator told him that Captain James Duncan, his former boss, had become a Rear Admiral and was working in the Pentagon.

It took Jason another hour to get to speak to Admiral Duncan.

"Admiral Duncan, this is Jason Darvish. Congratulations on your appointment."

"Thanks Jason, although I was in charge of ONI and loved it—now all I do is push papers around."

"Yeah, I know—but you are keeping us safe!"

"Thanks for the pep talk. How may I help you Jason?

Jason explained the complete situation and really got down to the finer points of his mission. He was sincere and Admiral Duncan stated he would try to help Jason.

"No promises Jason. If it works my assistant will contact you for more information."

At the end of the day Jason was contacted by Admiral Duncan's assistant for the important information. Jason thought, *That's number one!*

The next day Jason called George Matters, the Chief of Security for the Canadian delegation at the United Nations. He made an appointment to meet Mr. Matters for lunch for the next day. It was important to have Canada's help in order to accomplish his mission.

When both men sat down at a small delicatessen near the United Nations Jason did not know if George Mason could help him. He prayed that he would.

Jason explained his situation and in a most serious voice said, "George, I want to go to Afghanistan incognito as a Canadian business man. I really need your help."

"Is this about that prick, Ari Karem?"

"I can only tell you that it is about justice."

"I'll take that as a 'yes.' Okay it may take a few weeks. What about a passport?"

"The Pentagon is going to help me on that."

"What will your pseudo name be?"

"Roger O'Hearn."

"Okay. We have to get you a business, give you identity, set up a background, file a visa application to go to Afghanistan, get Afghan approval from their business minister, and prep you."

"How long will this take?"

"About a month if I push it."

"Please George, push it and press it—I've got to get into Afghanistan."

Jason thought, That's number two.

That evening Jason and Anna watched the eleven o'clock evening news and prepared to go to bed. Instead of their regular routine Jason went into the kitchen and asked Anna to join him.

"Hon, are you okay?"

"No, not since Ari Karem escaped and went back to Afghanistan."

"We are through with that, aren't we?"

Jason took Anna's hand, squeezed it, looked into her eyes and said, "No. I'm going to go into Afghanistan and get that man. He tried to kill us twice and now I'm going to get him."

Anna frowned and tears rolled down her eyes as she whispered, "You want vengeance." "Hon, I want retribution, I want revenge, I want satisfaction, I want retaliation, I want justice!"

'I know about your Navy record Jason and I know what you are capable of doing. Will you be able to live with your act after you do it?"

"I need your blessing. Without that I am gong to live with this current void of justice for the rest of my life."

Anna thought for a moment and took Jason's both hands and held them firmly. Her tears continued to roll down her eyes as she said, "I love you Jason—with my heart and soul. You are my man, my lover, my life and I will pray for you when you go."

She moved her hands to the side of each cheek, looked deeply into his eyes and gently kissed him on his lips.

Jason thought, *Thank God, that's number three.*

One week later the packet from the Pentagon arrived by registered mail, return signature receipt required. The letter carrier waited as Jason signed his name on the return post card. As he left Jason's office Jason ripped open the envelope and found a fairly worn Canadian passport with some pages stamped from the countries of Singapore, India and the People Republic of China. It was a beautiful job and looked authentic. He sighed a sigh of relief.

Jason called George Matters and asked, "Any news about my Canadian business?"

"Give it time Jason, my God its been only a week.'

"Sorry George, I just got my Canadian passport and it stimulated me to call."

"Damn it Jason, give it a bit of time, will you?"

"Sorry George."

Jason called his parent's in Florida to see how they were doing. His father had seen a cardiologist about some problems, but that seemed to be under control.

Jason's mother said, "Son, we have found a marvelous church only three miles away from us. The priest is a younger man who brings to our attention worldly problems as we see it during this modern era. We love his homilies. Have you been to church at all?"

"Not for quite awhile Mom, not for quite some time."

After their phone call Jason was moved to speak to a priest —perhaps in a confessional mode. He decided to go to the nearest Catholic church to the United Nations. It was called "The Church of Holy Family."

The church was across from the United Nations located on Forty-seventh Street between First and Second Avenue. Jason passed it many times and always liked the marble granite type of building. He checked their website and was surprised to see that they had services in Korean, Spanish and English. Jason checked the timing for church confessionals. He decided to do it later in the day. There was something in his mind, but he just could not get it centered.

When Jason was a kid he and his parents went to church regularly. He learned that confessing your sins wipes the slate clean with God and would make him spiritually stronger. The priest gives absolution to the sinner because he has been ordained. As a young person he never had to confess anything about a mortal sin, just venial sins. He learned at Sunday School that in the Catholic Church mortal sins were very serious and that if you committed a mortal sin you would forfeit heaven.

Jason was comfortable in the confessional. There was a screen between them. After gong through the rituals of making the sign; telling the priest how long it had been since he confessed; listing a few venial sins; he got into the true reason for his visit.

"Father, I work in security at the United Nations. My fiancée and I had two attempts on our lives from a former delegate from Afghanistan. Thank God the police saved our lives and the planner as well as the men who attacked us are now in jail. But the man who wanted this done escaped to Afghanistan because of diplomatic immunity. I intend to go after him. It seems to me that this is war and I have a mission to accomplish. I want to get to this man and provide justice."

"Son, in your mind and in your heart. Is this vengeance?"

"That is why I am here. I feel conflicted and I don't know why? Father, I think I am a good man. Yes, when I was in service I had to kill, but that was to protect the lives of my fellow SEALs."

"SEAL's—that is most dangerous."

"It was for national security and it was necessary."

"Go ahead young man, continue about this Afghanistan person."

"He represents what is truly bad about his religion and his people. There is nothing but hate in his heart against us. It seems that he believes that the ends justify the means. That's not only my view but our nation's view as well."

"My question to you again—is this revenge or vengeance?"

"Father, what does our church say about war and killing?"

"Are we talking about a Just War?"

"Yes Father."

"Ah let me think for a moment—the "Just War" doctrine that I remember from my studies are that the conditions must be grave; the conditions if not corrected, would cause serious damage to others; that all other methods were tried before the war; and that there would be an element of success for the mission. I'm sorry that I could not give you a dissertation about this aspect."

"This is heavy in my heart Father. I am conflicted in many ways and I think you have helped me with your short dissertation."

They both laughed at the same time.

"Bless you my son. I will pray for you. Come back and visit us. Come back to the church young man. We need worthy people as you."

"Thank you, Father, I will pray for you as well."

When Jason and Anna talked about his confessional she looked at him and thought, *I am so lucky to have such an honorable man to be my life's partner. He shares everything with me.*

Jason slept well that night. The talk with the priest about a "just war" made him realize what his true mission seemed to be. He was convinced that his mission would be successful.

There were a number of steps that were required, but he would overcome them.

However, Anna did not sleep well at all. She was troubled about the possibilities that she would live in regret by backing Jason's wishes. Anna felt conflicted because she learned early on from the United Church of Christ that the principles of the church was based on a "Just Peace Church." Many members were pacifists and believed that war would not have been Jesus's way. Anna felt closer to that doctrine than the "Just War" doctrine.

Anna thought about changing her mind and telling Jason that he could not go to Afghanistan. She thought, *I am in the horns of a dilemma. There is no easy answer.*

Chapter Forty-six

Ten days after Jason's conversation with George Matters, the Canadian, he was surprised to get word that George was ready to see him with some specific information.

"George, if you have all my stuff I'll buy you dinner anywhere in the city."

"Okay my friend, I'll meet you for lunch at Nino's two blocks away. They have the best lasagna in the city. One o'clock today. You make the reservations."

After a scrumptious Italian meal the men talked business. George opened up his large leather folder and started to lecture.

"Mr. Roger O'Hearn works at the Edward's Construction Company in Ottawa City. Here are your business cards. The fact is that you will be meeting with Delwar Busri, a middle official of the Afghanistan government. You are there to get specifications for a new school wing to be built. By the way Roger, this is legitimate so when you get back you better have all the specs ready for the Edward's Company."

"That's great."

"Further, give me your passport so I can get you a business visa. I can do that for you in one day since it is a very legitimate request from the Afghan government."

"When we get back to the office I'll have it sent to your office immediately." "Okay. Now it will be up to you to book your flights and pay for everything. May I suggest you use Air India since we Canadians tend to use them to go to Afghanistan. Buy one of those prepaid money debit cards, so you don't have to have any identification problems." "Great idea George. How come you know so much?"

"I was a spook in my early life." "What unit?"

"CSIS or as you Yanks would call it, Canadian Security Intelligence Service." "A good shop. I know it well."

"Thank you Yank! Oh, I forgot something else. Here is a Canadian burn phone. It has a Canadian number so when you call Mr. Busri he will see you are truly a Canadian. It's prepaid as well."

"I never would have thought of that."

"That my boy is because you were never trained to be a spook." They both laughed heartily.

Anna saw Jason at the kitchen table with a new cell phone at his ear. It was seven-thirty in the morning.

"Thank you, Mr. Busri. Just to confirm, we will meet at your offices in Kabul, Building Number six at ten in the morning on Thursday May eighth. —Yes, I will get my visa today. He said in Farsi, 'Mamnoon.' (Thank you.)"

"What is happening Jason?"

"I wanted to make sure I had all the information before letting you know what is happening. Kabul is eight and a half hours ahead of us in time so I had to call this morning. I'm going to Kabul the second week in May. I'll be undercover so not to embarrass the United States if I am caught."

"Are you sure about this?"

"Very sure. I have to finish this!"

"Jason, what would you do if I forbad you to go?"

"Then I could not go because we are partners."

"Are you saying that Ari Karem's life is in my hands." "No—you are saying it."

Anna ran into the bedroom without saying anything. She went into the bathroom and washed her face with cold water and looked in the mirror. She thought, *I am going to share Jason's guilt if he doesn't go or culpability if I say yes.*

Anna got ready for work and did not say anything to Jason. She was in a state of frozen disbelief that he really was going to go and dispose of Ari

Karem. The man she loved and adored was going to be a murderer or was he going to be a soldier? She had not reasoned it out as yet.

Anna looked at Jason and ran to him, hugged him and kissed him passionately.

She desperately said, "I believe in you. You are a good man so I will pray for your safety when you are in Afghanistan."

Jason's eyes teared up and he gulped as he said, "I love you with all my heart and soul

Anna."

Later in the day Jason went into Dr. Han's office and quickly closed the door. She looked startled.

"Dr. Han, I'm going to need the second and third week of May off. I'll be in Afghanistan to take care of a problem."

"Are you really sure you want to do this?"

"Dr. Han, he is a killer and tried to kill Anna and me twice."

"Jason, I cannot condone this. If you are caught there will nobody to bail you out. Not the United Nations, not the United States, nor any other government. Are you sure you have to do this?"

"I'll give the bastard a chance to defend himself. I'm sure Afghanistan law will have some sort of 'Stand Your Ground law', but it really doesn't matter. Why should Anna and I live in the fear that Ari Karem may try to do this again? I'm sure he feels a grudge against me now because he was forced to flee this country."

"I never thought of him retaliating against you again."

"He is a monster and I'm sure he hates Anna and me enough to try to kill us again. I never told Anna about my fear because she thinks it's over. It's over when the threat is over!"

"Jason, may I suggest you not communicate with any person in the United States when you are in Afghanistan."

"Don't worry. I'll be a Canadian."

"May I suggest you blend in for awhile before you make contact. Learn your escape routes. Learn the patterns of the city and of the police force."

"I thought you said you 'cannot condone this.'—now you are giving me advice." "Although I cannot condone this as your boss, I have been in your position as a young operative when I was in Interpol. Let me tell you that I was faced with problems that seemed to be insurmountable, but older and wiser people helped me out." "Any other suggestions?"

"When you do your surveillance find patterns and habits of your target. Make sure you have a place of hiding close to where the action will take place."

"I never would have thought of that."

"You will have to adapt to the culture, so start to grow some facial hair, buy appropriate Afghan clothing, shop in Afghan markets only and eat in only Afghan style restaurants. Become one of them. Blend in because it becomes easier when you are in the crowd."

"Thank you."

"One more thing, get rid of the weapon—destroy it in pieces and scatter it around. Jason—"

"Yes, Ma'am."

"This conversation never took place."

Jason had the weekend to himself because Anna, her Mother and Susan were shopping for Anna's wedding gown. They would be staying at Susan's apartment on Friday and Saturday nights in order to use the necessary time to shop and have some fun.

He decided to study the map of Kabul, research more Afghanistan customs, cuisine and culture in order to blend in more effectively. It seemed that there was a growing middle class in Kabul. Television was on at least sixteen hours a day and there were eighteen million phones all over the country. The schools were populated well into being over-crowded and that the atmosphere was positive even though there was a conservative government.

Fran Hopkins the wedding planner met Anna, Susan and Mrs. Mason at Bergdorf Goodman at five in the late afternoon. Taking the elevator to the seventh floor they had dinner to discuss shopping, style, budget, and stores.

Bergdorf Goodman always meant to New Yorkers the best of style, service and luxury. It showcased the very best designers, a wide variety of the world's fashion and was a shopping experience to the newcomer. It was on Fifth Avenue at Fifty-eighth Street and was one of the most visited department stores in the world.

They finished their dinner by six-thirty and visited the Bridal Salon.

Fran Hopkins said, "They close at eight tonight, but I wanted you to get a picture of the best gowns in the country. The prices vary from moderately high to out of this world, so don't faint when you look at the price tags. Look for style and what truly interests you. Tomorrow I will be with you all day to shop. Although I have been doing this for years it's fun for me."

The women had a great time and learned so much about quality gowns. There was one gown that had a very simple design that Anna tried on. She looked stunning and Susan took a picture of her on her cell phone. It was a Vera Wang gown.

They shopped all day Saturday and at the end of the day Anna knew what she wanted. It was a super weekend.

Chapter Forty-seven

The Air India flight would take over fifteen hours from JFK to Kabul. Air India was a good airline and he was bumped up to business class at the last minute. Jason was thrilled.

He asked the flight attendant, "Off the record, why was I picked to go to business class?" "Oh, it wasn't because of you personally. We had a last minute request for tickets from a family of four and in order to accommodate them we had to take you out of your coach seat and put you into business class in order for them to make the flight. Good fortune for you. Drink sir?"

"Sure, I'd like a ginger ale."

He was served a ginger ale and some vanilla wafer cookies. Jason looked at his watch. He would be landing in the early afternoon and hoped to get his apartment called Shahrak-e Aria, which was in an apartment house located near the airport. The rate was thirty United States dollars per day. Jason thought it was a bargain, but he decided to wait and see.

At customs he had nothing to declare. His passport was looked at for ten seconds, stamped and he was in a taxi headed for his apartment within one hour of landing. He arrived at a good looking off white six story apartment house that looked pretty good from the outside. The instructions were to go to apartment three and get the keys.

The manager was a large woman who said, "Passport."

He showed it and she gave him the keys to apartment five on the second floor. He inspected the apartment and was surprised to see a working television set, full kitchen and clean sheets plus adequate towels. Jason was asleep in ten minutes.

Kabul is the capital of Afghanistan. It has over four million-six-hundred thousand people living within its boundary. The capital is in the state of rebuilding itself. During the former administration the Taliban would send in suicide bombers to cause trouble. They bombed the markets, the mosques, the government and as many soft targets that could cause death. Added to this was a police force that was poorly paid and easily paid off. Crime existed openly.

Jason turned on the television set and immediately heard that a girl's high school in an adjacent province, near Kabul, was burned by masked attackers. They destroyed the labs, archives and administrative offices as well as killing the two guards who were standing watch. He thought, *The conservatives are at it again.*

According to his plan he decided to go out and buy some traditional Afghan clothing in order to blend in. Jason had researched clothing and knew that many male Kabul government employees wore western dress. It was about a fifty-fifty breakdown although Jason felt that traditional clothing would be better for his mission.

He found a small thrift shop down the street and bought a "perahan." It was to fit the top part of his body. The piece, which was sort of a tunic in style, was wide and loose with the sleeves also worn loosely. It ended at his knees and had small slits on its side.

The "tunban" or the lower garment had plenty of folds gathered into semi-pleats at the lower part of the legs. It had a massive amount of material although when you walked it was quite comfortable.

Jason bought a checkered sport coat to wear over the "perahan." He tried on a few "pakols" which is a round-topped men's hat made of wool that lays on the head as a beret. Sun glasses finished the disguise.

Walking down the street he spotted a restaurant called "Sufi." Jason decided to have an Afghan meal. He was greeted warmly by the waiter and he asked for black tea. Looking at the menu he ordered "Ashak." The menu described the dish as "Fresh pasta filled with scallions, leeks and cilantro, served with yogurt-garlic sauce. Topped with ground beef uniquely seasoned with coriander, turmeric and cayenne pepper, sprinkled with mint." It was served hot and it was delicious.

Jason took care of the Canadian Construction company's business the next day. After that he spent the next few days becoming familiar with the areas of Kabul. The government buildings were located in different areas of the city and Jason had to locate where Ari Karem worked. His method was simple, yet effective. Jason would call each of the buildings and ask for Karem. He was successful on his fourth call. Ari Karem worked for the Ministry of Defense located on a large avenue some seven minutes to the airport. It was in direct line to his apartment house but located the opposite the way. The good news was that it was ten minutes to the airport. Jason decided his apartment was okay to stay in.

He followed Ari Karem for three days making sure that he wasn't being seen. Karem had a set routine when he was working. He managed to pray five times a day and had his prayer rug with him. Ari Karem prayed on the north side of his building with about six other men. The best time for Jason to take him was on a Wednesday, right after prayer time. Prayer time was at five- forty-two in the afternoon, every day. Karem, normally would pray and then go to a tea house for refreshments. The walk took about ten minutes. That is when Jason planned to confront him. The weekend in Kabul was Thursday and Friday so Karem would be relaxed since Wednesday was his last day of work for the week.

Jason had gone to an open-air flea market a few days earlier and purchased a vintage WWII K-bar fighting knife. It cost him the equivalent of thirty dollars, but it had a good feel and was very sharp. He made sure that he could balance it and control it. His old Quantico training came into his memory. The USMC Master Sargent who trained him in knife fighting was brutal in his approach, yet Jason thrived in that atmosphere. Jason passed with flying colors.

His escape plan was to purchase two airline tickets. They were both evening flights. The first a simple flight from Kabul to Kandahar. The second was from Kabul to Dubai. The plan was to leave the country if there was no pressure in terms of surveillance after he eliminated Karem. If there was heavy surveillance then the short flight to Kandahar because he thought the police would be looking for the perpetrator to leave the country.

Jason decided to go to the tea room where Karem usually would go. At five-fifteen in the afternoon he ordered black tea and "Kulche Badami." It is an almond cookie which was crunchy on the outside and chewy inside. It was sweet and tasty. He took his time checking his watch.

Prayer time was five-forty-two. Jason planned to be walking by Karem at six in the evening. This was exactly what happened.

Jason was pleased to see that Karem was alone as he approached him. Karem passed Jason on the left. When that happened Jason spun around and hit Karem as hard as he could in the back of the head. Karem went down in a lump. After a minute he regained his senses. Jason was sitting on his chest. He took off his "pakol" and sun glasses to make sure Karem knew who he was. Jason really wanted Karem to look at him!

"You!" Ari Karem sputtered.

"Yes, me you son of a bitch. I'm here for you. Get up and defend yourself."

Karem sprang to his feet and backed off. He reached behind his back and drew out a moderate sized folded pocket knife and clicked it open. The blade was about five inches long and Ari Karem charged Jason.

Jason let him get to two feet of him and side swiped Karem with a simple judo move.

Karem went down quickly and lost his knife. Jason quickly hit Karm's face with the butt of his K-bar knife. He then sat on Karem using his full weight.

"Karem, this is justice for you killing your boss." Jason plunged the knife into Karem's heart.

As Karem was dying Jason looked down at him and said, "Justice for you trying to kill Anna and me!"

He quickly withdrew the knife, tucked it into his "tunban" and walked smartly to the main street. He had two hours to get to the airport. In a calm fashion he turned around and slowly walked to his apartment.

In his apartment Jason changed into his Canadian Roger O'Hearn disguise. He wiped the knife clean and walked up to the roof of his apartment house. Jason looked around and threw the knife down a ventilation shaft. He quickly left the building, taking a cab to the Kabul airport.

Jason decided to take the evening flight to Dubai.

When he arrived in Dubai, three hours later, he called Anna at her office.

"Hon, it's done."

"Did you give him a chance?"

"You bet. It was a fair fight—ended quickly, but fair and just."

"Thank you," she sobbed, "Jason. I love you."

"See you tomorrow at the apartment. Love you!"

He immediately booked a morning flight back to New York. Jason stayed in a nearby motel for the evening and had the shuttle take him to the airport. The flight left at seven in the morning. Dubai to New York took over fourteen hours but was eight hours ahead in time. Jason knew that his plane would arrive about one or two in the afternoon. He did not feel elated nor happy. The fact was that Jason felt numb. As he went over the events of the knife fight with Karem he felt some anxiousness. He ordered a vegetable plate and asked the flight attendant for coffee. Jason drank two cups of coffee which was uncharacteristic for him.

Jason thought, *I'm going to call Dr. Blackman at the V.A. to share my feelings. No— I'm going to call Dr. Wong, my psychiatrist at the ONI. I want to share my feelings with him and only him!*

Chapter Forty-eight

Anna took the day off. There was no way she would permit Jason to come back to an empty apartment from his trip to Afghanistan. She wanted him to feel safe, comfortable, and sheltered as she greeted him. Anna bought Jason's favorite ice cream and had baked an apple pie in the early afternoon. It was his favorite and she wanted him to feel at home and happy.

Jason opened the apartment door and smelled that wonderful smell of a pie baking. As he breathed in the smell of home Anna came out and hugged him and kissed him.

She held his hand as they sat on the couch, "Thank God it is done!"

"Yes, and he knew why as well!"

"Good. He was evil."

"Hon, I want to call Dr. Wong at ONI. I have some issues I have to clear up."

"Do you want me to go with you?"

"Of course, I do!"

"Okay—but first how about some apple pie ala mode?"

"You bet!"

That night their lovemaking was different. Both Anna and Jason never wanted to end it. They were considerate to each other; they were accommodating to each other; they stopped and rested for a time and just held onto each other. The couple kissed, fondled and loved every part of each other's body.

Finally, Jason whispered, "Hon, I'm so tired. Let's go to sleep." Anna nodded yes, "Just let me help you please—"

She took over the lovemaking and he finally groaned in pleasure as he said, "God I love you!"

They were asleep in two minutes. Locked with their arms around each other.

The next day Jason called ONI to make an appointment with Dr. Wong. He was told that Dr. Wong was on leave and would return in two weeks. Jason made an appointment with Dr.

Wong's assistant on the first day Dr. Wong would return to work.

Jason arranged to see his boss Dr. Han as soon as soon as he went back to work.

Sitting behind her desk she looked up and smiled as Jason walked in. She thought, *I'm glad he is back safe and sound.*

"Dr. Han, it's finished and I'm okay with it."

"You don't sound that you are. Are you?"

"Well, not really. I'll be seeing a friend—in fact my psychiatrist from the ONI in two weeks. I trust him and really have to speak to him."

"Is there anything I can do to ease your situation?"

"Not really. The good news is that we are in a slower part of the year right now so I don't feel guilty when I have to take off from work."

"Jason, I want you around our department for a long time. You take the necessary time when you need it."

Anna's work load lessened because not too many areas of the United Nations were operational. There was always an ebb and flow depending on General Assembly sessions and Security Council meetings. The major divisions as the World Health Organization, UNICEF, The World Bank and UNESCO still provided many reports for editing and distribution.

Fortunately, she and Jason worked regular hours and had enough time to plan for their wedding and enjoy each other.

Anna and Jason flew into Reagan National Airport on Sunday night and rented a car. The couple drove to a nearby motel in Suitland, Maryland to spend the night. Their appointment with Dr. Wong was for ten in the morning on Monday. Anna seemed relaxed although Jason was on edge. When they had dinner that evening he hardly ate his food.

"Hon, are you feeling ill?"

"No, I just am nervous and can't eat."

"Jason, you need some nourishment. Try."

"I feel like a kid and you're the mother pushing."

Anna leaned over the table, took her knife and fork and cut a piece of steak on Jason's plate. She placed the fork at Jason's mouth and said, "Eat!"

"Okay— okay—I'll eat!"

Jason's cell phone rang as they were finishing their dinner.

"Okay Dr. Wong, text me your address. Ten is fine."

"What's happening?"

"Dr. Wong wants us to meet him at his house tomorrow. It's about five miles from here. He thinks it would be better to see us there because we will have more privacy."

"He sounds very wise."

"Oh yes, he is wise and a good, a very good psychiatrist."

The house was a red brick two story structure with a large front porch and a small front lawn. As they went up the steps to the house Anna saw beautiful plants strategically placed on the porch. Dr. Wong opened the door and greeted Jason with a hug.

"Dr. Wong, this is Anna, my fiancée."

"Anna, it is truly my pleasure to meet you. I wish you great happiness for your marriage."

Anna instantly liked him. There was a great deal of warmth and caring in his voice. When she saw him embrace Jason she realized there was a strong bond between the men.

"Dr. Wong, Jason has nothing but the best to say about you. Any person who Jason honors so much is just fine with me."

Dr. Wong observed an articulate, pretty woman who obviously loved Jason and wished the best for him. He realized that she would have to be a part of his recovery. He suggested to see her first, "I want to hear from Anna and find out from her what the current situation is—is that okay?

"Of course."

"Anna, come into my office."

Anna told him everything. How Jason and she met; how they fell in love; what she discovered; the court case; the attempt on their lives; the attempt on Jason 's life again; the NYPD cooperation; the UN hearing; finally, she agreeing that evil had to be wiped out!

She cried, she wept heavily, she shook while telling Dr. Wong everything. Dr. Wong gave her a glass of water and suggested that she take a mild tranquilizer. Anna nodded and he gave her a light dose.

Jason came in and repeated the same story to Dr. Wong. When it came to the killing of Ari Karem, he was graphic and to the point.

"Well, why do you need me?"

"I feel conflicted. I feel sad. My moral compass is off kilter!"

"Why?"

"Well, I was brought up as a Catholic & maybe some of it is in me."

"Did you feel the same when you were in combat with the SEALs?"

"No, not at all. We had a mission and we knew why we had to go."

"Did you feel conflicted, sad, or any other negative feeling after the mission?

"No. Perhaps elated that I wasn't killed."

Dr. Wong asked Anna to come back to his office

"The story you both gave me lines up almost 100%. I understand the stress both of you had to go through and I compliment you. You could have stopped the investigation at any time and save yourself grief. Yet you were certain that an injustice took place. I'm going to ask you to think of what you did as a mission. Jason, you know about missions. Anna, when you committed yourself to this then it was your mission as well. It seems to me that good triumphed over evil."

Jason held Anna's hand, "Then why do we still feel sad and stressed?"

Dr. Wong let out a short giggle, "Your both civilians! It is not in your mindset to do things in such a way anymore. Jason, if I didn't know you so well I would have thought you could not operate anymore. Yet you did. Anna, thank God that you have each other. You did the right thing. You were justified. Hell, I would have done the same thing!"

Jason let out a sigh of relief, "Thank you Dr. Wong."

Dr. Wong asked them to stay for lunch. He told Jason about all the personnel changes at ONI and mentioned a few missions that were classified. He used fictitious countries although Jason and Anna recognized the action from the news stories they had see on television.

The lunch was a simple vegetable soup and a wonderful garden salad. It was simple and delicious! As they ate the dark cloud drifted away from Anna and Jason minds. They were in a wonderful mood and very happy.

Dr. Wong observed the couple and thought, *They will make it— just fine!*

When they were leaving Anna hugged Dr. Wong and said, "You will be invited to our wedding!"

Epilogue

Captain John Sparks and Mercedes Wright were married at New York City's City Hall on the last Friday in May. Officiating at the wedding was the Mayor of New York.

Before the ceremony the Mayor addressed John's parents, Mercedes' daughters and family plus Anna and Jason.

"Public service is hard, but sometimes performing a ceremony as this, is the best part of my job! I am particularly pleased that Captain John Sparks asked me to do this. He is the best of the best in our Police Force and I am honored to do this."

Mercedes and John read letters to each other as part of the ceremony and the Mayor did a perfect job solemnizing the marriage. He presented the couple with a Mayor's Proclamation scroll, designating the day as an honorary day to commemorate their wedding.

Later at Peter Luger's restaurant Anna looked at Mercedes wearing a beautiful coral wedding suit. It was a classic sheath dress and paired with a versatile open-front jacket. She had a trim figure and looked beautiful. John wore his dress uniform and looked handsome. His smile was constant throughout the day.

Jason clinked his glass to get the attention of the group. They all looked up.

"As best man it is proper to give the first toast. John told me to make sure it would be short. Please lift your glasses to wish a most perfect couple.

Mercedes and John, you bring out the best in each other—although that is pretty easy to do!"

They all applauded. It was a wonderful wedding day for everyone.

Jason Darvish and Anna Mason were married at St. Paul's Chapel on the second Saturday in June. Officiating at the wedding was the Chaplin of Columbia University. Since no Catholic Priest would be allowed to do a joint ceremony unless it was at a Catholic church and since Anna felt that the best compromise was to use an independent clergy person, they decided on using Columbia's University's Chaplin. She was terrific and responded to the couple with great enthusiasm.

Anna and Jason wrote almost one-hundred percent of the ceremony. They added elements of their religion and elements of working to make the world a better place to live. One- hundred and twenty people attended with some relatives coming in as far away as California.

The minister nearing the end of the ceremony said. "I have been a member of the clergy for over twenty years. This has been the most organized, understandable, well written and spiritual ceremony I have ever participated in. My compliments to this marvelous loving couple."

Later at Columbia University's Faculty House the wine flowed and laughter radiated throughout the reception and dinner. Anna's gown was so understated that it was a show stopper. It was a designer's gown with a low cut back, subtle pleats and a flattering A-line skirt. It took center stage, as it should have.

Jason was dressed in a white formal jacket with black dress pants. He wore a pleated white shirt, long sleeves with cuff links and around his neck a black bow tie. Jason was the perfect partner making sure that all eyes would be on the bride.

John Sparks clinked his glass a few times and everyone quieted down. He stood up and lifted his glass and said, "I am really happy that Jason invited me to be his best man. He was mine a few weeks ago and did a great job. Now it's my turn—Anna and Jason may your marriage be blessed with great happiness, wonderful health and joyful adventure. Knowing both of you that's easy to do!"

Everyone applauded and kept on clinking their glasses until the newly married couple kissed. The wedding was superb and lasted for many hours.

It was the culmination of a partnership that would not break under the most trying circumstances.

Jason and Anna rented a house on the island of Maui in Hawaii. Their honeymoon was an opportunity to get away from it all. Jason was able to scuba dive and Anna was able to snorkel.

On many days they would sun themselves on the beach and forget the pressures of their jobs and their most recent anxiety producing history. They had a gas barbeque on the rear porch of the house and they ate most of their dinners outside. The two city dwellers certainly enjoyed the outdoors.

On the plane going back to their apartment in New York, Anna looked at her husband and wondered, *I wonder what our kids will look like.*

She smiled at him and he smiled back as he held her hand. He thought, *I wonder how many kids she wants!*

End